In Bed With
A Stranger

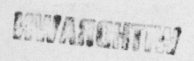

In Bed With
A Stranger

Mary Wine

BRAVA

KENSINGTON PUBLISHING CORP.

www.kensingtonbooks.com

BRAVA BOOKS are published by

Kensington Publishing Corp.
850 Third Avenue
New York, NY 10022

All Kensington titles, imprints, and distributed lines are available at special quantity discounts for bulk purchases for sales promotion, premiums, fund-raising, educational, or institutional use.

Special book excerpts or customized printings can also be created to fit specific needs. For details, write or phone the office of the Kensington Special Sales Manager: Kensington Publishing Corp., 850 Third Avenue, New York, NY 10022. Attn. Special Sales Department. Phone: 1-800-221-2647.

Brava and the B logo are Reg. U.S. Pat. & TM Off.

ISBN-13: 978-0-7582-3463-6
ISBN-10: 0-7582-3463-5

First Kensington Trade Paperback Printing: June 2009

10 9 8 7 6 5 4 3 2 1

Printed in the United States of America

Chapter One

Warwick Castle, 1578

"She shall not touch my pearls." The Countess of Warwick-shire was a beautiful woman but her lips twisted into an ugly expression as she glared at her husband's mistress.

"In sooth, she shall, Wife." The earl entered on silent feet; even his spurs didn't make any noise. He kept his voice even but there was the unmistakable ring of authority in it. Every servant in the room lowered their head in deference to the master of the house before continuing on with their tasks. But they listened to every word. The brewing discontent of the lady of the manor sent excitement through the staff. It had been growing since the day the lord's mistress had been discovered with child. A reckoning was long overdue.

"She shall wear the pearls and the new garments I instructed you to order made when the babe was birthed."

Lady Philipa bit into her lower lip as a scathing reply leapt to mind. She dared not voice it too harshly; men were such fickle creatures when it came to their cocks. She lowered her head to hide her frown as she curtsied to her husband. When she raised her face, her lips were smooth once more, a testimony to years of training at the hands of her governess.

Women had to be much more controlled than men, in the world where they were owned by them.

"My lord, am I to have no comforts? Shall I be reduced to seeing my own finery placed onto your leman? Will you see me shamed in front of my own household?"

The earl stepped in front of his wife, his dark gaze traveling over her face as he lifted one finger in front of her nose.

"You are a bitch, Philipa. A truly spoilt, pampered bitch, who doesn't even bother to perform the function of a true bitch." His hand closed into a fist that he shook in front of her alarmed eyes. "Hear me well, lady wife! There will be no dishonesty in this house! Declare to one and all that you are without comforts and I will have your chamber stripped of its tapestries and carpets. Your fine gowns and jewelry will be shut away and the spice cabinet locked so that you may, in truth, live without comforts."

The countess gasped but covered her mouth lest she spit out an angry retort and seal her fate. The earl nodded his head to himself before gripping her arm and turning her to face his mistress, Ivy Copper. Ivy was sitting up in bed with her new daughter at her breast. The babe kicked and pushed a plump fist against her mother's swollen breast as it suckled. She was a lively babe, in spite of the fact that no one had swaddled it. The strips of fabric cost money and Ivy didn't have any say over what she was given. The servants were Philipa's to command. She had not commanded that anyone spend time wrapping the babe in strips of swaddling fabric to ensure that its limbs grew straight. Only a long shift covered the babe, like a peasant child.

Ivy's hair was brushed into a soft shine over her opposite shoulder as she celebrated her sitting-up day. Philipa secretly hoped that her husband's mistress might die of childbed fever, but she sat there looking the picture of good health. Even her milk had come in to ensure that her bastard would be full and strong.

"Yet, you are shamed, Philipa, shamed by the fact of your own cowardice." Her husband turned her so she could stare up into his face. A shiver shook her as she caught a hint of his manly scent. Her weak female body enjoyed it. Avoiding his bed took discipline.

"Ah, you're a coward, Philipa. You left my bed for fear of childbirth. Look at my new daughter, Wife. God favors the bold." His gaze softened for a moment as he offered her a kind look. "You are my lady wife. Return to my bed and take up your duty as wife. If you do, I swear there will be no other taking your place. No bastard-born child set above your own children."

Her head shook back and forth as she pulled against his grip. Fear strangled her, trapping her words in her throat. Giving birth was deadly! Over half her friends had gone to their graves as fever engulfed their bodies or, worse still, their babes refused to be pushed from their wombs. They died in withering agony, with long hours of endless pain.

The earl snorted with disgust. Pointing his thick finger at her, his voice boomed so that it reverberated against all the walls of the chamber. "Then you yourself shall place that string of pearls around my leman's neck and follow her to her churching. You will stand as godmother to my new daughter."

"You mean to acknowledge the bastard?" In shock, Philipa felt her lower lip quiver. "What of Mary? I have given you a daughter, my lord!"

"And you were honored well and truly." Her husband released her arm and ran the back of his hand across her cheek. "I'd honor you again without holding a grudge if you'd return to my bed as a wife should." He lowered his voice so that Ivy could not hear him. "I'll set her aside, Philipa, for you and a legitimate son. Think on it. But I'll not turn to rape. You will not lay such a burden upon me. We are married and it is your duty to bear my child as much as mine to take you to my bed."

Her husband left her to join the group of visitors celebrating Ivy's survival of childbirth. Today was her sitting-up ceremony, and in another two weeks if she still lived, there would be the churching day when the new mother was cleansed by the estate clergy and allowed back into the church. The bastard would be taken from her at its baptism. The traditions were older than anyone remembered. If Ivy died before she was churched, she'd be buried in unconsecrated ground. If the baby died unbaptized, it, too, would be denied burial in church ground.

The baby's soft smacking sounds filled the chamber as Philipa watched her husband lean over to kiss his mistress. The bed was draped in lavish display. Thick wool tapestries covered the top of the bed and hung as curtains along the side of the bed. There were fine linen sheets, the stained sheet from the day of the birth proudly displayed by the window. The visitors all touched it for good luck as they passed. Ivy was wearing a shift taken from Philipa's own wardrobe. The fine fabric shimmered against her creamy skin. There was mulled wine at her command and cakes baked with spices from the lord's own private stock.

Everything was laid out as grandly as it had been when she was the mother and her daughter Mary first allowed to be seen. The only difference was that a wet nurse had suckled the child because as a noblewoman she could afford the luxury of not tending to a newborn's fussing. Philipa gazed at Ivy's breasts as the milk ran across the baby's cheek and the earl laughed. He wiped the milk away with his own hand. Ivy smiled as the lord bathed her with his attention, praising her and her whelp.

The sight left a bitter taste in Philipa's mouth. She shivered as she realized what it would take to win his attention away from his mistress. She couldn't do it. Not again. It had taken two days to force her daughter into the world. Days that had seemed endless as the pain wrung her body. In truth, she couldn't have suckled her child because she hated it so much for hurting her so greatly. That hate extended to her husband and his demands for more children. Her mother had had to endure such from her father, but it was a different time now. England had a queen and Mary could inherit everything. Elizabeth Tudor would see to that. Men were going to see an end to their absolute rule over their female relatives.

Turning in a flare of silk petticoats, Philipa left. Let the bastard be acknowledged! It would not change the fact that she was mistress of the estate. The earl would be called back to court and Ivy and her child would answer to her.

Warwick Chapel

"By what name shall the child be known?"

The congregation held their breath as they waited to hear the baby's name. A child was never named until it was being baptized to ensure that Satan couldn't send one of his demons to snatch the child's soul.

"Anne." Philipa spoke clearly as the clergyman looked to her as the godmother to decide on the name. "After the Queen's own dear departed mother."

The clergyman almost dropped the infant into the baptismal font as his eyes bulged out in shock. Philipa fluttered her eyelashes innocently at him. There was a mutter running across the congregation but she did not care. Let the bastard bear an unlucky name. Anne Boleyn had lost her head long before her daughter wore the crown of England. Her husband was forbidden to attend the baptism along with Ivy in an attempt to cleanse the child completely without any softhearted parents in attendance. Philipa glared at the clergyman and he dunked the baby with far less grace than he normally did.

Anne screamed as she was pulled out of the baptismal basin. Philipa frowned as the baby turned red and the congregation sent up a cheer of acceptance. If the baby hadn't screamed to release the devil, then it might have been shunned by its Christian community. Anne screeched loud enough to reach even the last pew.

At least she had managed to give the brat an unlucky name. The clergyman muttered a closing prayer before wrapping the infant in a towel and handing it to her. Philipa controlled the urge to sneer as she carried her goddaughter out of the chapel. The moment they entered the private hallway that led to her chamber, she thrust the child at a servant, turning her back on it. What she failed to see was the disapproving looks her maids gave her back as they cradled and soothed one of their own. Anne hiccupped before snuggling into the bosoms offered. The servants cooed to her as they stroked her dark baby hair.

The senior maid cast a look down the hallway her mistress had taken and frowned. "Some folks are mean hearted. Indeed they are! A baby is a blessing to the whole house! Everyone knows that. The mistress will poison herself with such meanness. It'll bring dark times to everyone living on the land. Mark my words."

The two under maids said nothing, holding their tongues in time-honored tradition. Speaking against the mistress of the house was grounds for dismissal. But not a one of them would admit to hearing anything from the housekeeper. Making an enemy of the housekeeper was bound to get a girl assigned the worst tasks. Instead, they reached up to touch the baby, smiling at the tiny rose lips. A healthy baby was good luck for everyone. Life was hard. Best to set your attentions on the good things when you could.

Warwickshire, the following spring

"Mother, come see. The swans have hatched."

Philipa smiled. Her daughter scampered down the hallway, her nurse on her heels.

"Of course mother shall come and see, my precious one."

Philipa followed her daughter toward the doorway. Looking down she smiled at the way Mary's hair shone in the sun. She was pure blue blood. Everything about her fine and noble.

Unlike Ivy's bastard.

Her daughter was perfection and legitimate. Joy filled her heart but it died in a sizzle when she gazed across the yard to see Ivy. The strumpet was big bellied once again and the gossips whispered that this time it was a male child. "Look Mother!" Mary pointed a chubby hand toward the swans but Philipa had lost all enjoyment of the moment. She glared at her husband's mistress. Alice, her lady companion, spoke softly.

"You must reconsider my lady and invite your husband to your bed once more."

Philipa turned on Alice in a sweep of the finest milled wool but her servant stood firm in the face of her displeasure. Alice had all but raised her and the disapproval drawing Alice's features tight was hard to face, even for a mistress of the house as she was now. Inside she was still a little girl who had answered to Alice and taken discipline from her hand.

"He might send you back to your father with a divorce, my lady. It's your duty. You need only give him a son."

"But what if I birth another useless daughter?" Philipa shuddered. "You heard the midwife, Alice. My hips are too narrow. If Mary had been a bigger babe . . . I might . . . have . . ."

It was too horrible to finish saying. Alice shook her head in sympathy. "My lady, the first babe is always the hardest. Give the lord a son and your position will be secure. Then let the Copper girl bear the rest."

Philipa's entire body shook as she pressed her thighs tightly together beneath her skirts. Just the thought of birthing made her body run as cold as an icy winter river. She could not do it. She wanted to live. Not die in a pool of her own blood.

"I will not, Alice. I shall not ever bed my husband again! I swear it! Even if it means he sends me back to my father."

Philipa felt her tears easing down her cheeks as she looked back at Ivy. Envy flowed into her heart, filling it. She welcomed it because it drove her fear away. Hate began to grow as she embraced her temper. An intense aversion for Ivy and her bastards and for everything they took from her, filled her heart.

She hated them. Hated, hated . . . *hated*.

Chapter Two

"**H**urry up with you, Anne. The mistress is in a snit today."

"As if that's any change."

Joyce shot a stern look at her charge, her nose wrinkling. "Mind that tongue, miss. She is your better, above you, placed there by God."

Anne lowered herself, while balancing a tray of morning offerings for the lady of the house. She did need to mind her tongue. However, not for herself. She had little care for her own comforts yet it was a poor child that heaped burdens on her mother. Lady Philipa wouldn't punish only her. The lady would cheerfully lay her wrath on Anne's mother as well.

With a sigh she followed Joyce toward the west wing, hurrying so that the tray would still be warm when the mistress was roused. Polished silver domes covered the mistress's morning meal. Each was ornately carved with flowers and birds, the precious metal heated over the fire before being placed on top of each plate to retain the heat.

She, herself, had risen with the first rays of dawn in order to be present when the lady of the house was ready to be woken. That duty had been hers since she began her woman's flow. The first few months, her wrists had ached from the weight of the tray with its silver, but now she was steady as she moved. Philipa had ordered that Anne dress her each morning to ensure that Anne slept in the maid's chamber behind the kitchens under the eye of the housekeeper. There would be no trysts. Her body was expected to remain virgin.

The reason was simple. Even bastard born, her blood was too blue. Philipa might detest the very sight of her and her siblings but she was also a keen mistress of the house. She wasted nothing, overlooked not one single resource. Anne's blood might be useful in some marriage negotiation. There were lesser knights who valued noble, blue blood in a wife. It was also just as likely that Philipa would see her as a courtesan, serving on the whims of some fat merchant. Whatever the lady had in mind, she had yet to unveil it.

So, Anne stood silently as the bed curtains were opened and Philipa turned her head to look at the assembled staff. Her eyes roamed each of them, inspecting their uniformed livery from pressed cap to skirt hem. Philipa missed nothing. Her lips never seemed to smile and her face bore the wrinkles to prove it. A painting in the lower hall showed her in her youth when she had been a bride, but there was little of that sparkle left in the woman before her. Anne watched Philipa through her eyelashes as the line of maids lowered their heads in deference.

"My feet were cold last night."

The covers were drawn back as the lady sat up. Plump pillows were moved behind her back as she adjusted her position.

"The fire was not laid correctly; the coals lost their heat."

None of the maids said a word. They lowered their heads each time Philipa spoke as they moved in a practiced team around the chamber. The heavy tapestry curtains were pulled aside with a care for how expensive such fabric was. The huge fireplace was quickly cleaned of its ashes and another fire built to warm the chamber. Anne waited until the lady looked settled before placing the tray across her lap. She was careful to make sure that the small brass legs of the serving tray didn't touch either of her mistress's legs but slid smoothly onto either side to hold the tray above Philipa's thighs.

The lady began to inspect what was hidden beneath the polished silver domes on her morning tray. Her lips pressed into a hard line as she dropped one dome back over whatever the cook had prepared.

"Tell the cook to present herself at noon."

Every maid tensed just the slightest amount because they had all been the unfortunate recipients of the lady's displeasure before. The cook would not have a pleasant day. Philipa began eating one of the offerings while she watched the servants with a critical eye. Every one of them had learned to move on carefully soft steps, so as to not bring notice to themselves. All eyes were kept downcast for fear that the mistress might single them out.

"I am ready to rise." Philipa dropped her eating wares with a clatter. The tray was removed almost in the same instant. Another maid pulled the covers down to the foot of the bed.

Anne joined the maids bringing in water to begin dressing the mistress. Depending on Philipa's mood, it might take up to two hours to dress their mistress. The maids flowed around Philipa cleansing her feet and hands before easing the knitted stockings up each of her legs. A fine chemise was lowered over her head and a quilted petticoat followed. It was a lovely garment, the harsher wool covered with expensive cotton from India and thousands of tiny stitches worked in pleasing designs to hold it together. Even in early spring it was needed to keep the lady warm. Warwickshire was the last estate under English rule before the land belonged to Scotland. The lord of the manor was constantly being summoned to court because of his importance as a border lord.

Anne missed her father greatly.

Times were good when the earl was in residence. Her lips twitched and she clamped them back into a firm line lest she offend Philipa. But her heart was happy as she thought about her father. Her mother was always filled with joy when he returned, even dancing at her age when the front riders burst through the gate to announce the approach of the lord of the manor. He had been at court all winter. Four long months of Philipa's sour disposition to tolerate without his loving attention. He did adore her and her siblings but clung to tradition. Philipa was the lady of the house, so Anne fell under her direction.

Still, it was better than many others had. She had a roof over her head and food on the servants' table below. There was a good wool dress on her back and shoes on her feet that had been made for her, not passed on from someone else. There was much she had to be thankful for. One unhappy mistress was less than many had to suffer.

At least Mary wasn't at home.

Anne shuddered. The legitimate daughter of the house was a mean-hearted bitch and she didn't feel a bit of shame for thinking it, either. Mary whined like a babe and could throw tantrums better than a madwoman. Even going so far as ripping good fabric because it was not as fine as something one of her friends attending court had. Philipa coddled such outbursts, finding money in the estate coffers to buy the things her daughter demanded.

Anne frowned as she faced away from Philipa. More rightly put, it was she who found the funds that made Lady Mary stop her howling. By tradition the ledger books should have been kept by Philipa and the duty taught in strictest detail to Mary.

'Twas not the case here at Warwickshire. After seeing to the
duty of dressing Philipa, Anne would spend the rest of the daylight hours and even more into the night ensuring that the estate books were balanced. Her lord father had insisted that
she and her siblings be educated. Yet Philipa was the one who
directed where their education was put to use. Anne's duty
was the estate books and making sure that the budget was
tight. Every time Lady Mary demanded more gold, it was Anne
who was set the task of finding it where the lord would not
notice. The funds were found either from the sale of lambs or
from the cloth woven by the household staff. Anne hated seeing the waste. Warwickshire would be stronger if it wasn't
being plundered so often for vanity.

A heavy thud came from the door. A maid hurried to open
it. As the wide wooden panel swung wide, the ringing of the
wall bells became clear.

"The master returns, madam."

Philipa scowled. "Well, finish dressing me you lack-wits."

Everyone hurried while keeping their eyes lowered. Anne
handed things to the other maids because she'd learned to
keep out of the mistress's reach when she was getting ready to
receive her husband. Philipa was quick with a slap when she
was anticipating a conversation with the earl. One of the girls
fumbled a shoe and there was a sharp pop of flesh on flesh.
"Get out."

The maid lowered her head even as she backed toward the
open doorway. A bright red splotch marked her face. Anne
tightened her courage and knelt to take up the shoe.

"Why is it I am cursed with the worst staff in England? These
Warwickshire families all breed idiots for daughters."

No one spoke but a few stares met behind the mistress's
back. Disgruntlement was shared with silent glares. Anne stood
up, grateful to have finished her task. Philipa eyed her when

she failed to lower herself promptly upon standing in her eye-sight.

"Bastard."

Anne hurried to give her deference. Philipa sneered at her. "Bastard born means conceived in sin. Better be grateful that the church has pity, else you never would have been baptized."

"Yes, madam."

Truly the insult didn't hurt. She had grown scars long ago from Philipa's lashing tongue. It was much easier to endure than her slaps.

In a flutter of silk skirts, Lady Mary flew into the room.

"Father married me off! Oh, Mother, I don't want to go to Scotland."

Lady Mary flung herself at her mother, crying on her chest loudly. "Tell me I don't have to go, Mother. *Please*." She began wailing loud enough to wake the dead. Huge tears flooded her eyes as she tore at her mother's dress.

"Tell him I won't go to any Scot's bed."

"That's enough out of you, Mary."

Everyone in the chamber turned as the lord of the castle entered. Even crowned with silver hair, he was no less powerful, no less the master of the home. Even Philipa lowered her head in deference, dragging her daughter with her.

"And I'll be damned if you will shame me, Daughter. It's a solid match with young Brodick. He's already a titled man."

"Of Scots." Mary's lip protruded as she whimpered.

"Times are changing, Daughter. We'll soon be a single nation, united under a Scot-born king. McJames will be a good match, better than many of your court friends will have."

The earl looked at his wife but his attention strayed to Anne. Anne couldn't stop her lips from curving upward in welcome even as she lowered her head. A sparkle lit her sire's eyes but there was a low hiss from Mary as she noticed the exchange. Anne's half-sister looked over her mother's shoulder, hate glittering in her eyes.

Her father stiffened, his gaze returning to his wife's. "The Earl of Alcaon's retainers should be here within the week. I was only granted leave to escort Mary home. I leave for court at daybreak." He pointed one thick finger at Mary. "You'll take your place as I've arranged it and there will be no more tears. Childhood is finished. See to it, Philipa."

"Must she marry?"

The earl scowled. "Good God, woman! She's twenty-six years old. This child has turned up her nose at every match I've laid before her. There will be no more discussion. It's my own fault for giving either of you a say in the matter. Mary should have been wed four years ago but I tried to wait until she agreed with a match or brought me one of her own thinking. Madam, it's been eight years since we placed her at court."

"But he's Scots, Father."

"He is an earl, madam." Mary sank back as her father moved toward her. "A man whose land borders ours which makes him a fine choice as husband for you."

Mary sobbed louder and her father made a low sound of disgust. He turned his displeasure on Philipa.

"You see there, Wife? This is the only child you had to see to and she is a whining whelp, ungrateful for the good match that's been made for her. What would you have of me, Daughter? Would you be a spinster? Or one of those disgraced courtier friends of yours with bastards growing in their bellies? There are not many lords who will have you due to the fact that your mother never birthed a son."

Mary shuddered and stood up, her eyes round with horror. Her head shook back and forth as her father glared at her. Anne did pity her half-sister; the world was most cruel to daughters because they carried the stain of their mothers. Because Philipa refused to give her husband an heir, Mary was suspected of being a poor choice for a wife as well.

"Aye, now you're seeing the truth of the matter. Another year and who will have you? It's time for marriage and children. 'Tis not an engagement, Daughter. You've been wed by proxy. Young McJames was not in the mood to be delayed by having to wait for a wedding to be arranged. The matter is sealed. You are now a wife with duties to attend to."

The earl turned and left, his spurs clanking against the stone floor. His men followed, having witnessed the entire event. But Philipa was oblivious to the maids in the chamber with her. Privacy was an extreme luxury. As wife to an earl, Mary would have to learn to deal with the many eyes that would know her every movement. Better now than on an estate she was expected to manage.

"Mother, you must give me Anne. For the books. I don't know how to keep them."

Anne's throat constricted as she caught the look her half-sister aimed at her. It resembled the way the lady looked at a new mare she was considering buying. Philipa turned to consider her and Anne lowered her head even as her temper began to simmer.

"Everyone, out! Except Anne, you stay."

Joyce cast her a helpless look as she herded the rest of the maids out the door.

"Come here, Anne." Philipa was in her element, her voice full of commanding authority.

Anne moved toward her without a scuff from her boots. She might be bound to serve the lady but she was not afraid of her. Fear was for children and fools.

"Remove your cap."

The linen head covering was held in place by a thin strap

running under her chin. There was a single button on the left side of it that kept the cap on her head and her hair out of sight. Removing it, she looked at the lady to see what she wanted. Philipa studied her for a long time, her eyes roaming over every detail.

"Leave."

Replacing her cap, Anne made it halfway to the door before Philipa stopped her.

"Have you been attentive in your studies, girl?"

Turning back to face the lady, Anne answered, "Aye, lady."

But not because of your dictates.

Her temper would be the worse for her but she couldn't stop it from rising. Still, she studied hard because learning was something that was a skill. It resided inside her and could never be stripped away.

"Take yourself up to the books and remain there."

Anne lowered her head because she didn't trust her voice to be smooth or anywhere near respectful. Lady Mary getting married wasn't any reason for the mistress to turn sour. Anyone with half a wit in their head had been expecting such an announcement for years. Having to be dragged home by her father—now that was reason for worry. Mary was fortunate her new husband didn't know what a brat she was; otherwise she just might gain her wish and escape consummating the marriage. But that would brand her a spinster and the gossips would have a heyday with it. Suspicion would grow as everyone wondered why Mary was so loath to commit to a marriage that would gain her a better estate than her mother governed. With her dowry to join with her husband's land, their children would live a better life than they did. It was a grand match.

Lady Mary was simply too childish to understand how food appeared on the table when she sat down for supper. Anne knew where the grain for every loaf of bread came from. She knew when the harvest was slim or the sheep not lambing as often as they should. It took a keen wit to balance everything and ensure there was enough stock to see the castle population through the winter. If you sold too much, there would be empty bellies. A true noblewoman was the mistress of the castle, shouldering the responsibilities of running the estate.

"What did she want?"

Joyce was hiding around the corner, the senior housekeeper wringing her apron as she waited to hear what had happened after she left the chamber.

"She ordered me to the books. I'd wager she plans to raid the coffers again for Mary's wardrobe."

"That tongue of yours came from your father. Only a noble would talk that way. Better have a care, girl; the mistress has no love for you."

"I know it well."

Joyce softened her stern look. "Oh, my lamb, I'm sorry as can be. She's a mean-spirited one. You've been a faithful daughter. Your father should be proud of the way you give that sour cow her deference."

Anne felt her face brighten. Her father was home. At least she might enjoy the secret that he'd be in her mother's chambers tonight. He always came when he was home, much to Philipa's disdain. Sometimes Anne suspected that he did it to annoy his fine-blooded wife.

After sunset

Anne hurried along the corridor; her duties had kept her late tonight. A smile brightened her face when she neared her mother's chamber. It was on the far end of the castle, facing north. It could be a bit chilly in the winter but Ivy refused to leave it even when the earl suggested it.

Ivy didn't want trouble. Her family had to live with Philipa while the lord was away at court. The lady had given her the chamber, so she would be content in it. Winter chill or not.

Anne opened the door. Yellow light shone out from several candles.

"There's my girl. My wife claims you're the worst maid she'd ever had to tolerate."

"Good evening, Father." Anne lowered her head, for once meaning the respectful gesture. Her sire nodded with approval. His face was unreadable for a long moment before he spread his arms wide.

Anne flew into his arms, laughing as he squeezed her tight. He released her and thumbed her nose.

"You're a good girl to not complain. Nothing pleases my wife but 'tis not your fault."

"I promise to try harder tomorrow, Father."

The earl smiled. "I know you shall. Just as I know that Philipa will still be unsatisfied. But I am not here to talk about my wife."

He laughed as he reached for Ivy. Drawing her close, he placed a kiss on her cheek. "I have missed you all very much."

"Tell us about court, Father." Bonnie, her parents' youngest child, eagerly awaited her father's tales.

The earl held up a thick finger. "I suppose I might tell you about the mask the Earl of Southampton presented last week . . ."

Bonnie wiggled with excitement. Anne enjoyed watching her younger sister. She reached for a dried fruit sitting on a plate. The humble table that often held only porridge and whey tonight offered fruits, scones and small beer. Brenda must have snuck the fruit tarts out of the kitchen in response to the tongue lashing Philipa had given her that morning. Such treats were only made for the mistress of the house but since the lady of the manor didn't know the first thing about how to prepare a meal, her servants could retaliate by using more than they needed. Philipa would have a fit if she witnessed Anne's children eating the same fine fare that was presented to her and Mary.

That fact made the tarts taste so much better.

Anne tried to reprimand herself for thinking so meanly but failed.

The rich fare made for a holiday humor but it was her father's attention that all the occupants gorged on. The chamber was lit well into the night, laughter spilling beneath the doorjamb. When Anne finally sought her bed, her heart was full.

No, Philipa's insults could never puncture such love as Anne had from her father. The mistress of the house might believe herself powerful but she could not break the bond Anne's sire had with her.

Everyone had something distasteful to bear in life. Philipa's disdain was hers to bear. It was nothing to worry about. It was, frankly, not important at all.

Sunrise

The Earl of Warwickshire swung up into his saddle with as much skill as any man riding with him. There were no fine clothes on him, but good English wool to keep the chill at bay. Anne watched from a second-floor window, the shutters pushed open, her sister Bonnie sharing the last view of their father.

"Do you think Father will bring you back a husband next time?"

Bonnie, at fourteen, was still unaware of the harsher realities of being born out of wedlock. Of course, the entire family went to great lengths to shelter her. Bonnie would grow up soon enough.

"I don't know, sweet, but I will try not to worry. Father always takes care of us."

Bonnie laughed, her blue eyes sparkling. "I think he shall bring you a knight. One who earned his spurs doing a noble deed for the queen and she dubbed him a knight with her own hands."

Bonnie sighed, lost in girlish foolishness. Anne couldn't help but enjoy the moment. Even she liked to believe that there was happiness for everyone. Tugging on Bonnie's hair, she smiled at her.

"Maybe that knight is waiting for you to grow up."

Bonnie's eyes glittered as her chin dropped and her mouth hung open in surprise. "Do you really think he might?"

"I do. Every town from here unto London knows what a treasure you are. You will likely have to choose between suitors."

"You are teasing me." Bonnie's lips twitched. "That isn't very nice. I might become vain."

"Now, sweet, I am but joining you in your daydream. You wouldn't deny me that pleasure, would you?"

Bonnie lifted a hand, waving to the earl. Their sire spurred his mount and started for the outer gate. Anne left her hands on the wooden window casing because she knew that her sire would not turn to look back. He never did. Philipa and Mary stood on the front steps, in their place as the ladies of the house. Her father never looked back at them when he left.

"You will have a husband, Anne, I dreamed it last night."

Anne pulled the shutter closed, ensuring the lock was secure. Casting a glance down the hallway and back the other way, she shook her head at her sister.

"Bonnie, you know what Mother has told you about your dreams."

Bonnie refused to be contrite. She raised her chin high in stubborn display.

"Well, I did dream it and I'm only telling you because you're the one he's coming for. By next spring you will have a baby growing in your belly. It will be a boy born before harvest moon. I saw it. Do not fear, you will not die."

A shiver went down her spine as Anne stared at her sister. Bonnie had the sight. The whole family knew it and tried to cover it up. There were men who burned people at the stake for less. With the queen so old, the local magistrates wielded their power with iron fists.

"You told no one else?"

Bonnie shook her head. "You know I promised Mother I wouldn't talk about my dreams. Only it was about you, and Mother did say no one outside the family, so I haven't broken my word."

"Very good, sweet, make sure you hold your tongue. Knights don't like women who act like ravens, chattering all day long."

"But he is coming for you, Anne. I saw him on a black steed. He has a huge sword that he wears on his back like the Scots we saw at the faire last spring."

Anne shook her head. "Lady Mary is married by proxy to a Scot, not I. That is what you saw."

"No, I saw you. I saw him riding into the lower courtyard looking for you. He has midnight eyes."

There was a part of her that was tempted to listen to her sister, but Anne silenced it. Life was hard. Taking solace in girlish dreams wouldn't help her. All that would do was make it harder to shoulder whatever burden Philipa placed upon her shoulders next. Joyce and the rest of the household staff could dream of love but not her. Bonnie would learn that soon enough. Their father's blood was as much curse as blessing and there was no way that she might ever have a true love.

None.

McJames land

"You're in a foul temper and that's for sure. I thought this was what ye wanted."

Brodick McJames snorted at his brother. Cullen snickered softly in return.

"I cannae marry for my own desires, Cullen. Her land borders ours. The dowry will increase McJames' land. And it's nae just land; it's fertile, rich farms with water. If her father has no more legitimate children, the entire estate will someday pass into our hands."

"Well, I still say ye sound mighty angry about it considering how good it is for everyone." Cullen reached for an oat cake but he didn't bite into it. "Maybe it's the bedding that has you so worried. You know, Brother, not every man is as blessed as I am. You shouldnae be envious of my skill with the lasses. That's a sin."

"So is bragging."

Cullen flashed his teeth at him. "Not so, I'm telling the truth. My cock is . . ."

"Save it for the lasses, Brother."

Cullen laughed as did a few of the men sitting nearby. Brodick stood up, pacing away from their campsite. Cullen had the right of it; he was in a sullen mood for sure. Fetching his bride should have been a duty that he took to in a lighter frame of mind.

It was a fine match, to be sure.

Good for his people, good for his children, but that didn't change the fact that he was dreading taking an English court lady back to his home. He'd been to the English court and would cheerfully go to his grave without ever setting foot in the place again. The women were conniving, deceitful creatures with more paint on their faces than the highlanders wore into battle. The dresses they wore were great hulking creations that hid the natural shape of a female, taking away any interest he might have had for them. Except for their breasts. His temper flared as he considered the way those court ladies had taken to painting their nipples because their dresses were cut so low that you could glimpse them. He wasn't a jealous man by nature but neither would he wear the horns of cuckold. His English wife would display her nipples only to his eyes.

And that only fouled his temper further. Looking down onto the border, he cursed under his breath. In spite of their land joining, he and his intended bride were as different as night and day to one another. He wouldn't allow her to behave shamefully and that would make her hate him. Their union held little hope of being peaceful much less pleasurable. Being the eldest, it was his duty and it weighed his shoulders down.

And Cullen didn't know why he was foul tempered. With a snort, Brodrick kicked a rock. He was saddled by tradition to take a wife who would enhance his peoples' lives. It was his lousy luck that that woman was going to be discontented in his home.

But he was the Earl of Alcaon.

Pride filled him as he drew a deep breath. Being an earl meant more than lowered heads as he passed. It was something he'd spent years earning the right to wear. His northern borders weren't as peaceful as his southern ones. When his father had taken an ax to his leg during a skirmish, it had fallen to Brodick to lead the McJames' retainers. In a lot of ways, he preferred battle to marriage. Stiffening his resolve, he looked down onto the English land that was shortly to become his.

In a way marriage was exactly like battle—only the strong became victorious. He'd claim his English bride and plant a

McJames son in her belly so that the dowry would remain his. He was the McJames, a McJames who didn't know how to lose.

Warwick Castle

"Lady Mary is taking a bath and you're to attend her."

Brenda the cook flung her words over the hissing of water as it was poured into twin copper jugs sitting on top of the stove. She poked the fire in the belly of the huge stove, adding a thick log.

"Wait for the water."

Rubbing her eyes, Anne looked at the stove. The flames mesmerized her tired eyes as she resisted the urge to let them close for a few moments of needed rest.

"Here now. No napping for you."

Anne laughed. "Oh 'twas a late night but a dear one."

Brenda grinned. The water boiled and Anne placed a wooden yoke over her shoulders to carry the two pots.

"Off with you and don't scald yourself."

Keeping her steps tiny, Anne hurried up the stairs to the top floor. The ladies of the house bathed in their chambers, which called for the hauling of water. Steam rose from the copper jugs as she knocked on the servants' door that would allow her to enter the lady's chamber from a small side entrance. It was even a secret from most of the castle inhabitants, only known to those the housekeeper or cook allowed to be told.

"Enter."

Mary was still completely dressed. Anne stared at her in confusion as she took the hot water toward the tub waiting near the fire. Lengths of linen were warming over a rack and more jugs of water were lined up on the floor for rinsing. Costly French soap was sitting on a silver tray, awaiting the lady.

"Bar the door, Mary."

Mary looked as shocked as Anne did when Philipa spoke. The lady frowned at her daughter. "Hurry up. We need secrecy here. Not whispers among the staff. Unless you have changed your mind, Daughter, in which case, you may bathe."

Mary shook her head and ran toward the door. She dropped the thick wooden beam across it before turning back around to stare at Anne.

"Dump that water, Anne."

"Of course . . ." Anne clamped her jaw shut as she realized that she was speaking. Philipa's eyes narrowed as a faint crimson colored her face. Anne reached for a jug, wrapping part of her skirt over the hot handle as she waited for the lady to blister her ears.

Nothing but the sound of water filled the chamber. Anne reached for the second jug and poured the hot water into the tub.

"Anne, take that dress off and get in."

Turning around, Anne stared at the lady, certain she had misunderstood. Philipa was staring straight at her. The mistress glared at her with firm authority.

"You're to bathe, Anne. Mary and I will help you."

"Here?"

Anne didn't care if her voice wasn't properly smooth and meek. Philipa was clearly soaked with wine.

The lady snickered. It was an eerie sound that sent a shiver down her spine. There was a smile on her lips as Philipa clapped her hands.

"Yes, here. You will get in that bath and wash from head to toe. You are finally going to earn every silver shilling I have been forced to spend on your mother and her whelps. Disrobe. Now."

Anne stared at the woman. Hate was an ugly thing and it

distorted Philipa's face. She now understood why the lady looked nothing like her portrait; her soul was rotten from hatred.

"Disrobe, Anne. You are going to take Mary's place with this Scots earl."

"I'll do no such thing." Anne spoke simply because shock kept her from tempering her response.

Mary gasped at the tone of her voice but Anne spared her little attention. Philipa smiled at her. A slow curving of her lips that sent a shiver down Anne's spine.

"You think not? You shall do my bidding or I shall turn your mother out. Tonight."

Anne gasped, horror flooding her. "My father will not allow such a thing."

"My husband is not here and if I turn your mother out, she'll be dead long before he returns."

Raising a hand to cover her mouth, Anne hid her disgust behind it. "That's murder, my lady. A deadly sin."

"I call it justice." Philipa shook with her rage. She recovered and raised an eyebrow. "It is a simple thing to avoid. Mary is gently bred and has no stomach for a man's touch. You, on the other hand, are the spawn of a light skirt so enduring a few nights with a man using your flesh should not be too difficult for you."

"My mother is a leman. She has no other lovers."

Philipa waved her hand, dismissing her words. "If she's a woman of some character, all the better. I expect that you might have been raised with some sense of responsibility if your mother is as honorable as you say."

Philipa reached for the strap holding Anne's linen cap in place. She popped the button open and pulled it off her head. "You will bathe and dress as I direct you."

"I cannot." Anne's voice did not shake only because of a lifetime of not arguing with the lady of the house.

Philipa snorted at her. "You shall. And mind me well, miss, you will play the part to perfection if you do not wish for your siblings to suffer unkind fates."

Anne felt her eyes widen. Philipa snickered as she noticed the horror on Anne's face.

"Now I have your attention. You will take Mary's place, or I shall see your two sisters wed before dark to the meanest men I can find! As for your brothers, I know a few prostitutes who need husbands. We need to think of their Christian souls. Marriage might be just what they need to make them repent their whoring ways."

"You are despicable." Anne refused to hold her tongue. Even God wouldn't condemn her for stating something so true.

"I am the lady of this house and my word is law."

Philipa waited, her eyes glittering with triumph. She pointed at the bathtub, her face set like stone.

"I am not a liar. I wouldn't know how to deceive a man."

Philipa waved her hand again. "There will be no need for lies. You are the earl's daughter. You are being sent to the Scot's bed. Simply keep your mouth shut and all will be well. When you find yourself with child, you will beg to come home to have your mother at your side when the birthing time comes. You see? Simple."

"Surely you do not believe this earl to be so slow witted as to not notice you have changed his wife for another."

Philipa waved her hand again . "The man is a Scot. I wouldn't expect a servant to understand but they are war-loving people. He'll likely plow you a few times, make sure you're breeding, and take off for more war among their clans. No man has any interest in a pregnant wife and Scots prefer their women uncivilized. He's got a mistress for sure, and your bed won't hold any interest to him once he knows his child is planted in your womb. By the time the babe is born and he comes to see his son, it will be more than a year. Changing places will be easy. The man will not even remember what color eyes you have. Besides, you and Mary look very similar. Mark my words, girl, you'd better set your mind to producing a son."

"I can't be a part of such a foul scheme. My father has bound Mary to this man."

"And I am giving him a daughter, a different daughter, yet still his child. As lady of this house, I can do that."

"You aren't given the power to lie about it. Dishonesty is a mortal sin."

Philipa frowned. "Make your choice, madam. Shuck your dress and bathe or prepare to watch your mother walking out of the gate while your siblings are bound to remain in the castle. The charge of theft should be enough to convince the guards to throw her into the road. With your father at court, whom do you think the captain will believe? The lady of the house, or you?"

Chapter Three

Evil

Anne stared at Philipa and knew that what was shining in the lady's eyes was pure evil. Not once in her life had she ever believed that any person might be so horrible. A glance over at Mary showed her another woman who placed her own comforts above the very life of the servants who brought them those comforts. There was no hint of mercy on the younger lady's face, either; only a slight fear that Anne wouldn't bend to the whim of her mother.

But to take her place in the wedding bed . . . Anne shivered, unable to grasp such an idea. To agree to such a bargain made her no better than a whore. A woman reduced to using her body to buy what she needed.

But there really was no choice to make. She would choose her love for her family above herself. Reaching for the button on the top of her doublet, she pushed it open.

"There. I am glad to see you behaving so reasonably." Philipa looked pleased. "Help her, Mary. We have to see this finished before any of the maids become wise."

Anne's doublet dropped away and Mary attacked the tie that closed the waist of her skirts. They dropped to her ankles, leaving her in her chemise and stays. Anne felt Mary's fingers on the ties that closed the corset, loosening them until her breasts hung free. Any other time, she would have savored the freedom from her stays, but Philipa's eyes dropped to her chest, inspecting her body. Philipa's lip curled in distaste as Mary grasped the hem of Anne's chemise and pulled it over her head. Philipa stared at her bared chest and grunted.

"With plump tits like those, you should breed quickly. I made a wise choice when I had you watched. You'd have a string of bastards like your mother if I hadn't."

"I am not promiscuous."

Philipa glared at her. "What you are is forgetful of your station."

Anne sat down on a small stood to begin removing her boots. She hid her fury as she looked at the boot lacings. It would be most unwise to continue to speak her mind. Her family would be left behind to suffer Philipa's temper.

But she wanted to voice every word she'd ever bitten back. The woman was horrible, an evil consort of demons. No one else could contrive such a plan or force it onto the shoulders of another.

"Hurry up." Mary dropped to her knees and began pulling on the other boot. "We haven't much time." Her eyes shimmered with glee as she removed the boot and yanked Anne's stocking down.

Anne was suddenly shy. She'd never stood nude in front of anyone. Mary got to her feet and went around back of her to pull her braid loose. For such a spoilt child she was better at the task than Anne might have guessed. Her half-sister picked up a brush and began working it through Anne's hair. It looked as though Mary had learned something at court while waiting on the Queen.

"Stand up. I want a look at you."

Anne rose, her hands covering as much of her body as possible. Philipa snapped her fingers at her.

"Stop cowering."

Anne bristled but let her hands fall to her sides. The lady swept her from head to toe, her lips pressing into a hard line.

"In with you, this Scot will never believe that his noble bride wasn't bathed before his arrival."

The water was still warm. It only made her angrier to sink into it and not be able to enjoy the moment. She always had to bathe in a chemise because the bathing tub used by the servants of Warwickshire was not in a private room. Besides, everyone needed help washing their hair or they tracked water across the floor when they went to fetch a bucket of rinse water. The sight of her own nipples was slightly distracting because she rarely looked at them.

The bar of soap landed in front of her, splashing water into her eyes. Her hand shot out, grabbing it out of reflex. Normally, no one simply threw such a costly item.

No one but Philipa, it would seem.

The soft scent of lavender teased her nose as Mary dumped a cup of water over her head. It was cold and tickled her nose. More followed until her hair was completely wet. But the fire was blazing, warming her bare skin. She had never had so fine a bath, never been allowed to wash with scented soap. The French soap glided over her skin. She suddenly understood why Philipa enjoyed her bath so much. If she were allowed such fine soap, she would linger in her bathing as well.

Mary rushed her through the bath, using hard motions of her hands to scrub Anne's hair. Within a quarter hour, Anne stood in front of the fire with the linen wrapped around her body. Despair tried to claim her but she resisted. It was not an easy task but panic would only aid Philipa.

"Surely this cannot work."

Philipa scoffed at her.

"What if the earl wishes to spend a few nights at Warwick-shire before returning to his lands?"

"He's Scots. The man will want to return home with all haste. I hear their clans raid one another when they hear the lord is away. Yet another reason why I will not send my only child to that barbaric land." Philipa shook out a chemise. "No matter if he does decide to stay. I shall tell him Mary is ill. You will remain hidden until he is ready to depart."

"Wear these." Mary handed her stockings. Anne stared at them. The tiny rows of knitted finery were something she had dressed Philipa in but never dreamed to don herself. "You must be ready at all times."

A fine chemise followed, as did an entire dress that was Mary's. It was good wool for traveling but edged in trim that was only for vanity. A quilted petticoat and stays were fit to her body as well. Mary drew a brush through her hair until it was dry and then she braided it.

"There. Now, you will wear a veil when you meet this Scot so that none of the household staff become wise. You will re-main in the upper alcove until I come for you. Make no mis-take, my girl. Cross me and I will turn your mother out without a loaf of bread or a cloak."

Philipa waved her toward the back stairs. Anne went but didn't lower her head before she moved. Instead she stared straight at Philipa, refusing to give her deference. The lady's face turned purple with temper.

"Get you up those stairs, and best you ponder what further defiance will bring on your family. Go."

"Mary, pick up that uniform. You'll have to wear that to leave Warwickshire. We can't have you seen or all our efforts will be for nothing."

The back stairs were dark. A flight of narrow stone steps led to a tower used by archers in time of siege. For the moment, it was where the books of the estate rested because there was no way to enter it except through the mistress's chamber. Hugging her arms around her body, Anne climbed as she felt the chill soak into her bones. It felt almost as though the chill was coming from inside her, and maybe it was.

Her heart ached. Never had she been away from her family. She slept in the maids' chamber, the furthest she had ever been from her mother. It might be foolishness to lament leaving the castle, but it was the only home she knew.

She shivered as she reached the small chamber. She could press her fingers against one wall and stick her leg out behind her to touch the opposite side with her foot. Very little light entered because there were naught but arrow slits in the stone walls. The wind whistled through the narrow openings, sending more shivers down her spine.

Surely she must be dreaming. A nightmare that she would awaken from soon. Her fingers stroked the front of her skirt, finding the lines of trim carefully sewn down the center front. She had helped to make some of it with her own hands, sitting with the other maids after the fires had been banked for the night. With Mary's love of fashion, every pair of hands helped with constructing her wardrobe.

The dress was fine but had not been made for her. The stays were a tiny bit too long in the waist, poking into her hips. She would have to alter it, but dared not do it now. Mary's husband might arrive at any hour.

Actually, her husband.

Anne considered that. She wasn't afraid of men but she was ignorant of them. Having been kept under a strict eye, she had told herself to not look at the boys who tried to gain her attention. It was an unnatural thing to not flirt, and now it seemed it was also unwise. What if the Scot didn't like her? She didn't know how to entice him into her bed.

A shiver shook her as she considered that duty. Maybe she should avoid it. If she produced the baby Philipa demanded, there would be no further need for her. Icy dread closed around her heart as she contemplated the deception Philipa was set on using her to achieve. The lady wasn't above murder. Swallowing the lump in her throat, Anne ordered herself not to panic. She had to think. She needed to figure out a way to get the news to her father. She couldn't tell the Scot about the deception; he would send her home and into Philipa's keeping. The idea of her sweet sister Bonnie being wed made her stomach twist sickeningly. Her father was the only one who held the power to protect her and her family.

He would. She believed that. She had to, it was her only hope.

She would write him a letter. Turning around, she looked at the desk she'd spent many an hour at doing the estate books. Yes. There was parchment and ink.

Yet, how would she have it delivered? Court was an uncertain place with nobles crowding around the Queen. Only an experienced man could see any letter into her father's powerful hand. His secretary often had letters for months before gaining the chance to present them to her noble sire.

Still, she refused to go meekly to her own slaughter. Philipa would kill her, she felt certain of it. If she lived there would always be the danger that the truth might be discovered.

Sitting down, she pulled the cork out of the small inkwell. Made of pottery, it held a generous portion of dark ink. Lifting a quill, Anne dipped it before laying the tip against a new sheet of paper. She wrote carefully, forming her letters with skill. She listened closely for steps, fearing to hear a tread upon them that would interrupt her task.

She sealed it with wax but not the seal of the house. Tucking it carefully into the estate books, she prayed that her father would be home for quartering day, when the household staff was paid. It was still four months away but the master was expected to pay each servant with his own hand. Her father had kept that tradition as long as she could remember, laying her own earned silver in her palm when she had grown old enough to deserve it. She couldn't get the letter to him, but she might leave it where he could discover it. Without the seal, no one would know where the letter came from and hopefully it would be left for the master to open. For once Philipa's laziness might just be a blessing.

Anne prayed as she had never prayed for it to be so.

In the meantime, she would have to employ every tactic she could imagine to keep the Scot from consummating his union. She needed time. A twinge of guilt assaulted her but she shrugged it away. The man was an innocent, but she could not treat him fairly. It was the first time she had planned to be unkind to a stranger but she had no choice. She would lead him on a merry chase, avoiding his touch as long as possible, and she prayed that God might grant her the ability to keep the man at arm's length.

It was by far the strangest prayer she had ever sent to heaven.

Time passed slowly. Anne paced once the books were in order, unable to sit still. She wasn't used to being idle. Her belly rumbled for hours before Mary appeared with a meal near sunset.

Her half-sister shrugged. "I'm not used to serving so I forgot to bring you something at midday." Setting the tray down with a clank, she turned and looked at the small alcove. "Mother says you have to sleep here. I'm to fetch you some bedding. It's so boring waiting for this husband to show himself. Mother

says I cannot return to court until you have a baby. I wish he'd
hurry up."

Selfish brat.

Anne waited until Mary was on her way down the stone
steps before muttering. To the pampered legitimate daughter
of the house she was little more than a strip of fertile land to
be planted and harvested.

Still, she'd be wise to hold her tongue. The alcove would be
very cold at night with no fire. Anne just hoped that the witless
creature remembered to bring her something to keep her warm.

There were no silver domes to keep the food warm. It was
poor fare as well. A bowl of porridge, 'twas cold and con-
gealed. The end of a loaf of bread was lying near the bowl, its
center stale. Two tarts were sitting among the fare, their rich-
ness a stark contrast to the rest of the meal. A tear stung her
eye as she recalled sharing one with Brenda just a few hours
ago. Wiping her tear aside, she refused to indulge her pity. Life
was hard and crying was for children who hadn't learned that
fact yet.

Her belly grumbled and she reached for the porridge. As
hungry as she was, the taste was bearable. There was no serving ware with the food, so she dipped her fingers into it. A
small pitcher of whey sat next to it. Anne frowned as she drank
it. Whey was the weakest part of the morning milk, after the
cream had been skimmed off for butter. But at least it helped
wash the cold porridge down her throat. There was no ale or
cider, nothing else to drink at all.

Steps on the stairway interrupted her meal. Mary huffed as
she appeared at the top of the stairs.

"This will have to do. I can't go hauling pallets from the servants' quarters without raising suspicions."

She dropped whatever was in her grasp on the floor and
turned around, leaving quickly.

Rather a blessing that you don't have the care of any of the horses . . . Anne frowned. *And now you're talking to yourself.*

Washing her fingers in some of the whey, she wiped them on the hem of her skirt. She hated soiling the garment but couldn't think of a better solution. Anne walked toward the heap of cloth on the floor, picked it up and shook it out. Made of thick boiled wool, it was a traveling cloak fashioned with a deep hood to shield the wearer from the weather. The wind blew in the arrow notches, making the alcove as cold as the yard below. Even with the cloak, she would shiver half the night.

At least you have a quilted petticoat . . .

Turning in a huff, Anne looked at the tarts and bread. Her mouth watered but she resisted the urge to eat them. Who knew when she would have more food. It was best to save some. A half filled belly was easier to endure than an empty one.

The sun set and with it the light faded. Candles were locked in a cupboard near the kitchen. They were handed out carefully, to conserve resources. Standing near an arrow slit, she watched the yard below. Light twinkled in the stable as the last chores were done. The retainers walked the walls, guarding as they always did. She was tempted to sneak down the steps and set her letter into the captain's hand but it was such a great risk. Philipa did hold the estate tight in her grip. She'd turned more than one person out without a care for their plight. The captain might take the letter to his lady instead of her sire. With the earl at court so often, many at Warwickshire coveted Philipa's good will.

Despair wrapped around her as she picked up the cloak. Icy fear gripped her heart as she pulled the wool around her body. She was so close to everyone she held dear and yet separated from them. Loneliness sent tears into her eyes despite her efforts to remain strong. With nothing but darkness to keep her company, she didn't have enough strength to fend off crying. Sinking down against the wall, she pulled her knees closer to her body as the night grew colder. Somehow she slipped off into sleep, her mind full of dreams of the fire burning in Philipa's room. She tried to get closer to it, straining toward the warmth but couldn't seem to move, her body shivering so much she was stuck next to the stone wall.

She awoke more tired than when she'd fallen asleep. Her eyes burned as her hands ached from holding the front edges of the cloak tight against her chest. Her body was stiff from sleeping against the hard floor. Her toes felt like ice in her boots. Moving hurt. But remaining still did too.

The first rays of dawn were hitting the arrow slits, filtering in to where she lay. Standing up, she raised her face into those rays to feel the heat lick across her chilled cheeks.

"Riders ho!"

Her eyes opened wide as the call filtered up from below. With a rush toward the arrow slit, Anne searched the courtyard but the gates were still closed. Beyond the outer wall, a blue and gold banner was waving in the distance. It was tiny and dancing because the rider was moving quickly. The captain hurried up the ladder to the top of the walls in his shirt, clearly fresh from his bed. He used a looking glass to study the banner for long moments.

"Alcaon retainers. Sound the muster."

The sergeant rang a large bell attached to the stone outer wall. Men began rolling out of their barracks, buttoning doublets and sheathing swords as they appeared in the courtyard. The banner was still some distance away because the castle was built on high ground.

So the moment was here . . .

May the Lord forgive her enough to allow her to live.

* * *

"Hurry up."

Mary was out of breath and didn't even climb to the top step. She gestured with a frantic hand for Anne to follow her down to Philipa's chamber. Her stomach knotted as she descended, sure that her soul was going lower into damnation with each step.

"There you are. I hope the night has improved your attitude." Philipa was already dressed and looking nervous for a change. "Yes. Good. We are agreed. Mary, fetch her that French hood with the veil."

Mary pulled a brown French hood from a chair. The brim would wrap over her head and down low enough to cover her ears completely. There was a long veil hanging from the back that would reach her waist. It was made of lightest weight wool to keep her neck warm. A second piece of fabric was sewn to the front of the hood. This was light cotton from India. She would be able to see through it but not well. Ladies often wore face veils like it when the snow was flying to protect their makeup. Face powder smeared when the snowflakes melted against the skin.

Mary pushed it down onto Anne's hair, uncaring how the edges cut into her cheeks. She flipped the veil into place, shutting out most of the early morning light.

"Perfect. That shall keep the staff from discovering us." Mary smiled in triumph as Anne allowed her lips to press into a hard line. Out of habit she started to lower herself but froze before completing the respectable movement. Mary frowned, displeasure tightening her face.

A hard thump landed on the door.

"Hide yourself, Mary. Quickly, my lamb."

Mary turned and ran toward the stairs that led to the alcove. Philipa smiled at her back, rare happiness glittering in her eyes. It vanished the moment she looked at Anne.

"Best you recall what I have instructed you to do. As soon as you are with child, tell the Scot you must return to your mother. Even an uncivilized Scot will not deny you that comfort."

The door thumped again. "Enter."

The captain of the guard appeared, lowering himself before Philipa.

"The Earl of Alcaon awaits you in the courtyard, my lady."

"We are ready." Philipa gripped Anne's arm, her fingers digging into the flesh. "Indeed we are."

Indeed she was not nor would she ever be.

"God's breath."

Anne froze as she got her first look at the men awaiting her. They were huge. She might not have risked Philipa's wrath to indulge her whims with a lover but she did know what men looked like, more or less anyhow.

They were much larger than any man she might name, aside from one or two of the villagers. Their bodies were cut with muscle as well. Her eyes lingered on their rolled up sleeves and the amount of bare skin on display. The morning chill didn't seem to bother them; in fact they looked as though they were in prime health. Several wore kilts, pants being the oddity. Instead of shirts, they wore some type of undergarment that had wide sleeves without cuffs. Their doublets were made of leather and most of them fastened only a few times across their bellies. Boots laced up their calves to the knees, with antler horn buttons to twist the strips of leather around. Instead of fashionable livery, every bit of clothing appeared to be constructed for utility. The exception were the kilts, made from long lengths of fabric, woven with several color hues to form plaids. These were blue, yellow and orange plaid. The only uniformity in dress among them was the corner of those plaids resting over each man's shoulder. The fabric was held in place by large metal brooches with pins tucked through them. There didn't appear to be an unfit man among them, and thick swords were strapped to each and every back.

"He will come for you . . ."

Bonnie's words echoed through her mind as one man broke away from the others. His hair was as dark as midnight and his eyes dark blue. His shirt sleeves were tied up at the shoulder, displaying how powerful his arms were. He looked like a Roman statue, all muscle.

"I am Brodick McJames."

Philipa lowered herself, tugging on Anne's wrist to ensure that she followed suit.

"Welcome to Warwickshire, my lord. Please accept our hospitality." Philipa curtsied lower and more meekly than Anne had ever witnessed. But the Scot wasn't interested in her show of deference, his gaze looked past the mistress of the manor to settle on Anne's silent form.

He studied her lowered head, trying to see past the veil. She secretly prayed that the man would take Philipa's offer and linger a few nights. That might undo Philipa's foul scheme before it got a start.

"I regret that I dinnae have time to enjoy your kind invitation. I must return to my land."

"I understand." Philipa spoke almost too quickly but she covered up her glee with a loud sniffle. "Truly I do."

He looked surprised but shook off the emotion quickly. "Good."

His voice was rich and deep, his tone showing he was no stranger to commanding. "I give you my word that your daughter will have safe escort." He climbed the front steps, growing larger with each one. When he stood even with them, his shoulders were above her nose.

"Thank you, sir."

In all her life Anne had never heard Philipa sound so meek. She turned her head to stare at the woman, stunned to see such deception being played out. Philipa's eyebrows rose slightly. "Now, Mary, mind your duty and greet your lord respectfully." A flicker of temper appeared in her eyes. Anne knew that look well.

"My lord."

Keeping her voice low, Anne lowered her head, remaining there for a long moment.

"My lady."

He held out his hand, the palm facing up. A quiver went through her as she stared at it.

Eve must have felt the same quiver when she faced the serpent.

Philipa gave her a pinch and she placed her hand into his. With controlled strength, his fingers engulfed her hand. His large hand completely capturing her smaller one, he pulled her toward him, his eyes trying to peer through her veil. The fact that he could not seemed not to be a reason to linger. He turned, leading her down the steps. One of his men stood with a mare, holding it firmly as the earl walked her to it. Grabbing her skirts in order to lift her foot to the stirrup, Anne gasped when his hands unexpectedly grasped her waist. Her feet quickly left the ground as he tossed her up onto the back of the mare. His men sent out a cheer, their voices chuckling in the morning air. The earl flashed her a grin that transformed his face into that of a boy for a moment before it faded back to the confidence of a man. He watched her grip the front of the saddle and adjust her hips so that she was balanced on the horse side fashion.

"Mount."

He bellowed the command as he swung up on his own mount. The horse was coal black, its eyes flashing.

"I saw him on a black steed . . ."

Anne lifted her eyes to the man on the horse. He wrapped the reins around one powerful hand, commanding the horse expertly. His eyes were focused on her, trying to penetrate her veil as his kilt rose up to show his legs. They were just as sculpted as his arms as he clasped the horse between his thighs. Wheeling about, she stared at the sword strapped to his back. Bonnie's words sent a shaft of apprehension through her.

"You'll have a baby before next harvest moon."

She mustn't.

There had to be a way to avoid it. The man holding her reins kept them, mounting his own horse and pulling hers along. She shivered as the household waved good-bye to her, calling out good wishes. She stared at the wide backs of the men in front of her, each one powerful. Their leader radiated strength as he rode back through the gates. Her mare followed, gaining speed as they cleared the outer wall.

Stiffening her resolve, Anne didn't look back. Instead she looked straight at the wide back of the man she had to outwit. Where there was a will, there was a way.

That was the only thing she had time to think about. Bonnie's dream would have to pass away this time.

She would make it so

There were not enough saints.

Anne gripped the saddle horn tighter, lamenting the lack of heavenly ears to lay her pleas on. Considering her plight, she needed more holy patrons to intercede on her behalf. Her gaze wandered over the shoulders of the earl. He was so powerfully built, she might not have believed it without seeing it herself. She wasn't even sure that it was natural for men to grow so broad.

Yet he appeared in harmony with the huge steed beneath

him. Confidence radiated from the pair as firm hands held onto the reins. He clasped the sides of the animal with his thick legs, his back remaining straight as the horse climbed the steep trail.

Keeping this man at arm's length was going to prove a challenge. To his way of thinking, she was his wife.

Yes, many more saints.

Anne frowned. Praying was all well and good but she needed a firm plan if she was going to give her father time to discover her plight. Her belly grumbled as her horse was tugged further along the trail. Warwickshire Castle grew smaller as the sun moved over them in an arc toward the west. The corset dug into her hip where it was too long. Shifting about only moved the pain from spot to spot until her entire side throbbed. She tried to keep her motions small or at least to mask them by adjusting her seat when the horse moved. Every man accompanying the earl found a reason to look her way. They were clever about how they did it, looking over the trail beyond her or inspecting their dirks sheathed in the top of a boot.

Their curious eyes found a reason to look her way.

Yet she was as drawn to them as well. Their bare knees mystified her. Warwickshire was on the borderlands and considered chilly by English standards. The last pair of English knees she'd seen outside the bathing room were on one of the young groomsmen in the stable, who was still more of a boy and prone to forgetting to dress appropriately. Every man with her now didn't even have their doublets closed. The edges of the leather flapped open, allowing the afternoon air to ruffle the linen of their shirts. The protective sleeves attached to those doublets were tied behind their backs, obviously unneeded to ward off the chill. She shivered just looking at their bare collarbones.

But none of them looked cold. That drew her attention. Each man seemed at ease, most of them eager to be heading home. Their mounts took to the rocky trail expertly. Each horse confident as it picked its way. Not that she might blame them for being jovial. Knowing that you were returning home must be a wonderful feeling.

One she wished she knew. Envy took root in her chest. She hadn't even been allowed to bid farewell to her family.

She resisted the urge to look behind her. Gazing on Warwickshire so far in the distance just might be more than her composure could bear. At least she might keep herself from tears. Crying would be useless. She had so often considered Lady Mary to be weak for all her sobbing. That doubled her resolve to remain calm as the day drew longer. The earl only drew his men to a halt twice. Both times he did it near a river so that the horses might drink.

Her feet were asleep and dismounting sent prickles of pain up her numb legs. She had never sat on a horse so long. There had never been any need to. Horses were expensive and they generated further cost in stables and feed. Besides, her life had been Warwickshire. The villages and the castle proper. Her feet served her well enough for traveling between them. She didn't earn enough in an entire year to even buy a horse as fine as the one she was riding today. Giving the mare a pat, Anne smoothed her fingers over its shiny coat.

"She's a fine animal, to be sure." Turning her head, Anne found one of the McJames' retainers a few feet behind her. He studied her with eyes the same shade as a summer sky. He was fair-haired as well; quite the opposite of the earl.

"Indeed, she is very beautiful."

He lifted a hand to firmly pat the horse on its hindquarter. "Strong. That's what matters."

Releasing the reins, Anne let the mare have her freedom. With a soft nicker, the mare followed the other horses toward the edge of the river.

"My brother bred her from his own stock. McJames' horses are the best in Scotland."

"I can see that."

The Scot peered at her trying to see past her face veil. When she didn't lift it, his gaze slid down her frame, inspecting her exactly as he had the mare.

"I thought English ladies wore gloves to keep their hands soft."

Anne was grateful for her veil because it hid the sudden widening of her eyes. She curled her frozen fingers into fists.

"I forgot them this morning." She cringed because she made yet another error. As a lady, her maid should have seen to the task of fetching her gloves. "When you were spotted approaching, I became flustered."

A grin appeared on the Scot. "Now don't go telling my brother that. His ego disnae need any stroking." He actually winked at her. The playful expression stunned her because she'd never quite pictured Scotsmen relaxed.

"Well then, you'd better take care of your needs before we mount up again." He pointed to a large outcropping of boulders and her face burned scarlet.

"Yes, thank you." Her voice squeaked as her blush deepened. She felt like every pair of eyes was focused on her as she walked toward the rocks. Returning took a great deal of discipline as she ordered herself to stop being so childish. The body had needs; it was no reason for blushing.

More of the men were turned her way now, studying her as she drew closer to the water. The earl was already back on his steed, watching them from several feet above. He scanned the horizon, his face set in hard lines. He wasn't relaxed or jovial. Solid determination radiated from him as he swept the entire surrounding area before letting his gaze settle on her.

Her cheeks warmed again, the tiny response tingling as it went through her flesh. She worried her lower lip as she found herself staring back at him, unable to break the connection. He actually frowned before looking away. Her pride bristled, the hot stain on her cheeks annoying.

How could she blush for him?

And why did he find her unpleasing?

Her anger stunned her, numbing her mind as she tried to decide why she cared what the man thought of her. If he found her ugly, all the better. It would certainly make avoiding the bedding easier.

Yet she could not deny the surge of disappointment that went through her. It was as real as the kilt-wearing men near her. Quite unexpected but still a firm reality.

"The two of you will just have to wait."

There was a male chuckle as the earl's brother returned leading her mare. He smirked at her while offering her a hand to mount. Anne reached for the saddle horn instead, lodging one foot in the stirrup and pushing her body up into the air on her own.

Humph, she'd be very well and good on her own.

"Well now, I've never seen an English lady who could do that. Maybe my brother made a better choice than he thinks."

Looking down at the Scot, Anne was tempted to flip her veil back so that he might see the frown she was aiming at him. It was another impulse, one that was very hard to resist. She found the man grinning from ear to ear, his sky blue eyes sparkling with mischief. Her anger fled as she noted how much he reminded her of Bonnie.

"You know a great deal about English women, do you?"

His lips lowered into a pensive line. "I've attended yer queen's court with my brother, so aye, I know a wee bit." His eyes flickered with something that looked like distrust. "Ye're not exactly what I expected when my brother told me we were off to fetch ye home."

He looked at her with a critical eye that made her wonder just what she was lacking in his opinion.

"As we are strangers, I declined to form any opinions of you or your brother before I met you both."

One of his eyebrows rose. A soft scoff pasted his lips and his eyes glittered with amusement.

"Och well, there's a tone I recall well. Ye English lasses must be descended from Valkyries because ye have the north wind living inside ye. Icy as snow ye are when ye're of the mind to freeze a man with your words."

Anne bit back an apology. Philipa's words rose above her impulse. Becoming too familiar with any of these men was unwise considering the precarious position of her family. Still, she was not the one casting rude comments about. No matter the situation, she was not weak willed.

"My name is Cullen." He offered her a folded cloth. "Here's something to eat. It's a two-day ride to Sterling castle. Ye'll need yer strength."

"Thank you." Her voice was low as she took the offering. Cullen hooked a leather cord attached to a full wine skin over the saddle horn. Her cheeks heated again, this time in shame for being so outspoken. She shouldn't allow Philipa to turn her into a bitter-hearted person. But she held her comments, sealing them behind her lips for fear of what might yet happen to her family. She had to play her role, at least until her sire discovered her plight.

Cullen nodded. "Welcome to the family."

His voice was gruff. She deserved it for being so haughty.

Regret pierced her as he walked toward his own horse. She had regret for so many things that weren't in her power to change. Everything about where she found herself was frustrating. She'd heard a lot of sermons on kindness being the key to unlocking good solutions, but today she was hard-pressed to figure a way to deal with her dilemma in a Christian way.

There was nothing virtuous about her position. It was steeped in sin and the stain was smearing with each word she spoke. Philipa had truly poisoned herself with hatred because no woman with a heart could send someone into such a situation.

But being correct didn't help her. All of her reasoning and justifications of being the victim failed to fend off the guilt chewing on her. Truly, speaking to the saints was unlikely to bring her any help. Not when she considered that all of those holy figures had martyred themselves rather than act unchristian.

Even knowing that didn't open her lips. She kept them sealed and sat, firmly resolved to play her assigned role as the earl motioned them forward.

Her counterfeit role.

Chapter Four

The earl didn't call a halt to their travel until the sun was almost gone. Only a pink stain colored the horizon when his hand rose and the horses all stopped. His men seemed to know exactly what his gesture meant because they dismounted and began making camp.

The spot he'd chosen was sheltered in trees, their branches forming a camouflage of sorts. There were few leaves on them but several large boulders rose up out of the earth to join them. One rock was smudged with dark black soot. Two of the retainers set about building a small fire in the same spot, while another couple of men gathered up the horses. They removed the bits from the mouths of their mounts, but made sure each bridle was secure. They knotted a length of rope to each bridle draping several feet between each horse to keep them from wandering apart during the night. One man climbed up onto the rock outcroppings, propping his back against some of the tree branches. He pulled his sword from its scabbard and propped it against one thigh.

The rest of the men talked in low voices but she couldn't miss the lightness of their tones. There was also the distinct Scottish sound to their words. Loneliness clamped around her like a steel vise, tightening with each foreign detail she noticed. With a sigh she turned and walked toward the river. She could hear the water rushing and babbling but it wasn't in sight. She had to walk over a rise and the water was below her. Paying close attention to her footing, she made her way down the slope. The wine skin hadn't been filled with sweet wine but water. Still it had been welcome as her lips dried out in the winter air. Propping a foot on a rock, she was mindful to toss her skirts over her thigh before leaning down to refill the skin. The night air brushed her bare skin above the edge of the knitted stocking, raising gooseflesh. Once full, she straightened up, placing both feet firmly back on the bank. Giving the top a twist she secured it before looking up.

She gasped as she came face to face with the earl. He was only two feet behind her, his huge body impossibly large. She jumped away from him without considering how close the river was. Her heels sank into the moist soil, the wine skin dropping into the mud as she tottered off balance.

His hand snaked out, capturing her wrist. Warm, hard fingers curled around her limb, jerking her away from the river. She slammed into his chest, unsure if she wouldn't have preferred the cold water behind her. Her eyes widened as his arm slid right around her back, securing her in place.

"Are ye actually intent on running off into the night?"

There was no mistaking the anger that colored his voice. He frowned at her, distrust etched into his face.

"I simply wanted to refill the skin."

He snorted at her. "And ye just did that little chore without telling anyone where ye were going. Slipping off into the darkness quiet as may be."

"I certainly didn't think of it like that."

But she should have. It was another error. Mary would have sent someone to fill the skin, never mind that there were the horses to tend to.

"I'd appreciate ye staying with my men. We don't need to be fetching ye away from the men of any other clans that stumble upon ye without escort. If ye've no care for the harm they might do ye, have a bit of concern for the blood that will be spilt when we have to fight to take ye back."

Her mouth formed a little round expression of horror. "I want no one fighting over me."

His face was as serious as an executioner. "Be very sure of that. I dinnae let anyone take what is mine, madam. Run away and I'll fetch ye back."

His words were as hard and unrelenting as the arm binding her to him.

"I wasn't fleeing."

He snorted, clearly doubting her. Anne snapped her lips shut because her temper was rising. Labeling him a presumptuous clod wouldn't help matters. However, she could at least take solace in the fact that insulting him was definitely something Mary would have done. His lips pressed tightly together as she failed to answer.

"Are ye ever going to take that thing off yer head? I thought it was against the law to be a nun in England."

Anne raised her chin to find the earl frowning at her again. His eyes were a darker blue than his brother's.

Midnight eyes . . .

She shivered, a chill shooting down her spine. His eyes narrowed as the hand pressing across her back felt the ripple of reaction. Heat bled across her cheeks once again as she inhaled the scent of his skin. Her belly suddenly tightened with the oddest sensation. With a hard shove she tried to escape from his hold.

He scoffed at her. A soft sound of male disgruntlement. "Since ye've been at court, I don't see the need for feigning innocence, Mary. I'm nae the first man that's held you."

Her eyes widened as he retained his hold. His arm was like steel, binding her to his body.

How presumptuous. "I pretend nothing, sir."

His gaze narrowed once more. A moment later her French hood was tugged off her head, pulling her hair as he plucked it free. He studied her face for a long moment before releasing her.

"I'll be the judge of that matter myself."

One foot plunged into the mud as she placed distance between them. A flicker of amusement entered his eyes as he stood blocking her path, using the river and his larger size to keep her at his mercy.

"If ye've become accustomed to loose morals at yer English court, best ye ken that I will not be shamed."

Her chin lifted, no amount of better judgment interfering. "You've made yourself clear."

She pushed past him, uncaring of how close she was to his body anymore. There were very few things she had the right to call her own, but she wasn't a lightskirt.

"Good." Command edged his voice. He followed her up the bank. "It pleases me to find yer face beneath that veil instead of a courtesan's, all covered in paint."

He reached out, stroking a finger over one of her cheeks. "Aye, I am pleased."

She shivered again, this time in some odd response to the way his tone had softened. He was no longer angry with her.

Anne turned quickly to hide the strange reaction from his keen stare. Her face was hot where he'd touched it, the skin oddly alive with sensation. There was a part of her that liked hearing that he approved of her. A man such as he was far above any that she might hope to have of her own.

"Face me, Mary."

Hearing her half-sister's name was like icy water being tossed onto her feet. She turned slowly, struggling to conceal her emotions before facing him once more. This man would not take being deceived very well. Now that her face veil was gone, she needed to be more attentive to concealing her feelings.

"I've no taste for timid women."

The gruff tone of his voice annoyed her once again. "You may always return me home." She looked at the ground, doing her best to look like a coward. For one brief moment hope flickered in her heart that he might reject her.

"You should take me to my father. He is returned to court."

A hard hand cupped her chin, raising it to lock stares with him. "It's clear you've been at court. That place is ripe with schemes." His lips lost their hard line as he stepped up closer holding her jaw in a firm grip. "Do I really look like a man who would cry surrender so soon after greeting ye?" He chuckled, the sound sending a quiver through her belly. His warm scent filled her head with each breath as he tilted his head so that his breath teased her lips.

"You dinnae know very much about Scotsmen, Wife. We're nae intimidated by a few cold glances. In Scotland, we're more practiced in the arts of warming up our women."

He touched his mouth to hers and she jerked away from the contact. It burned clear through her, all the way to her toes. Her freedom was short-lived. With a twist of his larger body, he snaked an arm around her waist. He moved toward her in the same moment, surrounding her and pinning her against his hard body.

"Now that won't do." He pulled her flush against his frame, tight enough to feel his heart beating. His gaze settled onto her mouth as he slipped a hand up the back of her neck to hold her head. "It won't do at all. Kissing my new wife is something I'm nae in the mood to miss."

He touched his mouth to hers again, this time slowly. She

twisted in his embrace, too many impulses shooting along her body to understand. The few kisses in her past had been stolen ones and brief. Brodick lingered over her mouth, gently tasting her lips before pressing her jaw to open for a deeper touch. His embrace imprisoned her but not painfully. He seemed to understand his strength perfectly, keeping her against him with exactly enough force, but stopping short of causing her pain.

She shivered as the tip of his tongued glided across her lower lip. Sensation rippled down her spine as she gasped in shock. Never once had she thought that a touch might be so intense. Her hands were flattened against his chest and her fingertips were alive with new desires. Touching him felt good. She opened her fingers wider, letting them smooth over the hard ridges of muscles that his open doublet had allowed her to see. Pleasure moved through her in a slow cloud that left a haze over her mind. Forming thoughts became slow and cumbersome as he teased her upper lip, tasting her.

"Much better."

His eyes were full of male enjoyment now. It was mesmerizing, so much so, she stared at him, forgetting that keeping him at arm's length was in her best interest.

"I see the pair of you dinnae seem to be interested in supper."

Cullen's voice was full of glee. Anne felt her eyes widen in horror. She pushed against the hard chest beneath her fingers. Brodick frowned, a dangerous look entering his eyes. His arms released her a moment later as he turned to glare at his brother.

"You don't look like my manservant."

Cullen smiled like a boy. "You don't have one."

"Oh, but I do, Cullen. Ye see, the man is wise enough to be invisible—like ye should be."

Cullen began walking toward them in spite of the growl in his brother's voice. He winked at her as he drew closer.

"Now is that any way to act in front of the English lass here? She'll be thinking we're uncivilized."

Brodick snorted. Anne stared at him, trying to decide if she'd really heard such a sound from an earl. "Most English think the word Scots means uncivilized."

The earl looked back at her, his words sounding like a challenge. His lips were set in an arrogant expression of enjoyment. The man wasn't sorry about stealing that kiss. Not one bit.

"No one might label you indecisive, that much is for certain." Anne glared at him, unsure if she should be annoyed at him for being so bold or herself for enjoying it.

Cullen laughed his amusement out loud against the darkening night. "Are ye sure ye want to keep her, Brother? I think I like her."

Brodick lifted one dark eyebrow as he clasped his arms over his chest. He looked more formidable than Goliath must have—a mountain of undefeatable muscle and brawn.

"I was working on getting to know her when ye so rudely interrupted."

"Och well, ye can let the lass have some supper before ye get around to consummating yer union."

Shock slammed into her as she listened to the word "consummate."

"Surely not tonight!" She shook her head, wrapping her arms around her body. "Not here!"

Brodick returned to brooding, suspicion coating his features.

"What reason would ye have for denying me, Wife?"

She was in dangerous waters now, that place that she had fretted about all day. How did she put the man off when he held all the legal right to claim her? Brodick's gaze shifted to her mouth for a moment, and the tender skin on her lips tingled. Her hand rose to cover them as she tried to understand why his kiss had been so pleasurable.

"Ye didn't seem to be minding all that much when I was kissing ye." He stepped closer and she shivered, the damned impulse sending a ripple along her spine in spite of her need to think of a way to avoid his touch.

"Maybe the trail doesn't meet yer standards, my lady." His voice was full of mocking scorn now. The Scot in him was clearly offended that she didn't care for his country. "Perhaps it's too primitive."

"I find your country quite pleasing but there are standards expected and we must make sure to follow traditions." Her mind was working frantically as she held a hand out in front of her. "Yes, traditions."

"I heard ye the first time."

Taking a deep breath she forced her heart to stop racing while she considered her next words. "My lord, I meant no inconvenience; however, I have but one maidenhead and must be careful that it is intact for my husband."

"I am yer husband." He stepped toward her, his arms uncrossing.

Anne held her chin high, refusing to cower. Little David had felled Goliath after all.

"Yet, I have not been inspected and it is possible that after that task is seen to, you may wish to rethink our union."

A smirk appeared on Brodick's face. "Well lass, that's exactly what I was getting to doing when my brother showed up. I'll be happy to inspect every bit of ye. Personally."

Cullen frowned, his face darkening. It almost looked as though he might be jealous.

"Now that is ludicrous."

"I disagree." The earl was back in full commanding form now. "I believe that inspecting my bride has full merit."

"I'll not be inspected by you."

"And why not?" He glared at her as formidable as she'd always heard Scotsmen were. This was not a man who would bend simply because she told him no.

Anne stiffened. "Because you are not a midwife. What could you possibly know about a woman's body?"

His lips twitched up again as his attention dropped to her chest. Heat snaked along her skin until it touched her breasts behind her stays. Her nipples actually tingled as her lips had done. A sudden picture of him kissing the tip of her breast blossomed inside her mind, sending a torrent of heat through her blood. It was heavy with dark temptation to allow him to do it, to discover if it felt as delightful as his kiss had against her lips.

"I assure ye I know a great deal about the gentle sex."

A flame of jealousy touched her as she listened to the mocking tone of his voice.

He has a mistress for sure . . .

Philipa's words rose from her memory as she raised her chin stubbornly, determined to not allow herself to be used without a struggle.

"Lust has no bearing on a woman's fertility. Inspection of a bride is done by a senior midwife and sometimes the groom's mother, but it is not something to be mocked, sir. I might spend tonight as your leman and find myself on my way back to my father at sunrise with no one to defend me."

She moved a few paces up the hillside, toward the camp and its many pairs of eyes to offer her sanctuary.

"Yer mother should have seen to having ye inspected."

"It is customary for the groom's family to choose the midwife. Everyone knows that. You could easily refute my mother's midwife." It was a tradition that went back for centuries. She should have recalled it sooner. When a woman was married by proxy, her dowry was legally in the hands of her husband's family. If he sent her back to her father, it might take years to fight through the legal system to regain the monies and lands. By the time the battle was over, the discarded bride was often too old to marry and ended her days a pauper, dependent upon her relatives for everything.

The tradition of inspection protected a woman because if a senior midwife pronounced her fertile and strong, there was no court that might annul the marriage. In a world run by men, it was a woman's saving grace when fate took babes to death early or worse still, a bride failed to conceive. Some midwives even boldly suggested that some men might be sterile. Such a charge was rejected among men of course but midwives still maintained their authority on the subject of whether or not a woman's hips and womb were correct for bearing children.

"Inspection before consummation is custom in both our countries."

Brodick's expression darkened. Clearly the man was not accustomed to having someone else upset his plans. Anne stood tall, facing his displeasure. It was something she was going to have to become familiar with. Becoming compliant would land her on her back in his bed.

"Now I know I like her." Cullen sounded gleeful, exactly like a younger brother teasing his older sibling. The only thing missing was a governess chasing after him, to tug on his ear.

"With family like ye, I dinnae need enemies."

Cullen didn't flinch under the force of Brodick's words, instead he grinned. But the earl stared at her, trying to buckle her under his fierce displeasure.

Oh, he was angry. Even if she was a virgin, she instinctively understood what was flickering in his eyes. It was as old as time and part of her in a way she didn't truly understand yet. But she felt her belly tighten and her nipples draw into hard points. Something inside her was awakening.

"Leave us, Cullen." There was an edge of undeniable authority in his voice. The playful expression melted off Cullen's face before he nodded his head in acknowledgment. The younger brother turned and left them, moving up the hill and into the darkness. The sun was completely gone now, leaving her alone in the night with Brodick. The sound of the river would mask their words as well.

"What game are ye playing?"

He spoke quietly but she wasn't lured into thinking that he was relaxed. She'd heard her father use that tone before and nothing good had ever come from it. There was a hardened nobleman in Brodick who managed his people with an iron hand.

"Answer me, lady. Why are you avoiding our union?"

"I'm not."

He snorted. "Are ye a coward?"

She held her denial behind clenched teeth. "I have displeased you. You should send me to my father."

A soft male chuckle was her response. He was half in shadow in the moonlight, his frame lit with silver light. For a moment, it felt as if they were in some fairy ring. She watched his hand move, fascinated by the play of night shadows.

"Clearly that is what ye want."

His hand landed on her waist, the fingers hooking into the thick cartridge pleats that formed the skirt. With a jerk, she tumbled into his embrace. He locked an arm across her back, securing her as he captured the back of her head in one hand.

"But I would never have survived very long as the Earl of Alcaon if I gave up so easily. Fortune favors the bold."

He kissed her again. This time it was a demanding press of lips. The hand on the back of her head held her in place as he took a deeper taste, his kiss pushing past her protesting lips until her mouth opened to allow his tongue to delve inside. She twisted in his arms, unable to sort out all the impulses racing through her. His scent filled her senses, unlocking desires she'd never encountered before. She wanted to touch him. Her fingertips felt sensitive and longed to discover what his bare skin felt like. She sought out the opening of his shirt where she'd glimpsed his flesh. His tongue invaded her mouth, seeking out hers. He teased her, stroking along her tongue until she allowed hers to tangle with his. It was a wicked dance that sent pleasure through her, the sweet intoxication sweeping aside all thoughts of what she needed to do. All that remained was what she wanted to do.

His mouth broke away from hers, trailing kisses along her cheek. She shivered as the skin of her neck begged for a touch from his lips. Her fingers pushed deeper beneath his shirt so that her entire hand might be flush against his body. Her heart was thumping hard, working hard.

"Ye shall have your inspection, lass, but ye'll also have a taste of frustration."

A tiny bite was placed on the column of her neck before he released her. She stumbled as he let her go and the night air cruelly swirled around her. The separation of their embrace made her shiver. He cupped her chin, a hint of a scowl on his lips.

"Ye'll take the same longing to sleep tonight that I will, and maybe by sunrise you'll cease talking about returning to yer father."

He clasped both sides of her face, holding her for his kiss. This time he didn't begin with teasing touches. His mouth took her, pushing aside her effort to hold him off. His tongue thrust deeply inside, stroking the length of hers. A tiny moan caught between their joined mouths as desire pounded through her. It didn't begin softly this time but rose instantly. His mouth left hers, trailing hot kisses along her cheek and onto her neck. Never once had she noticed how sensitive the skin of her neck was. Each kiss sent a shaft of need through her. But Brodick didn't just press his lips against her; he used his teeth to gently nip her. Her hands curled into talons on his shirt, an insane impulse to tug the fabric away from his skin making her shove away from him. She didn't understand such an idea or why it was so vivid. Her breathing was rough as she staggered back several paces from him, fear actually tingling through her.

But not fear of him; it was far worse. She was frightened of what she wanted to do to him.

He followed her but forced himself to stop. His body shook as she heard him draw in a ragged breath. He crossed his arms over his wide chest, almost like he needed to keep himself from pulling her back into his embrace.

It would feel good if he did.

"Best ye ken me now, madam. Our bed is not to be a chilly one. Ye can have yer inspection, but when that's past, ye will have done with yer standoffish nature. I'll have none of it."

"Or what? You cannot change who I am. You should take this night to consider how ill matched we are."

"Why would I do that when ye have such passion locked behind that cool exterior?" He stepped toward her and she retreated without thinking. A warm hand cupped her chin, allowing her to feel his strength once again. "I dinna need to change ye, lass, I just need to do my part of introducing ye to yer own nature."

Horror flooded her as she shook her head. The fingers cupping her chin tightened, stilling her denial.

"Aye, lass, ye kissed me back and that is all I needed to ken. We'll learn to make our union work. But feel free to deny that yer body is burning with need. Tell me yer nipples aren't hard."

They were.

"You shouldn't say things like that."

"I shouldna state the truth? We're married, it's nae a sin to discuss passion."

He ran his hand over her face, clicking his tongue as his fingers stroked the blush the night covered up.

"Ye're blushing for me. It's a basic form of communication. Yer body is trying to attract my attention and I find it very pleasing." His thumb pressed down onto her lip and her breath caught as sensation erupted from the touch.

"Most couples in our station aren't so lucky."

He removed his hand, slowly, and her skin begged her to lean forward just a tiny amount to prolong the contact.

"I've been negotiating with yer father for over two years and I'm nae going to give up just because ye don't value a union between us as much as I do. Our marriage is for the benefit of more than just the pair of us. Better set yer mind to thinking about all the people that will have better lives." He moved closer again, curling his hands around her upper arms. He leaned close so that she could see his face clearly in the dim light.

"Best ye ken that Brodick McJames will nae be told no by his own wife. You are mine, madam. We shall share a bed . . . often, and I intend to kiss each of yer nipples."

He turned her loose, giving her a push towards the camp. She stumbled but regained her footing.

"I belong to no one." The words left her mouth before she thought about them.

"Well now, that's something I'm going to enjoy showing ye the error of yer ways."

Her words were far too bold for any woman, even a queen. Women did have a harder life and their male relatives held a great deal of authority over them. That was the law in both England and Scotland. Brodick wasn't abnormal in his thinking that she belonged to him. Every court in the land would agree with him.

"Up to camp with ye, as ye have a mind to see tradition honored. I agree that it is the custom in a marriage such as ours. Once the midwife pronounces ye fit to bear my children, maybe ye'll settle down. I suppose a maiden is allowed to be a bit nervous the first time her husband kisses her. Even if ye do learn the art of kissing quickly."

"'Twas more than a kiss . . ." Anne shut her mouth quickly before her ignorance showed any further. She'd never known that a man used his tongue when kissing.

His teeth flashed in the moonlight. "Aye, that it was and such a delight when our tongues mingled."

Heat speared through her as she stared at him. She was frozen in a moment of shock mixed with excitement, her lips tingling and clamoring for another moment beneath his.

"Does that look mean ye've changed yer mind?" He hooked her around the waist once again, closing the gap between their bodies so that the chill of the night was cut off. He handled her so simply, his strength far superior to hers. "Ye don't appear to be very interested in returning to camp."

"You're distracting me, my lord. I'm not accustomed to turning my back on someone who is speaking to me. I was taught that to do so is rude."

"Leaving yer lord with unrelieved desire is also unkind."

Her eyes widened but her chin rose, too. Brodick gritted his teeth before baiting her further. It was his duty to act with honor, not taunt her into a passionate tryst. At least that was what he had heard. When it came to marriage, he was inexperienced. Now women, he liked them and didn't enjoy waiting to claim what he desired.

He didn't give a damn about a midwife's inspection. But it was the custom and he'd be acting like an uncivilized ruffian to refuse her request for tradition to be honored.

"Join the others. Now."

She pulled in a harsh breath, clearly annoyed with his tone. But she kept her lips sealed and even lowered her head slightly before turning and climbing to the top of the hill. Brodick remained where he was, taking a moment to fill his chest with the night air. It didn't do much to cool his blood.

But that wasn't something to lament. Or so most of his fellow noblemen would say. Having a hard cock for your wife was surely the least of worries considering how ill matched most noble unions were.

He shrugged as his own thoughts failed to fend off a sour disposition. His cock was hard and he wasn't in the mood to be placated by counting his blessings.

What he wanted was to investigate just how much more passion was locked up inside his English bride. That damned face veil had hidden quite the surprise. Her unpainted face was like discovering ripe strawberries in the dead of winter. Her kiss was just as sweet as those same tempting fruits. Letting her go was a test of his discipline and he'd come very close to failing it.

Still . . . it was a fine feeling indeed to know that he craved his wife. Even if his cock was throbbing and bound to ache for the next hour, at least he wouldn't have to worry about how he was going to breed her. Too many grooms made wedding contracts that benefited their people but ended up with limp cocks when they got a look at their brides.

His was standing stiffly at attention, eager for the consummation.

He chuckled as he began moving toward his men.

Well now, it was a surprise that he was going to enjoy full well.

That it was.

She'd never guessed that a man might feel so good pressing up against her, never even considered such an idea since she was forbidden lovers. It was like discovering a hidden treasure of feelings locked deep inside her.

Anne snorted.

'Twas more like stumbling across Pandora's box. Keeping everything inside was the best course of action. Failing to do that might seal her fate.

Still, she couldn't quite banish the memory from her thoughts. Maybe that proved Philipa correct; she was like her mother.

A wanton.

She scowled, grateful for the darkness. Her mother loved her father. It was a curse, that emotion. Love wasn't a wise choice for anyone. It drove men insane and drew women away from their families. Many doctors labeled it an affliction similar to insanity.

She couldn't think of her mother as deranged or her siblings as the product of insanity. There had to be more to it, something that was yet to be understood. It was the age of understanding after all. Men were sailing the ocean and bringing back tales of new lands inhabited by savages.

She should be able to resist the longings twisting her belly. Every inch of her skin was alive with heightened sensation.

She was keenly aware of how soft the fine chemise was against
her. For the first time in her life, she detested her stays. They
felt too tight against her swollen breasts.

Lust . . .

She lifted a hand to cover her mouth, her breath lodging in
her throat. Arousal was nipping along her body, flowing through
her blood like a slow-acting poison. Being a virgin didn't
mean she was ignorant. She knew the realities of the marriage
bed, and had since she was half grown. But lust was another
matter altogether. It led many a woman to ill consequences.

So why did it feel so good?

She should be able to ignore the tingling in her breasts.
Banish from her mind the memory of the way it felt to be held
against his body. Instead the sensation persisted, dancing
through her mind like fairies intent on leading her into the
forest where she would dance forever.

Supper was a quiet affair. The night closed around them,
the fire a welcome friend. More oat cakes were offered to her,
their dry texture making her grateful for the full skin of water.
She shivered as the wind whipped through their campsite.
Most of the men had buttoned their doublets now, including
the sleeves. They pulled part of their kilts loose, wrapping the
wool around their bodies to keep warm. As far as practicality
went, she was beginning to understand why they wore kilts.
The Celtic standard dress required no sewing and could be
adjusted for warm or cold weather. All-in-all a rather inge-
nious way of dressing.

"You'll be wanting this tonight, ma'am."

The thick cloak that she'd spent last night huddled in was
offered up by another man. This one considered her with dark
eyes. She took the cloak and he tugged the corner of his knitted bonnet in respect.

"I'm called Druce and we're cousins now by yer marriage."

He watched her wrap the cloak around her shoulders, his expression pensive. "On account of yer husband's father and mine were brothers."

So he was a noble-blooded man as well, yet still riding with the rest of the men without any finery to set him apart. She found the lack of arrogance in her escort a refreshing change. Each man earning respect instead of expecting it because of who his father was. They were every bit as strong and capable as their retainers.

She found it quite admirable.

Possibly too much so, because she was battling the urge to like them. As a people, she found the Celtic men more appealing than she had ever thought she might.

"Thank you."

"No need to fret about sleeping out in the open. There'll be a good watch posted. Scotland isnae as wild as you might have been led to believe."

"I have faith in my father's judgment."

Druce offered her a grin. "That's the way to think of it. You're a good daughter to trust yer sire. He's nae sent yer off with barbarians, no matter what ye may have heard."

Her cheeks warmed slightly. "Well . . . gossip should not be believed. It is rarely true."

He chuckled at her. Druce pointed towards the ground. "Ye'll want to settle in and get some sleep. Brodick will have us up at dawn. Mark my words."

All that much better for getting me to his bed.

Her thoughts were sordid. She laid the blame on Brodick. Before he'd touched her she'd never known lust. Now it wove along her bloodstream like wine, diluting her better sense.

She walked over a spot a few times, feeling for stones with her feet. She kicked a few of them out of the way before lying down, using the cloak to shield her from the dirt.

There was the sound of metal being drawn and she sat up, her heart freezing. The flicker of the campfire flashed off the blade of the earl's sword. He held the thick handle in one hand while untying the strap that held the scabbard to his back. It came free and he replaced his weapon in the protective leather before taking a last look around. He was deadly serious as he noted each of his men before nodding approval. He turned, aiming his attention toward her. Anne was suddenly grateful for the deep hood of the cloak; it gave her means of shielding herself from his probing eyes. His lips were pressed tight as he sat down next to her.

Too close to her.

He placed his sword on his right side before jerking his kilt up to cover his back.

"Relax, wife. It is the normal custom for married couples to sleep alongside one another. I don't see why ye're so tense considering yer fondness for traditions."

His lips twitched and she shot a glare at him that she didn't even care if he disliked it or not. His humor was misplaced.

Brodick lay down but rolled onto his side facing her. He propped an elbow against the ground and let his jaw rest in his hand. He lifted a dark eyebrow before using his free hand to pat the dirt next to his large body.

"Come lay by me, Wife." Thick amusement coated his voice as his lips twitched again. He patted the ground, taunting her reluctance. His brogue had thickened and mischief sparkled in his eyes.

"Unless I frighten ye too badly."

She lay back, shutting her eyes to ignore him. He chuckled at her and the sound ruffled her pride. She lost her will to keep her eyes closed.

"You think too much of yourself, my lord. You are but a man, no different from many, many others."

She kept her voice low but he heard her. Instead of taking offense at her insult, he grinned. He reached across her body, keeping her shoulders pinned to the ground as he leaned close to her face, hovering above her lips. Tense anticipation tightened around her as she felt the brush of his breath on the delicate skin of her lips.

"It will be my pleasure to introduce ye to the differences, lass." He pressed a firm kiss against her mouth. It was hard and inescapable, his chest keeping her in place as his mouth took what he wanted from her.

But it felt good. The kiss blew against the coals of the passion he'd sparked in her by the river. When he lifted his lips away, her breath was uneven.

"I'm looking forward to being in a more private place tomorrow night. There be a world o' difference between knowing the men around ye and knowing a husband."

He lay down beside her but remained on his side. She felt his stare on her as she tried to banish the feel of his kiss from her lips.

She forgot to pray as her body tingled and longed for more kisses.

Along with ones applied to her nipples.

Her thoughts made her sleep restless, and she turned and twisted on the hard ground. She opened her eyes half a dozen times during the night, staring at the shapes of the men around her. Her mind tossed about the idea of escape but she conquered that weakness by thinking of her family. If she ran away, she was abandoning them to Philipa's wrath.

A soft grunt filled her ear as Brodick shifted. He reached across her body and hooked her around the waist. Pulling her snug against him, he kept her still as she wiggled in his embrace.

"You need some rest and so do I," he whispered into her

ear as his front pressed against her back. She was a great deal warmer with his body sharing his heat with her. But she also caught his scent and it awakened the need that had been so hard to resist while he kissed her. She shifted, trying to find some way to escape the smell of his warm skin.

"Keep rubbing against my cock and ye'll have to live without that inspection."

She gasped, looking around them, but his men had lay down several paces from them. His lips grazed her neck. His hand slid down to her belly, keeping her still as his lower body remained in firm contact with her bottom. Even through all the layers of her skirt and cloak, there was the unmistakable bulge of his cock. It was hard and her passage suddenly felt empty as though she would enjoy having it invade her sheath.

"Ye see how well suited we are."

"Lust does not prove compatibility."

He raised his head so that their eyes met in the dark. "It is a fine place to start." He rubbed her mons, boldly touching it for the first time.

"*Stop that.*"

"Ye're my wife, mine to touch by blessing of the church and yer family. Why would I stop doing something that yer face tells me ye're enjoying?"

Pleasure burned up her passage as his hand moved. His eyes glittered as his lips thinned. There was no mercy on his face as his hand remained over her mons, moving in a steady motion.

"Close yer eyes and sleep or I'm going to take ye back to the riverbank to settle this question. Keep waking me up and it will be yer duty to entertain me, Wife."

She closed her eyes in spite of her temper. Several retorts formed in her mind and she bit them back. A soft kiss landed on one cheek before he pulled his hand away from her mons.

He settled it around her waist, clamping her against him from toes to chin.

"I'm nae a brute, Mary. But avoiding me will nae make this adjustment any easier. Some things are best done quickly. That way ye nae have time to dread them."

She scoffed at him, the sound leaving her lips without thought. He chuckled, nuzzling against her neck for a long moment before settling back behind her, his scent keeping her passion alive and hot. She tried to sleep once more but her body wasn't interested in rest. It longed for more touches, more pleasure. Her clitoris was pulsing softly with need as her passage craved penetration. There was no escape from the lust as long as Brodick held her tight against him. Her body wanted his and she couldn't escape thinking about him while he held her. Time stretched, the night longer than any she had ever endured.

Chapter Five

Brodick rose before the sun. He huffed as he got to his feet, his expression disgruntled. With one hooded-eye look, the earl walked away to rub the neck of his horse.

"That cloak is too bulky for riding." Druce held out a hand for it.

Surrendering the garment took courage because the morning was chilly. But the Scotsman was correct. If she tried to sit side-saddle on the mare with the fabric beneath her hip, she'd likely land on the trail in a heap.

"Here, lass. You have thin blood." Cullen draped a thick surcoat over her shoulders, pausing to wink at her. "We only left your trunk behind, nae your clothing. It's all tied to the back of one of the mares."

Anne fingered the surcoat, grateful for its warmth. With deep slits up the sides, it allowed for riding while wearing it. It was wool, edged in true velvet. The expensive fabric was neatly sewn around the openings to the arms and where the front closed. Carefully knotted silk cord frogs ran down the front of the loose gown. She noticed a loose thread and plucked it free. Staring at it, she looked down the front of the coat to see others sticking up. All were evenly spaced, denoting where pearls had been placed. Mary must have spent several hours removing the pearl beads from the clothing that had been sent with Anne. All of her court-loving sibling's garments were embellished with pearls, gold, and even some gems.

Cullen had rejoined the men, their voices gaining volume as the sun rose. Clutching the surcoat close, she enjoyed its warmth. Even if the pearls had been removed, it was a fine garment, thick and sturdy.

The black steed was missing. Lifting her chin, she scanned the trail, searching for the earl. There was something very comforting in keeping the man in sight. She found him sitting much further up the slope, his eyes on the horizon.

"Will ye stop undressing the man with yer eyes, lass? I'm becoming jealous."

Cullen led her mare to her, his voice full of mockery.

"I am not . . ." The idea of undressing Brodick got stuck in her throat.

"Nae what?" Cullen smirked at her.

"I simply am not." Reaching for the saddle horn, she lifted her foot and lodged it in the stirrup. A hard hand pushed her up, square on her bottom, making her gasp.

Cullen wasn't repentant a bit when she cast a disgruntled look at him from atop the horse. He tugged on the corner of his knitted hat.

"You're welcome."

He swatted her mare on the flank and she took to the trail. The mare eagerly climbed toward the earl, as the rest of his men mounted. They surrounded her, keeping her mare between them, Brodick watching from his position above them. As they drew closer, she thought she noticed a satisfied smile on his lips, but he turned, showing her his broad back before she decided.

"Sterling." Brodick's voice echoed in the early morning as his hand rose, the fingers clenched tight in a fist.

"Sterling," his men answered, their cheer almost deafening.

Even the horses appeared to catch on to the enthusiasm of their riders, picking up their hooves faster. A flicker of excitement surprised her, washing through her as she looked up at the back of the earl. His men followed him happily and without fear. It was a stark contrast to the years she'd served Lady Philipa. Every servant under her spoke against the lady when they were below floors. She hadn't truly realized just how bleak Warwickshire was until she saw the opposite displayed by Brodick's men. For a brief moment, Anne allowed herself to enjoy the tide of contentment. But she couldn't take solace in it too long.

Her position was not going to improve once they arrived at Sterling. It was only going to become harder to avoid Brodick and his expectations. A little ripple of guilt hit her. She didn't want to disappoint him. Shocked by her own emotions, Anne tried to resign herself to following her plans. Postponing the consummation was critical to her survival.

Yet a flicker of passion flared up as she considered Brodick's back. His hair was slightly curled, and long enough to brush the top of his shoulders. His shirt was tied up at the shoulders, displaying the hard cut of muscle along his arms. Her memory offered up exactly how good that strength felt.

Pandora's box . . .

Tension pooled in her belly as she recalled how his kiss had awakened her flesh. It made her bold, those kisses. The sort that sent good women down a road paved with disgrace. With a shake of her head, she chewed on her lower lip, trying to concoct some reason to delay the inspection.

There had to be a way . . . she just had yet to think of it.

Warwickshire

Ivy Copper hugged Bonnie tighter than normal.

"Mother, is something wrong?"

Cupping Bonnie's fair cheeks in her hands, Ivy smiled. "No, sweet, I am just a mother and we always see our children as babes."

Bonnie gave her another hug before dancing off across the chamber. "I must go or be late. We are weaving today. No more spinning or carding wool."

Ivy waved her towards her duty, waiting until she heard Bonnie's steps diminish before allowing her guard to drop and worry lines to appear on her face.

Anne was gone from the castle.

Worry filled her as she began to pace. None of her children had ever left Warwickshire. Perhaps she was foolish to let it unsettle her, for the young often traveled, but she could not stop her mind from turning and twisting. She feared that something was amiss even though her common sense told her that she was only enduring a mother's grief.

She wished the earl were in residence.

At least that thought brought a measure of calm to her. She always wished that Henry was near. How could she not? She loved him too much. Yet she was not alone in that insanity. Henry adored her and had always treated her well, far better than most lemans. He had never strayed from her side even when her belly was swollen, even now that the years were passing too quickly.

Love . . .

It was their gift.

Everything would be well. Even if Philipa had taken Anne to town with her and Mary, there was nothing amiss. Henry's wife might harbor meanness toward them but she would not risk the anger of her husband by doing anything that was truly evil.

Anne would return in the summer, and she would hug Bonnie tighter each day until her family was reunited.

That was a mother's path.

Sterling

Sterling rose up from a hillside. Its towers were great polished round structures, each one six feet wide and three sto-
ries high. There were five of them, spaced out in a line. Behind
them was a drop-off that protected the back of the castle from
invaders. Thick walls connected the towers, the blue and gold
standard of the McJames flying from it. The men sent out a
cheer as the distant sound of bells drifted with the afternoon
breeze. There were two gates set into the stone walls. That was
a curiosity, since castles were constructed to withstand sieges.
Having two gates meant you needed twice the men to protect
the weakest spot.

Villagers began appearing from their homes. They called out
to the men, cheerfully welcoming them home. The fields were
still only carefully turned plots of earth, but the sun was warm
on her face, hinting at springtime. The villagers' homes dotted
the land around the castle, telling her that Sterling was a pro-
ductive land. In another few weeks there would be work aplenty
for everyone as planting began. For now, the villagers emerged
from their homes where they spent the winter months working
with leather and cloth, producing goods that might be traded
or sold.

Brodick headed for the north gate, his men close on his
heels. But he did not ride through the huge opening. He
turned and caught her in his sight. There was a chuckle from
the men in front of her before he kneed his mount. The black
beast surged toward her, a magnificent display of power. Brodick fit with the picture, every bit as strong—master and steed
were well suited. He pulled the horse to a stop only inches
from her, reaching out to grab the reins of her mare. He controlled the nervous sidesteps of her horse, keeping the bridle
down until the mare stopped prancing.

A wicked gleam twinkled in his eyes as he released the reins. He stood up in the stirrups and leaned over. A hard hand hooked her around her waist before he pulled her across the space between the horses. She clutched at his hard shoulders, desperate to avoid falling. His men laughed, their voices hearty.

Brodick laughed as well, but his voice was deeper and right next to her ear as he settled her in front of him. His arm clasped her to his body, securing her tightly. Her body became alive with all sorts of tiny impulses. Each breath drew his scent into her head. She'd never noticed that men smelled different or that she might have a preference for one in particular. A little wave of enjoyment went through her as she drew in the warm scent of his male skin.

"What are you doing, my lord?"

He leaned down until she felt his breath against her ear. Gooseflesh spread down her neck and beneath her stays in response.

"Practicing a few of my own traditions. The McJames brings his wife into the castle for the first time." His fingers spread wide, covering her belly. "Mind you, the situation hasnae always been this . . . civilized."

She shivered. The kitchen at Warwickshire had often been alight with tales of Scotsmen and their raids on fellow clans. More than one marriage had come about due to the bride being carried off. A wedding after the bedding was often the case among the Celtic clans.

"I confess that there are some traditions I like more than others, lass. Riding off into the night with you is something I believe I'd enjoy. The negotiations with yer father were dull."

"But dealing with my father ensured you the dowry you sought."

The hand on her belly moved, rubbing over her torso. Her breath caught in her throat as she felt the brush of his breath on her neck and the skin became abnormally sensitive, anticipating the touch of his lips.

"Ah, but having ye sitting on the front of my horse, pressed against me, is far more stimulating." His lips grazed her neck and she started as sensation coursed through her. There was a soft chuckle beside her ear before he pressed a second kiss to her sensitive skin.

"It feels like ye agree with me, Wife."

Brodick didn't wait for her reply; he wrapped the reins tightly around his knuckles and dug his heels into the belly of his steed. He leaned forward as the powerful horse leapt forward, moving in fluid motion with the animal, his hips thrusting gently forward. The arm clamping her to him ensured that their bodies moved in unison. A blush burned across her face as her body instantly connected the motion with that of being intimate. Brodick would ride her as smoothly as he was riding the horse, his motions steady and strong.

She had never been one to believe completely in the Church's teachings about keeping women ignorant to keep them from sinning. Since meeting Brodick, her mind was shifting to better understanding of why the Church believed that way. Just knowing that the man intended to take her maidenhead was giving rise to thoughts of lust. In sooth, she had difficulty banishing the heated ideas from her mind. All she seemed to do was linger in thoughts of how his kiss felt or how much she enjoyed the steady thrusting motion of his hips behind her now. Heat spread down her neck and across her body, the skin on her belly begging for contact with the hard hand lying on top of her doublet. The strange sensations didn't stop there either; they flowed down lower, touching her sex.

She drew in a ragged breath as she felt her clitoris flicker with need. Never once had she felt so interested in entertaining a man.

"Welcome to Sterling, Wife."

Brodick rode through the gates, keeping her tightly clasped against his body. She felt more like a captive than any sedately negotiated bride. People filled the lower courtyard, their voices raised in a cheer as Brodick galloped toward the steps that led up into one of the stone towers. He pulled the horse to a stop, a cloud of dust rising up around them.

"I bring ye yer new mistress."

Brodick's voice was full of command as he dismounted. She was suddenly the center of attention, every set of eyes on her. Unused to the attention, her chin began to lower, but she caught herself and held her head firmly in place.

She was not a coward and would not shame her father by acting as one.

Two hands encircled her waist, pulling her toward the lord of the manor. She reached for his shoulders, letting her hands grip him. The onlookers cheered as Brodick brought her to the ground. His gaze flickered with heat as he held her for a long moment.

"Welcome to my home." His voice was gruff, and guilt assailed her. She was helping to steal the moment from him with her deception. The man deserved better.

Suspicion clouded his face as he watched her, but the crowd wasn't in the mood to wait. They jostled Brodick in their quest to get closer to her.

"Later." There was a warning contained in his voice, one that pierced her heart because although she might not know very much about him, she trusted that he was not a man who would allow anyone to dupe him without retribution. She suddenly dreaded the day he discovered the deception.

He turned around, keeping her hand in his grip. Striding

forward, he took her up the stairs and into one of the round towers.

"Sterling is larger than Warwickshire. Mind that ye don't get lost." He turned his keen stare towards her. "Or wander off. The neighboring clans are not as welcoming."

"Listen to you." A dark-haired girl boldly interrupted Brodick, aiming a finger at his chest. "Ye'll have her cowering beneath the covers of her bed, thinking Scotland is full of bloodthirsty savages."

"And that's what I love about it." Cullen added his comment as he hooked the girl around the waist to pull her into a hug. She hissed at him, wiggling.

"Stop messing my hair, you oaf."

Brodick squeezed Anne's fingers, and returning her attention to his face, she stared at the unguarded expression. It reminded her so very much of her father when he was behind the closed door of her mother's rooms. There was an enjoyment of the banter that hinted at family intimacy.

"This is my sister, Fiona. She's vain concerning her hair."

Fiona tossed her head, settling one hand on her hip. She looked formidable, much more so than any titled lady Anne had ever seen.

"I am only vain if you don't have standards above those of the stable animals, Brother dearest."

Brodick frowned, aiming a hard look at his sister. "I take pride in my horses. Best kept animals in Scotland."

His stern reprimand made Anne laugh, a soft sound escaping her lips before she stilled it. Brodick's eyes narrowed.

"I don't need the pair of ye uniting in an effort to annoy me." His tone was stern but his eyes glittered with amusement.

"But I appreciate it full well. I've been the lone woman at this table for far too long." Fiona offered her a bright smile that drew a groan from Brodick.

" 'Tis a fine season for weddings."

Fiona lost her teasing look. "When pigs smell nice." She stood up enjoying the way all the men at the long table stopped talking to tug the corners of their bonnets in respect. The ease that the younger woman dealt with so much male attention was admirable. Fiona sent her a smile. "I'm too young to wed. Convince my oaf of a brother for me please?"

Anne couldn't resist the teasing mood. With a sigh she shook her head. "Better to take yourself to the chapel for I am learning that your brother is as set in his ways as an old man."

Cullen and Druce laughed. Fiona smiled. "Well that is a fact. I do hope for the best for yer union in spite of it."

She strode away, her body a tightly leashed bundle of energy. Cullen clicked his tongue.

"You know, that sister of ours is going to drive some poor man insane."

"She's already doing it." Brodick shook his head. "To me."

Cullen smirked. His brother offered him a deadly look before his midnight eyes returned to Anne. His mood changed instantly, heat entering his gaze as his eyes settled on her lips for a moment.

"It seems we have some traditions to observe, my lady. I wouldnae want to keep you waiting."

Yet I must keep you waiting . . .

Anne didn't like her own thoughts, not a bit, but she held her chin steady. "I am not so old that you need to rush, my lord."

A soft sound of amusement passed his lips but it wasn't a cheerful one. He used his hold on her hand to pull her closer, watching her eyes as he did it. He lowered his voice so that it remained between them.

"And I am not so young as to be led about on a merry dance.

I went to England to fetch a wife and that is what I intend to have in my bed this night."

Brodick stood. Half the room did too. Men lifted tankards to down a last measure before leaving with their lord. He lingered for a long moment, almost as though he wanted her to see his power. Even if such was arrogant Anne could not discard how admirable it was.

"I'll set off to fulfill yer request, madam."

Anne rose to her feet. Something inside her demanded she meet his show of strength with steel in her spine. "A safe journey to you, my lord."

With a slow curtsy she quit the room, conscious of how many eyes watched her. Anticipation drew her belly tight but the thing that made her walk fast was the pulsing tempo filling her blood.

It was excitement.

This night . . .

Anne paced the entire length of the chamber, turned and moved toward the opposite wall. She barely noticed the room, so intent on the coming battle with Brodick. She needed to find a solution, some way to push off his demands yet again.

A small bell attached to the door rang. Looking up, she stared at the tiny silver bell. It looked like something she'd seen in the church, used only to enhance the service. This one was hanging from an iron hook with a string tied to the top. That twine passed through a hold in the door.

Someone on the other side of the door pulled the string which tugged the bell to one side. When they released the tension, the bell swung allowing it to ring. The door opened slowly, a middle-aged woman peeked in.

"Ma'am, I'm Helen." She pushed the door wide, hesitating as she stared at her.

"Good day."

Helen nodded before looking over her shoulder. "This way."

There was a scuff of boots before two lads entered with their arms full of clothing. They muttered greetings as they passed.

"I'll see to getting yer things in order. I fear that tying them to the saddle has left most of yer skirts crushed. But it's nothing that cannae be undone."

"Traveling is always hard on clothing. Even with a trunk." Anne followed the boys, reaching for a heavy skirt. Giving it a hard shake, she froze when she noticed the gaping looks being sent her way.

Another error. Lady Mary would have never seen to her own garments.

Her temper rose as she thought of her half-sister. She did not care. She could not change who she was, and she was not pampered nor lazy nor was she going to be able to start behaving as such.

"Thank you for bring my things to me." Giving the skirt another shake, she turned and spread it over a chair. She reached for another item, smiling as she did it. Helen watched her, studying her for a long moment. With an approving nod, the middle-aged woman pointed at the young men.

"What's the matter with ye? Do you think all English ladies are whining babes that don't know a thing about running their own homes?"

Helen sent Anne a smile. "The lord sent me to maid ye, at least until ye decide who ye prefer among the staff. The cook has set some water to boil and the lads here will be bringing the bathing tub up for a bath afore the midwife arrives."

"There's no need to bring the tub up. I will bathe in the bath room."

Helen looked stunned. She opened her mouth but shut it before speaking. Anne snapped another skirt to cover the awkward moment. She had to appear confident in her every motion, else no one would believe her.

"The lord told me to have ye bathe in this chamber as befits yer station, ma'am. It just wouldn't be fitting for ye to join the staff in the bath house."

"I am not accustomed to taking direction from your lord." Anne froze for a moment, attempting to calm her temper. Brodick was the master of the house. A fact that she would be wise to remember. Maybe she wasn't his true wife but there wasn't anyone to stand between him and her should she raise his anger by being peckish in her words. Even Philipa minded her tongue when her noble husband was sharing the same roof with her.

"I am simply not one to waste time, Helen. Hauling water and tubs is wasteful when I'm very capable of walking myself to the bathing facilities. I'm sure that the staff has plenty of tasks and don't need me adding one."

Helen looked surprised, stunned into a moment of silence. She recovered, smiling.

"Now that's a fine head ye have on those shoulders. Indeed, I'm pleasantly astounded." Helen turned to address her helpers.

"Go down and tell Bythe to make sure the tub is ready for the mistress. You two can stand at the door to make sure no one interrupts her bath."

Helen waved them both out the door, command sitting comfortably on her shoulders. She crossed the floor and scanned the piles of clothing.

"Well now, what we need is a clean chemise for ye and maybe that sturdy surcoat ye were wearing. No need to tie ye back up in yer stays if ye're going to be inspected after yer bath."

Anne turned around to hide her uncertainty. It wasn't that she was overly modest, but she was unaccustomed to having her body seen bare.

"Is there a senior midwife at Sterling?"

"Nay. Not one that ye might consider very experienced. The earl and his brother set out for Perth to fetch Agnes. She's been delivering babes for decades. Her wit is sharp as a pike and her eyes still keen."

So he was taking no chance on her disapproving of the midwife. Anne felt the walls closing in on her, Philipa's trap pressing in, making it harder to breathe.

Helen pulled a chemise free, smiling as she held it up. "This is so lovely. I believe the earl will find it quite fetching on ye. We'll brush out yer hair, and won't ye make a pretty bride when we put ye to bed with yer new husband."

Helen pulled the door open, waiting for Anne to precede her toward the bath. Tension knotted Anne's belly but she forced her feet to move.

"There now, no need to be so worried. The earl is a fine man. Yer wedding night willnae be anything to work yerself into knots over. By sunrise, ye'll be lamenting having to leave his bed to see to the day's chores."

That was exactly what she did fear. Developing a taste for Brodick's touch wasn't wise. She was so tired of being caught in the middle. Her life had always been unfair and today she felt the weight of that more than ever before.

But that changed nothing. Placing a corset back on the bed, Anne turned to follow Helen to another bath that wasn't meant for her.

The chamber was on the second floor, the stairs set into the rounded wall of the tower. There was a sturdy hand rail, placed on the open side to keep a missed step from turning to disaster. Looking up, she saw a ceiling that was also the floor of the chamber she'd been pacing across. There was another set of stairs that led to a third floor. With five of the large structures, an enemy would find it impossible to approach Sterling without being seen.

Helen led her to the bottom of the stairs. There was more noise here, the sounds of conversation and steps on the hard floor. She was slightly surprised to see carpets. Everything she knew of Scotland said the Celtic people were less advanced than their English neighbors. She had expected rushes to be covering the floor. The wool carpets were a pleasant discovery. Dry rushes turned musty during the long winter months, collecting mud and dirt as they were walked on. There was no way to clean them until spring when you had them completely hauled away and new ones set down.

Carpets could be taken out into the yard and beaten. At Warwickshire, she'd helped with the task and watched a great cloud of dust rising as a crop was applied. The hall smelled far better, without the stink of months of grime.

"We have a fine bath house. The lord has made sure it's as modern as any in England."

Helen moved past the kitchens, and the maids turned to cast curious looks their way.

"We don't even have to haul the hot water by bucket anymore." Helen preened as she entered the bath house behind the kitchen and pointed eagerly at a wooden trough.

"The lord had that added when he saw one at the house of one of yer English nobles. Ye ring the bell and the cook pours the water and . . . .there ye are. Almost as modern as the Romans had."

It was such a simple idea but one that would save a lot of sore fingers. Anne touched the wooden spillway, shaking her head at the simplicity of the idea. The trough extended over a large slipper tub. A peek inside showed her that it was clean, not sporting rust. As bath houses went, Sterling was no shame. But something near the bottom of the tub caught her attention. A round piece of expensive cork, pushed into the metal side.

"Is there a hole in the tub?"

Helen reached for an iron ring hanging from another hook. She pulled it several times before turning to answer.

"Yes, ma'am. The lord calls that a stopper. Look at the floor and ye'll see another wooden track constructed to let the water carry itself away when ye're done. That's why the tub is set up on blocks, so that the water can flow."

Anne hurried around and sure enough there was another pair of boards waiting to guide the water toward a missing stone in the floor. She couldn't see where it went from there but the idea was immensely ideal. No hauling of water at all. Simply scrub out the tub and bathing was suddenly a simple matter.

Now that was modern thinking.

Water began splashing into the empty tub.

"There now, let's get yer dress off before Bythe sends the hot water."

Helen was already reaching for the buttons that held her doublet closed down the front of her body. She made quick work of it, moving behind her to gently tug the open garment down her arms. There were rows of pegs set into a long piece of wood that ran the length of the walls. Helen hung the doublet on one as Anne began unlacing her skirts. Her fingers were slow as she tried to think of a reason to avoid getting into the tub and thereby put off the coming inspection.

But she could think of nothing, so her skirts were lifted over her head and hung on another peg.

" 'Tis glad I am to see that ye're not padded. The lord didnae care for the court ladies he met. He said you couldnae even tell that they were women for all the steel and padded pieces they strapped to themselves beneath their dresses."

"The queen does love her fashion."

Anne watched Helen take her small hip roll away. It wasn't any larger than her fist and considered modest by most. Worn around the hips, it helped carry the weight of the cartridge pleated skirts. There was the added bonus that it kept your hem away from your feet, making it far simpler to carry a heavy tray because you didn't need a hand to pick up your skirt.

"I heard that the English queen padded her hips a full foot on either side of her body. As if anyone would believe a woman could be so broad."

Helen shook her head on the way to a peg. Anne smiled because it was true that many women wore large hip rolls to give the illusion that they were good child bearers. Prenuptial inspections had become popular in the last decade due to the practice.

" 'Tis glad I am to see that ye're not suffering your monthly curse. That would have put the lord in a nasty humor indeed."

Standing in only her stays and chemise, it was easy for Helen to notice the lack of stain on the cream cloth.

"But it would have been his own fault for not giving you any notice of when he was going to be arriving to fetch ye. I imagine that ye are a wee bit tender having to leave your family without time to truly prepare for the separation."

Helen pulled on the lace securing Anne's stays in place. She tugged and loosened each eye until the stiffly boned vest released its hold on Anne's breasts. A little mutter of delight escaped her because she didn't sleep in her corset normally. Freedom from the steel-stiffened garment was very welcome, her breasts rejoicing in it.

Helen tsked. "You need a better tailor. This corset has worn a hole clean through yer lovely chemise and skin. It's too long on the side." She shook her head as she frowned.

"I wasn't thinking when I wore it."

Helen clicked her tongue again. "I'm glad ye left yer maid behind. The girl obviously lacks a good eye for dressing her mistress."

Yet another little error that proved she was not born to noble station. Mary would have blamed her servant for any discomfort caused by an ill-fitting corset. Such attitudes were the reason that the staff banded together. It took everyone to ensure that the nobles weren't unhappy because if they were the staff would suffer for it. Every new piece of clothing that was delivered to Warwickshire was inspected by the housekeeper and measured to check for accuracy before it ever made it into the chamber of the mistress.

"Sit down, so I can get at yer boots."

Anne made use of a stool. Her chemise billowed up as she sat down. A shiver shook her as the cool air rushed over her skin.

"Don't ye worry, ye won't be cold very long. The lord will tend to that."

Her face burned as Helen pulled both boots off. The maid winked as only an experienced woman could, a saucy smile appearing on her lips.

"Well now, no need to be blushing. Ye're a married woman now."

"As everyone keeps telling me." She leaned down to cover

the disgruntled expression taking root on her face, reaching for one of the finely knit stockings and gently rolling it down her calf.

"Och now, you couldnae have been so surprised to hear of yer marriage. I wager yer governess has been telling ye to expect such news since ye grew enough to need a pair of stays to hold up those breasts."

Anne crossed her hands over her chest. It was a fact that most women understood that they would marry and that they would not choose their groom. In that respect, she was the spoilt one. Lady Mary's governess had often lectured her on the importance of being poised and ready to hear that her husband had been selected.

Helen propped both her hands on her hips. "Ye're a bit of a shy one." Her eyes studied the way Anne covered her nipples. "If I might be so bold as to instruct ye, that modesty will not please the lord."

He's got a mistress for sure.

Philipa's words rose from her memory. "Does he bring many women to his bed?"

"Och well, there's nothing for ye to worry about. What a man does afore he's wed is only natural. Ye can't be holding that against him."

Helen's tone turned guarded as she averted her eyes. She busied herself with placing the stockings carefully over pegs.

"No, 'tis only a woman who is expected to remain virgin."

Helen's posture stiffened. She turned, aiming a mature look at Anne.

"That's only due to the fact that it's important to be sure that children are born into the family that they were fathered from."

She didn't apologize for speaking so strongly, but Anne didn't want her to.

"You enjoy serving in this house, don't you, Helen?"

It wasn't truly a question. Anne could see the loyalty, even hear it.

"Aye, that's a fact. I suppose I've got a bit of passion in me due to knowing that I serve a good man."

"Your lord is fortunate to have you among his staff."

Helen glowed under the compliment. Clasping her hands together, she rubbed them, her eyes sparkling.

"Well now, listen to me chattering away when ye've got important things to be preparing for. Ye'll be right as spring rain once the formalities are finished. Tomorrow morning ye'll have forgotten all about being timid."

Helen stopped and pulled the ring for water once again. This time steam rose from the water that spilt into the tub. Helen picked up a large wooden paddle and stirred the contents of the tub a few times. She stuck her hand in the water to test it.

"Ye'll have to tell me how ye like your bath. For now, it's warm enough to take the winter chill out of your toes."

Anne forced her stiff fingers to release her chemise. Her hands had fisted in the fabric but Helen grasped the hem and lifted it away. Standing up, Anne tried to not dwell on the fact that she was bare. She really had no idea if she was built for bearing children or not. It was very possible that the midwife would find her lacking. Noble daughters were often inspected several times by their own family's midwives before marriage negotiation progressed. It brought shame to great names when a bride was found by her husband to have deformities. Even Queen Elizabeth had been displayed to ambassadors when just a babe because it was rumored that she was misshapen. As the illegitimate child at Warwickshire Anne had never seen the midwife. It was quite possible that her body was not the same as other women. Anne snuck a peek at Helen, to see what the woman's expression was. Helen was quietly studying her with a knowledgeable eye. The servant shook her head.

"Stop lingering and worrying. Ye're well put together, nothing at all to fret over." She motioned her forward.

The tub was inviting with its high sides. It was better than standing in the center of the room at least. The water was warm, delighting her stiff toes. Helen began pulling the pins from her hair.

"I dinnae ken the English. Men don't care for a woman to tie her hair up. They like it soft and flowing."

Did they? Anne bit her lower lip as she looked down at her breasts. Her nipples were hard from her anxiety. She studied the pink buttons, shivering as she considered seeing Brodick's head leaning toward one to kiss it. Her nipple drew tighter with her thoughts, hardening into a pink berry.

He'd promised to do that.

"There. Much better. We'll give this a rinse to make it perfect."

Helen moved around, fetching a bar of soap and cloth. The woman was good at her job, bathing Anne with confident hands. She rang for more water, catching it in a pitcher before it poured into the tub.

"Beware yer eyes, lass."

The water trickled over her head a moment later, drawing a gasp from her because it was cold. Helen clicked her tongue as she gathered up the wet mass and applied some soap to it. Using the cloth, Anne scrubbed at the marks two days of riding had left on her hands. Dirt had made its way beneath her fingernails and she worked diligently to clean it away.

"Beware."

Anne squeezed her eyes shut as more water landed on her head. Tension knotted her belly as she felt like a pig being readied for roasting. Knowing the traditions surrounding marriage had somehow failed to impact her with just how it must feel to be taken through the steps. There really wasn't so great a difference between what she was enduring and what a stable master did before presenting a mare to a stallion.

More precisely, before the mare was mounted.

Her face flamed but the heat didn't remain in her cheeks. It traveled lower until her breasts were rosy and warm with anticipation. Lust coiled through her, spreading to every bit of her body. There was a portion of her that looked on her situation with happiness. At last she would understand what it was to be a woman.

She had enjoyed those kisses.

She lifted her eyelids and felt her clitoris flicker with excitement. Heated lust was curling up in her belly, drawing attention to her sex. There was a hypnotic feel to it, a mesmerizing need that hooked her attention. The water felt so smooth as it flowed across her skin, almost as if she'd never taken the time to really feel. All of her senses were heightened. She smelled the soap; this bar had rosemary oil in it. Her sense of smell was so keen, she even noticed what the water smelled like . . . fresh and full of life. Everything filled her, touching off a storm of longing. Her lips tingled, craving a kiss.

Brodick's kiss.

His midnight eyes sprang to mind as Helen held out a length of toweling. Standing up, Anne stepped from the tub trying to banish Brodick from her thoughts. She still hadn't thought of a way to keep him from her bed tonight. Dwelling on her lust would certainly be no help. More like a pixie leading her on to ruin.

Perth

Brodick stewed as he was forced to walk his horse in a zigzag pattern to allow for the cart to keep up. Agnes didn't ride horses, claiming the beasts were noble and too fine for her. She was the matriarch of her village and had been present at his own birth, but only when she was still a young undermaid of Sterling. Now half of the lowlands snapped to attention when Agnes spoke.

"Why are ye doing this?" Cullen had lost his teasing tone. His brother kept his own horse under a tight rein near him.

Brodick muttered under his breath, his patience already strained. He didn't have much left to deal with his own brother thinking him a brute.

" 'Tis nae my idea."

Cullen shot him a hard look that cut clean into his temper. Pointing a finger at his brother, he snarled softly. "Do yerself a favor, Brother, thank God that ye were nae born first."

With a snort, Brodick turned and let his horse pace a wide circle in the dirt outside Agnes's home. The stone cottage had dried bundles of herbs hanging from most of the rafters. Two men were working a sharpening stone under the eaves. They stood up as he and Cullen rode into view.

Making his bride suffer through an inspection had never crossed his mind even if it was the custom and in his best interest. Mary's own mother had a stench attached to her name. One girl child wasn't a very good reference for her daughter. Marriage was for union and dowry, but he would be stuck with Mary as his lawful wife. If she didn't produce children, he'd never have any legitimate ones.

"I just never figured ye'd be so hard on a little lass."

"This is her idea. Use that head of yers and remember that I was more than happy to take care of consummating our vows last night. It's my bride who seems to be unwilling."

Cullen frowned, his features darkening. Most people didn't think he had a temper but Brodick knew better. Light hair aside, his brother was pure McJames—fierce and unrelenting.

"Now why would she be wanting an inspection?" Suspicion coated Cullen's words. "Inspections are done for the groom's family interests. She has nothing to gain from it and much more to lose."

"Except time or the possibility that I'll send her back after hearing what the midwife has to say."

"Will ye?"

"No." Firm and resolute, Brodick shot his brother a determined look. "She stays."

"But at what cost? I'll nae see ye stuck with a wife who isn't going to honor yer union."

"Suspicion's an ugly thing, Cullen. Be wary of it." Brodick kept his voice low to hide the uncertainty in it. He was unsure of his bride and her attempts to leave him, but he was also very intent on keeping her.

"Does she love another?" Cullen stroked his chin with one hand. "I hear that the English ladies are marrying for love with the queen too old to keep them from running amuck."

"I dinnae know." Yet he should have considered it. His bride had been at the English court for many years. "She wanted me to return her to her father at court."

"Maybe you should." Cullen sounded dangerous. "Ye dinnae need a discontented wife. She'll turn against ye. Possibly be barren."

Many men would agree with Cullen. A sullen wife often didn't conceive just to spite her spouse. Everyone knew that a woman controlled her fertility. Still, the taste of her sweet kiss clung to his lips. He'd touched something inside of her that was beautiful. She hadn't complained even once on the journey home, never muttered a cross word for sleeping on the ground.

"She's nae a spoilt lass."

Cullen nodded, some of his temper fading. "She was pleasant enough on the way home. I know a few Scottish lasses who would have quarreled with sleeping on the trail with a bunch of retainers."

"Maybe she's truly afeared that I'll send her back to her father, disgraced, after bedding her. I hear that happens in England now that the queen is too old to care."

"I'd have to thrash ye if ye even thought of it."

Brodick grinned, showing his teeth to his sibling. "That's providing ye could. I hate to remind ye of how ye fail to measure up to my strength."

"But I make up for it in cunning."

"Ye've got that confused with blustering." The men who'd been working the stone tugged on their hats as they recognized the earl.

"I've a need to fetch Agnes to Sterling."

A moment later the midwife appeared. She still walked straight, even if her pace was a bit slower these days. Her hair was silver but still hung in a thick braid down her back. The McJames' plaid was pulled proudly over her right shoulder and secured with a silver brooch that had been a gift from his own mother.

"My lord." Her voice was sharp and only a bit graveled by age. "How may I serve you?"

Brodick swung out of his saddle, showing the woman respect by speaking to her on an equal footing. She lowered her chin as he stepped closer, acknowledging his title. When he'd been a boy, she'd swatted his ears when he got into mischief.

"I've come to ask ye to return to Sterling with me." He stopped, his next words sticking in his throat.

"I heard in the market that ye'd gone to the border land to claim a wife." Agnes paused, choosing her words with care. "Do ye have a concern with her?"

"My bride has asked to have the custom of inspection carried out."

The two men looked at one another as Agnes took to stroking the silver brooch.

"It is her wish, my lord?"

"Aye."

She nodded, still fingering the broach. "I didnae know that the custom was so practiced in England these days."

"Nor did I."

Agnes lowered her chin. "Bring out my cloak, Johnny. I'm off to Sterling."

Brodick frowned as he headed back to his horse. He didn't like it. Not a bit. Agnes allowed one of his men to help her into the cart. She sat back in the straw as her son handed her cloak in to her. Cullen had a good point; it was possible that his bride loved another man. He didn't like the idea of it. In fact, he was jealous. The surge of emotion was surprising. Never once had he been possessive of a woman. Not even with the mistresses he'd enjoyed so well and completely. He liked women, enjoyed the way they felt when there was nothing between them but skin and passion. Some of them had accused him of being a demanding man.

That was a fact.

A quick fuck wasn't his idea of fun. He'd never placed a woman's back against a tree because his cock was hard and time short. Well, maybe he'd been in a hurry a few times when he was a lad still trying to grow a full beard because he thought it would make him a man. He'd left that impatience behind along with his youthful whiskers. As long as his eyes were still sharp, he would be a clean-shaven man. He had no love for facial hair.

When he took a woman, he took the time to raise her passion. There was nothing more intimate than being lovers. Getting his cock inside a willing female wasn't nearly as good as the experience of feeling his partner climaxing while he rode her. His memory offered up the way his bride had shivered in his embrace. Aye, that was what he was talking about. Reaching out to touch that passion was the thing that drew his attention to a woman. Spread thighs weren't enough.

Wanting that from his marriage was risky. He should have expected Mary to want to be returned to her father. He was Scottish. In spite of the coming union between the two countries, the people still harbored many ill opinions of each other. On both sides. There were titled Scots who believed him daft for seeking the union.

Maybe he was.

Yet thinking that didn't seem to be killing off his growing attraction to her. Perhaps hiding behind her veil had been a crafty ploy, but it had succeeded. Hooking his attention as completely as a well-turned ankle would have. That first day had been a long one as he hoped the wind might give him a peek at her face, or the heat might see her raising the fabric.

Beneath his kilt, his cock was hard, his thoughts having raised it. It wasn't his last mistress's face he saw in his mind, it was his bride's. It was the sound of her sigh when he kissed her neck. Looking back at the cart, he saw that Agnes was well settled.

Raising a fist into the air, he commanded his men.

"Sterling."

His wife would have her assurances and then she would learn that he kept what was his. By tonight, she would be installed in his bed so that he might begin teaching her exactly how much he wanted her. His erection kept him company as they rode back towards Sterling. He enjoyed the burn, savoring the need before he appeased it. He was a lucky man to harbor passion for his bride.

She would not be returning to her father.

Brodick McJames never surrendered. No, it would be his little English bride who cried quarter. That was going to be his personal pledge and his pleasure to see done.

Chapter Six

Sterling

The saints had truly deserted her.

Brodick returned as the sun set. Helen pulled her down the stairs and into the double doorway to watch a cart being pulled into the yard by an ox team. McJames retainers flanked it, their plaids proudly pulled over the right shoulder of each man. There was an air of celebration among them. Each one tugging the corner of his knitted cap when she looked at him.

Helen pointed at the wagon. "There. The lord has brought Agnes. She's delivered more babies than anyone could keep track of. She's more skill in one hand than I have in both of my own. Everything shall proceed smoothly now."

The midwife Brodick brought her was formidable. Agnes was helped from the cart by two burly Scotsmen but she walked towards Anne on steady steps. She walked right up the steps without a quiver, pausing for a moment to consider Anne.

"Good day to ye, mistress."

There was no possibility that she might challenge the experience of the woman in front of her. Agnes radiated confidence and mastery of her skill. Her eyes were the sort that looked straight into a person's soul. Anne found herself shifting slightly as she feared that the veteran female might just see through the entire façade.

Such a thing was impossible, of course, but the emotion welled up inside her anyway.

Brodick stepped up, catching her attention. He was in his commanding element, not a hint of weakness on his face. He captured her hand, keeping her close so that their words remained between them.

"I've done what ye wanted, Mary. But I want to make it plain that I am not demanding this inspection. It makes no difference to me if this custom is carried through or not. I'll honor our proxy marriage without it."

That was very generous. Far more so than most women, even high born ones, might expect.

He stared at her, waiting for her reaction. Part of her wanted to melt at his feet. She'd rarely ever had such kindness offered to her. It was certainly something that she'd never expected from a man.

It reminded her of the way her father was with her mother.

Tears stung her eyes as she thought of the way her parents looked at each other. Loneliness made her heart ache. But guilt weighed down on her shoulders so greatly, her knees wanted to buckle. Brodick could love, she saw it in his eyes. She didn't want to be the cause of him being shackled to her sister.

"You should send me back to my father. At court." There was a plea in her voice that she could not disguise. "Please." To return to Warwickshire was to risk being turned out along with her mother. Her father was her only hope.

His features drew tight, displeasure flickering in his eyes. He tugged her forward, back into the tower. Keeping her hand prisoner in his larger one, Brodick held her near. "Do you love another?" He spoke through clenched teeth, the grip on her hand tightening.

"No."

"Explain yerself, Mary. No more of this game. What is it about our marriage that ye find unacceptable?"

Fear gripped her, squeezing her throat until she felt as though even a breath of air wouldn't pass. She did not know him and could not place the safety of her family in his hands. If he discovered Philipa's deception, he might simply leave her back at Warwickshire and wash his hands of the entire affair.

"It is not so simple a thing for a woman, my lord. With my queen so aged, many women find themselves returned to their fathers as unfit. Men rule this world, so I must be careful. You shall increase your land holdings while I have no hope for happiness."

Pushing his hand off hers, she remained still so that he wouldn't reach for her again. "You have not sought me out for any tender feelings; only a matter of making a good match. We know nothing of one another."

"Tis normal enough, madam, for our station," he said, his eyes full of suspicion. "Which is why I dinnae ken yer asking me to return ye to yer father. That smacks of cowardice, and yet ye stand up to me with steel in yer spine."

The compliment stunned her. She couldn't help but enjoy it. The man in front of her was not one who handed out praise lightly. It was something you had to earn from him.

He cupped her chin, his grip solid but unpainful. "Make yer choice, madam. Ye may join me in our bed with or without yer inspection, but be very sure that ye will be passing the night in my bed."

He stepped away from her, his body tense. But he controlled his frustration, never hinting at physical chastisement.

That only made her respect him, even like him. Many a man raised his hand to a female who challenged his will.

"Knowing each other takes time, madam. We've made a fine start on it but I didnae fetch ye here to court ye like some youth. I'll nae be content with a few kisses. Ye're past that age as well."

"But we could spend a few months before celebrating our wedding. Your people would enjoy witnessing their lord taking marriage vows in the church. It would serve as good Christian example."

"This is Scotland, madam. I'll have to fend off the thieving attempts of half my neighbors if they hear ye are here and still a maiden."

Shock held her silent for a moment. "That is barbaric."

"It's as Scottish as I am."

And the man was proud too. Anne saw it shimmering in his eyes along with a lurking glimmer of amusement. The sight intrigued her because he was so large and strong that she would have thought there was no hint of boyish mischief left in him. That glimmer said there was a part of him that still enjoyed playing.

"I see."

He pressed his lips into a hard line. "No ye don't."

Anne felt her patience grow thin. That was the problem with noble peers . . . they always believed that they knew everything. Well, she was her own person, her thoughts hers and none others.

"You can not know what is in my mind, sir."

One of his eyebrows rose. "I've a fair idea of what is churning inside, behind that pretty face. Ye've a mind to run back to court where some whelp has turned yer head with his poetry."

"I am not in love with anyone."

His expression hardened. "Then ye are discontent because I am Scots."

Anne shook her head before thinking. Rejection shot through her so quickly, she could not hold back her denial of his charge. It would have served her better to let him believe she detested his heritage, such attitudes were common.

Yet she could not do it. There was too much of him that she found admirable, too much that she found worthy of praise. It was the truth that she was beginning to like him.

Brodick made a low sound of frustration. He propped his hands on his hips, looking even larger. The sword hilt rising over his right shoulder added to the formidable picture he presented.

"Ye are making me daft," he announced.

"I'm trying your patience because I don't dislike you for being Scots?"

Brodick stepped closer, instantly drawing a response from her flesh. She backed away from him without consideration and he kept coming until her back hit the wall. He pressed his hands against the cool stone. There was a mere finger length between them now. Her heart began to race as she caught the faint scent of his skin. Never had she noticed that men smelled enticing. Behind her stays her nipples drew tight. His gaze centered on her lips and the tender skin tingled with longing. Time froze. She felt suspended in that moment, aware of nothing but Brodick and his body. Needs rose from every inch of her skin to be in contact with him, stroked by him.

It was insanity.

"I'll be waiting for Agnes to let me know what ye decide." His voice was thick with hunger. He leaned down and pressed a kiss against her lips. It was over almost before it began but the sensation burned all the way to her toes.

"Make no mistake about what I have decided, madam. I will have ye tonight."

He pushed away from her and strode across the main floor

of the tower. The castle folk were watching from the yard, their necks stretching out to see into the tower. The confused looks on their faces told her that no one could tell what was happening inside the wall. Brodick stopped to have words with Agnes. The midwife nodded her head, casting her attention toward Anne.

The earl left on long strides, clearing the front entrance as their audience looked between his wide back and her set face. The curious crowd watched the midwife as she made her way to stand in front of Anne, her face pensive. She said nothing for a long time, inspecting Anne from head to toe with her keen stare. She fingered the silver brooch that held her tartan securely on one shoulder.

"Do you have need of me, my lady?" She spoke softly, each word carefully delivered. "Or may I return home?"

Temptation needled Anne. She was caught so completely in Philipa's scheme that even the smallest possibility that she might be found lacking was something she could not cast aside. Preserving her modesty could not take precedence.

"I would be grateful for your opinion."

Agnes frowned but Anne held her head level. "A marriage such as this should never proceed forward if there is any doubt. An earl cannot be so lax in his choice of bride. He needs an heir. If I cannot provide that, it would be best to dissolve our union now before there is disappointment."

The midwife lost her disgruntled expression. She nodded in agreement.

"Ye're a fair woman, to be sure."

Fair . . . hah!

Agnes began walking toward the stairs that led to the upper floor, clearly knowing the castle.

"Come along, mistress. Let us attend to this matter. I see yer thinking. More noblewomen should be as astute." Agnes swept her from head to toe again. "Indeed it would make for a happier world. The lord's mother was inspected before her wedding night as well. Yer mother was wise to teach ye to respect the tradition. It has its place."

Anne forced her feet to move. Each step was an effort and she was suddenly very aware of how little clothing she had on. Her surcoat was closed up over a chemise. The only other thing she wore was a pair of slippers. The tapestry footwear was meant for her dressing chamber and felt very thin. Walking allowed the air to brush all the way up her exposed skin.

She was convinced that the flight of stairs took longer to climb than any other she had ever mounted. Helen had built a fire in the chamber and fed it far more wood than normal. It blazed high, filling the chamber with heat. Helen came forward, intent on removing the surcoat.

Anne stood still and straight, refusing to allow her modesty to buckle her resolve. It took mere seconds to bare her body, once the surcoat was removed, yet it felt like hours. There was only her chemise and shoes. Each second swelled into time that felt as though it were standing still.

Agnes was still for a long time, her eyes moving over her body in slow motion. She circled around Anne, lingering behind her. When Agnes returned to stand in front of her, the midwife reached out to cup a breast. She handled it with a knowing hand as Anne bit into her lip to still her protest. Her grip was firm, judging the weight and texture. She finished by pinching the nipple and leaning closer to look at it.

Agnes didn't make a sound as she left off and moved her hand to the opposite breast. After pinching the nipple, she withdrew her hand.

"Lie down on the bed. I need to see if yer womb is sitting correctly in yer belly."

"Of . . . course." Anne snapped her mouth closed as her

voice cracked. What Brodick wanted from her was far more in-
trusive. She had better adjust to allowing the midwife to make
a detailed inspection. That would provide her with all the
more opportunity to gain the woman's disapproval. Getting to
her father was the key. He would deal with Philipa.

Agnes pressed her hands against Anne's belly, moving in an
arch from one hip to the other. Anne watched the woman's
practiced manner, the knowledgeable touch something only
experience taught. There was something she might admire at
least. Agnes continued until she'd felt every inch of Anne's ab-
domen with careful hands.

"Ye may dress yer mistress," Agnes instructed Helen.

The midwife stood back and Helen brought Anne's chemise
forward. Anne held her tongue because Agnes was still contemplating her. Standing up, she helped pull her surcoat on,
shivering as it warmed her. The midwife stepped close again.

"Let me see yer teeth."

Agnes didn't miss any part of her. She even made Anne
cover her eyes so that she might test her hearing by snapping
her finger near one ear and having Anne raise the hand on the
same side of her body.

"Ye are more than fit, mistress."

She gasped, but Helen clapped her hands together with
glee.

"I'm going to fetch ye some supper. Ye'll need all your
strength tonight." The maid hurried from the room, excitement making her steps lively.

"Oh, but—" Helen was gone before Anne decided what she
might say to stop her.

"Marriage is always a time of uncertainty for a woman. Ye'll
settle in, mistress, as we all do."

There was a firm parental expectation in Agnes's tone. One
that made Anne close her lips. For a small moment she felt like

a child caught snatching a piece of sweet bread from the kitchen between meals.

"I do not want to disappoint the earl."

The midwife slowly shook her head. "Ye willnae. I've seen many a girl less built for bearing babes than ye, push children into this world. Save yer worrying for things that have already gone bad."

The trap was closing tighter around her again, crushing the breath from her. Agnes was watching her, observing the play of emotions that crossed her face. Anne turned, pacing toward the far side of the chamber.

"Did yer mother tell ye some tale of painful duty associated with consummating your marriage?"

Agnes was trying hard to understand her dilemma. More guilt piled on top of her for putting the woman to the trouble of trying to help her. She dare not trust anyone but she wanted to. The desire to blurt out everything was growing stronger with each kind person she met. But just because a person wanted to help you didn't mean that they could. Brodick might shelter her at Sterling but Philipa was still mistress of Warwickshire. Even an earl did not have the right to remove servants from another holding.

"No, I understand the way of a man and a woman."

"Yet ye clearly dread it." Agnes followed her. "Are ye truly so feared of not producing a son? I hear yer mother never did."

She was more worried about conceiving but Agnes had hit upon a perfect excuse for her to hide behind.

"Of course I am. Doubts fill my heart. Surely given my family background you can understand why I believe it would be best if you informed the lord of our mismatching. He could offer for a woman that has many brothers. A far better situation for him."

Agnes didn't look convinced. She pressed her lips together, aiming her keen stare at her.

"I disagree, mistress. Ye are healthy and large enough to bear the lord's children without concern." She took a deep breath, letting it out slowly. "Ye are simply nervous. If I send ye home, ye'll never face yer fears. No one should live life that way. Ye English need to ken the value of boldness in a girl. That also has its place."

The midwife nodded firmly, clearly settled in her decision. "Daughters do gain things from their fathers as well. Do not dwell so much on what yer mother didn't do."

Agnes lowered herself in a stately manner before she turned and left. Anne sighed, feeling her strength bleeding away.

Philipa's plan was proceeding and she had no idea how to stop it.

None.

Brodick was tense.

Far more worried than he'd been in a long time. He hadnae wanted to let Agnes near Mary. The surge of emotion worried him because it was so strong. It was the sort of thing he'd heard tales about but always considered it nothing that could really happen to him.

"I've never seen ye pace."

"Go away, Cullen. I'm nae in the mood for jesting."

His brother didn't leave but his mocking grin melted as he moved closer. "Nor am I. This marriage business is more complicated than I figured."

"There is a great deal riding on what Agnes says." And Brodick wasn't just thinking about the dowry. He wanted Mary in his bed. Knowing that she was bare up in that chamber right now was slowly burning a hole in his discipline.

"Ye don't have to send her away even if Agnes says she's nae strong."

Brodick nodded but returned to pacing. "By tradition I should."

"Ye're the McJames, no one will take her anywhere without yer word."

"True enough," Brodick said. "But it would be unkind. I've no wish to see the lass suffer."

Cullen snorted. "It's clear to one and all where ye wish the lass to be. In yer bed and right quickly, too."

Brodick froze. "Is it that obvious?"

"To one that knows ye, aye." He returned to smirking. "Ye're so pathetic I can't even find the heart to tease ye any-more. I never thought the day would come when I'd watch ye beg for a taste of honey."

"What I crave is a family, Brother. It's something that comes with manhood. Chasing a wildcat for a few rounds of blister-ing passion is no longer what I need. I want to lay awake on the trail and know that there is a woman waiting for me in my bed. Maybe even praying that I'll arrive home safely. I want to see her cradling our babe, suckling it with her own breast, be-cause she's happy being my wife, and mothering my children."

Brodick smiled at his brother. They had always enjoyed taunting each other. The only one who needled him better was his sister. Fiona hid behind her feminine grace, trouncing both of them when it came to verbal attacks.

"I hope ye gain that, Brodick." Cullen was serious, his face pensive. "Yet I'm suspicious of yer bride. Something is nae clear about her."

Brodick agreed. "It disnae matter. Once Agnes is finished with this inspection, I'll get on with welcoming my bride to the family. It won't make any difference what she was thinking. All that will be important is our future. She's in a foreign place surrounded by strangers. It's expected that she'll need time to settle in."

"Spoken like a true McJames."

Brodick felt his anxiety fade. He was the McJames and Mary would adjust. Agnes appeared at the top of the stairs and he felt his shoulders tighten in spite of his resolutions. Mary was correct about one thing. Men didn't know a great deal about a woman's body being sound for marriage. What a man sought were things that nature designed to attract his interest. That was the main reason that marriage was more of a business transaction. It was the wiser course of action. Letting lust lead the way was bound to land a man in a poor match both in dowry and children. He was a large man; taking a petite female to his bed would be like a death sentence for her. Inspections had begun to prevent uneven pairs. It made sense, but his lust was trying to argue with logic. He should be disciplined enough to ignore his rising attraction.

But he wasn't.

His cock was straight and swollen again. The thing demanded he cut through all the formalities and get down to what he craved. The idea of tradition was beginning to sound foul as customs blocked his path. Desire was ripping through years of practiced discipline and it was the honest truth that he was enjoying the burn.

He moved toward Agnes with determination. The midwife approached him but stopped, waving her sons away when they stood to go to her side.

"My lord." She lowered her head, waiting for him to ask her for her findings. That was the time-honored way of lord and vassal.

"Is my bride fit to assume her duties?"

"I believe she is."

Satisfaction surged through him but Agnes held up a wrinkled hand.

"She is most concerned that her mother didnae produce any sons and that she may follow in those footsteps. Disappointing ye. She considers the production of children a serious responsibility."

"Life is full of uncertainty. You cannae spend yer days never trying. Any bride I take would have that worry to contend with."

Agnes pursed her lips, disliking his tone. The reprimand hit that spot inside him that was still a boy when it came to her. The midwife aimed a hard stare at him.

"A bride who plans to avoid disappointing her husband is as valuable as one who's eager to please the desires of youth. I found yer new wife to be a woman of forethought."

"Ye have my gratitude."

Agnes lowered herself, just a tiny amount, before gesturing to her sons.

"May yer union be blessed with healthy children. I will look forward to being summoned to the lady in the fall."

Brodick offered Agnes a small pouch. She looked at it but only stroked the silver brooch at her shoulder.

"Ye're a stubborn woman, Agnes."

"Thank you, my lord."

With a cheeky grin, the midwife turned to join her family. She'd never accepted payment from the lord's family. His mother had ordered the brooch made and gifted it to her in order to get around the stubborn streak. Agnes might refuse payment, considering her service owed to the noble family who owned the land her family farmed, but she could not refuse a gift from the lady of the house. That would be rude. It would be interesting to see how Mary dealt with the woman.

Because his bride would be staying. God willing, Agnes would be back.

"Why are ye dressing?"

Helen looked disappointed when she returned to discover Anne halfway into her dress. It was only the stays that she needed help with lacing.

"There's no need for anyone to bring trays to my chamber. I shall eat below."

"Och, ye're such a considerate one."

Helen moved behind her to begin tying her corset in place. "It will please the folks greatly, too, I'll no deny that. They are a might curious about the new mistress. There were a few rumors of how English ladies like their pampering that had us wondering."

"I don't wish to be a burden to anyone."

" 'Tis a delight to have one of those men marry up. This house needs life, mistress."

The title of mistress made her smile. She simply could not help it. It was a word that she'd never expected to hear applied to herself. It wasn't pampering that she coveted in the position, only the respect. The chance to be judged solely on what she did.

"Into yer doublet. Cook has the supper out."

Her belly was empty, but that wasn't what motivated her. Anne gratefully quit the chamber with its large bed. Besides, she would have no one's wrists aching from bringing a tray to her.

Helen led her down the stairs and into a long hallway. The evening light streamed through small openings in the stone walls. Helen kept walking until they reached another of the large round towers. There was a buzz of conversation floating into the hallway. When they reached the arched opening, she stared at a wide expanse of tables. Fires were blazing in the hearths that circled the room. It was exactly like the great hall at Warwickshire, only round. Long tables filled it and there was a raised dais at one end with thick chairs set on more carpets. Beneath the tables there was only stone, but it had been swept clean. Anne nodded approval, seeing the sense in it. Spills and crumbs might be swept up easily.

Many of the tables were already full of the earl's retainers. They talked freely as the food was passed between them. A hush fell over the room as she entered. The servants paused in their duties to cast inquisitive looks her direction.

"May I present Mary Spencer, daughter of the Earl of Warwickshire. My wife."

Brodick's voice bounced off the walls, surprising her with its volume. He stood at the dais, one foot propped on the top step. He looked completely confident there, a vision of strength. The room erupted in a cheer that startled her. Brodick smiled, holding out a hand in welcome.

Guilt showed up again to crush her with its weight. Every step across the hall was pure torment because she felt like an actor. Men tugged on the corners of their bonnets in respect, while others raised their tankards with good wishes.

She was worse than a charlatan.

The good cheer filled the room, conversation resuming. Brodick didn't climb the remaining step to the dais. Instead, he met her on the main floor. Satisfaction was shimmering in his midnight eyes. Her throat went dry. He closed his hand around hers firmly, clearly confident that all obstacles had been removed from his path. Excitement ripped through her, sending a surge of emotion along her limbs. His eyes narrowed as he felt the shiver in her hand. His thumb reached to rub across the tender skin of her inner wrist. She gasped softly as sensation rippled up her arm. It was such a simple touch, but so intense, her knees weakened.

"Would the pair of ye mind waiting until supper is over?"

Anne jumped, shocked at her own inattention. Fiona was eyeing them from the nearest table. She fluttered her eyelashes while smiling so sweetly a nun couldn't have taken exception to her.

"Those simpering looks might make me lose my appetite."

Brodick grunted. "Ye remember my sister. She's the talk of half of Scotland, even if our father spent a fortune on tutors to train her better."

"Gossip should never be believed." Fiona offered a mischievous smile along with her comment. She reached for a round of bread and pulled a piece off. "No one truly cares what I do."

"Not so, Sister. I am very interested in what ye've been about." Brodick stepped over the bench and sat down across from his sister. Cullen was seated a few feet away, joking with other young men. Unlike Warwickshire, there appeared to be no finery laid out for the nobles. They broke bread with their people, ate off the same platters.

Brodick left the fine chairs on the dais empty choosing to sit with his men instead.

"That was my father's table."

Anne turned her attention back to Brodick. His expression was solemn. "I will nae sit there until I've earned the right, as my father did. Until I sit there with my family, showing the McJames name to be one that will continue." He gazed at her. "I hope you dinnae mind."

He lifted one foot and straddled a bench.

Brodick watched her, waiting to see what she made of his table. She sat on the bench, choosing the end nearest him and brought her legs about to be beneath the table.

"This is a fine table, I am honored to sit at it." The scent of warm food drew a rumble from her belly. Brodick groaned.

"I've been remiss in feeding you. Now that we're home, Bythe will take delight in stuffing ye."

He began piling food on her plate, much larger portions than she could eat.

"Enough, Brodick, do I look that large to you?"

He stopped, turning his gaze toward her. " 'Tis the first time ye have used my name."

Anne bit into a piece of bread to avoid answering him. He was pushing close to her, overwhelming her personal space. The intimacy was bold and there was a part of her that enjoyed it. Somehow, it made him seem more powerful, that determination. Her pride was ruffled, too, but that did not stop the tingle of anticipation that flowed down to her breasts. Laced up once more, the tender globes protested their imprisonment. Behind the steel stays, her nipples drew taut.

Fiona sighed dramatically. Brodick turned to look at his sister. She only wiggled her eyebrows at his temper. Fiona shrugged before smiling at Anne.

"Men are thick-headed. They canae disengage their minds from their lust."

"Mind yer mouth, Fiona." Brodick reached for a tankard. "At least give the lass a few days to become accustomed to yer brashness."

"More like ye're thinking to get her settled into yer bed and stuck as yer wife before she learns too much about Celts."

"We're soon to be one nation, sister. I, for one, do not long to hold onto the wars that have taken so much blood." There was a solid reprimand in his voice, but not anger.

Anne held her breath. Warwickshire had always been such a formal house, she wasn't sure what Brodick would make of his sister's words. He shook his head, his expression turning jovial again.

"And aye, I'd like to show the pleasant part of living at Sterling afore she hears what a bold female I have for a sister."

They both laughed, enjoying the jest. She was drawn to the family camaraderie. Hidden from Philipa's eyes, her own family enjoyed the same ease. Teasing was the one thing that truly said she was among family, because every other aspect of her life was governed by rules and her station.

Sterling was a welcoming house, indeed. The maids were not standing with their platters, attempting to be unnoticed. There was no lowering of heads before the food was presented. Conversation flowed freely instead of each word being measured before it was uttered for fear of those higher than yourself becoming offended. Her appetite returned with full vigor as she watched the supper tables, enthralled by the contentment displayed. It radiated from everyone around her, warming up that spot in her chest that had turned so cold when she was separated from her family. She still longed for them but happily enjoyed her meal with such company.

It would be simple to slip into the role she'd been thrust into. She was tempted, sorely so. Her eyes strayed to Brodick. His jaw was newly scraped clean of whiskers. His face was firm and hard, like the rest of his body. The doublet he'd worn on the trail was missing. He wore only his shirt and kilt. The tartan was flipped up along his thigh, displaying the thick muscle of his leg. She should have ignored it, but her eyes were drawn to it.

So intent was she on him she missed the fact that one of his hands was beneath the table. He gently squeezed her knee through her skirts and she jumped, knocking the table.

"Thick, cloddish, with only one thing on their minds." Fiona waggled a finger from side to side with each insult she tossed at her brother.

Heat crept into Anne's cheeks as Brodick turned his gaze onto her. Suspicion was clouding his expression again. He gripped her knee once more, keeping his hand there. "Maybe ye are as innocent as ye say. Ye certainly are not used to being touched."

He had lowered his voice but it still lit her temper. Pushing her foot off the floor, she drove her knee and his hand into the top of the table. The thump covered the swift intake of his breath.

"And you wonder," she gritted out, keeping her voice low, "why I am intent on following traditions that protect my good name."

Several men had stopped talking and were silently chewing as they tried to listen. Rising, she bobbed a quick reverence before striding across the hall. She didn't care if it was unwise to be angry, she was out of patience with performing to everyone's expectations. She had no more tolerance for charges against her chastity.

A hard hand caught her elbow once she entered the hallway. Brodick spun her around to face his displeasure.

"Ye're right, Mary, I dinnae ken why ye're avoiding my bed."

"Your bed . . . all I hear is your bed." She raised her chin and let him see the flames in her eyes. "Yet it is my virtue you question. I am not the one who speaks of lust so often. Attending court does not make any lady a strumpet."

"I've been to your English court, madam, and it was full of titled ladies who held no reservations about anything." He pointed a finger at her. "They fucked in the hallways outside the Queen's own chamber. I won't have it in my wife."

The word fuck was blunt but it also sent a shaft of need through her. Her heart was racing, driving her blood at a fast pace through her. It seemed to accentuate each of her senses.

"Then why did you enter negotiations with my father, if you have such a low opinion of English ladies?"

Her rapid breathing pulled his scent into her head. She was instantly distracted from her purpose by rising lust again. She wanted to find out what all that muscle felt like, smooth her hands over it. She could not stop the impulses and tried to thrust away from him. His arm shot around her waist the second her palms slammed against his hard chest, and with a hard jerk, she ran into his body, her fingers clenching at his shirt.

"We are ill matched—" She gasped behind Brodick's hand as it slapped over her mouth.

"Dinnae say it! I'll be taking ye to my bed and no other place." He lowered his voice as his arms tightened, holding her prisoner when she squirmed. "Tell me true, Mary," he said, removing his hand, "have ye been with another? Let us begin our marriage with honesty."

"You've already made up your mind about me. Nothing I say will make any difference."

"It will. I can trust. But it disnae come for free. Ye have to be honest with me first."

His hand moved up her back until he threaded it through her hair. His grasp tightened and she was forced to stare into his eyes. Suspicion stared back at her and hunger so fierce it stunned her. Her words melted away as she forgot what she was fighting with him about. His attention dropped to her mouth and her lips tingled, anticipating his kiss.

It never came. With a growl, he released her. His shoulders shook as he stepped back.

"I'll nae be distracted. Ye'll answer me before yer kisses drive thought from my mind."

Her body shook with the loss of his support. A dull ache ran through every inch of her flesh. Clasping her arms around herself, she tried to remove the feeling of his hands by rubbing her arms.

"You doubt me. That will never change. Even after my innocence is proven you will continue to doubt my word." She shivered. "This is why I ask you to send me back to my father."

"And I have told ye that I willnae do so." He spat his words at her, pointing that finger toward her once more. "Have ye known another man?"

"No, and that won't be changing tonight." She had no way to enforce her words but they flew out of her mouth born from the flames of her temper. How she wished she were enduring her woman's flow. Her eyes widened.

Her monthly flow . . .

"Since you doubt my innocence, it is only prudent to wait until my monthly curse happens before consummating this marriage. Only by doing that will you never doubt the parentage of any babe I may conceive."

His expression darkened but she didn't wait for him to demand compliance from her again.

"Yes. That is the way to end this quarrel." Taking a deep breath into her lungs, she curtsied, dismissing him with the gesture. "Good night, my lord."

She turned her back on him, the hairs on her nape rising as she did so. Her shoulders were tense as she began walking away, expecting to feel his hands on her at any moment. She made it the length of the hallway without any interference. Disappointment slammed into her, making her aware of how much she enjoyed his touch. Tears clouded her vision as she climbed the stairs and she wasn't even sure why she was sniffling.

She had gained what she wanted. There was no reason for her to despair. Her monthly curse would not come for another fortnight at least. It was a much better plan than asking for an inspection.

So why did she not feel relief?

Chapter Seven

Helen was cross with her.

The maid hid it well but Anne knew from personal experience what the tight set of her lips meant. How many times had she done the same while tending to Philipa?

The maid was holding back the words that she wanted to lecture Anne with. She performed her duties efficiently but without the friendly banter she'd added this afternoon. There was little to do after Anne's dress was removed and hung up. Helen returned with a silver brush. Anne heard her pull in a stiff breath as she drew it through Anne's hair.

"The lord will adore yer hair."

The brush slid along the waist-length strands. Anne rarely let it hang loose. That was something girls did and she'd passed such a stage when it came time to begin earning her keep in the kitchen. Tight braids were far more practical. Warwickshire servants wore linen caps, too. The required head covering kept flour out of her hair. Pinning her braids up kept the ends from frizzing when she leaned over to poke up the fire.

"He's a good man, the lord."

Anne sighed, unsure what to believe anymore. Had she truly only left Warwickshire three days ago? It felt so much longer.

"If yer mother were here, she'd explain how men can be suspicious when they are thinking about their wives." Helen was silent for a long moment. "Ye really should not take it to heart. It only shows how much they value a good reputation. That's nae something they feel is needed in a mistress. It's a compliment, setting ye above the women in their past."

"Should I risk him reproaching our first child? Wondering if I was carrying before he knew me?"

"The McJames would nae do such a thing." There was an edge to her tone now. "Besides, Agnes would have known if ye were breeding."

"He doubts my purity."

Helen stopped. She walked in front of her, aiming a steady look that reminded her very much of her mother's.

"Go to his bed and prove the matter. Pride is poor company once the bed curtains have been pulled."

Anne bit back her longing to do exactly that. Helen saw it and sighed. She curtsied.

"Good night, then, mistress."

"Thank you, Helen."

She hesitated before leaving, looking back at Anne. With a nod, she left the room. The crackle from the dying fire was suddenly loud. Heat braised Anne's cheeks as she felt her hair shifting softly around her shoulders. She felt so pretty, something she wasn't accustomed to. Vanity was another one of those things she had never had time for. Her skin was creamy and smooth from her bath, practically glowing in the firelight.

As a noble bride should be . . .

Yet she had sent her groom away.

The bed curtains were drawn along the sides to catch the heat and hold it. Reaching out, she fingered one of the thick panels. It was a luxury that she had never thought to sample. The sheets were smooth and soft, too. Running her hand over them, she remained on her knees, ill at ease among such finery.

Her guilt robbed her of any enjoyment. She had not earned the place as mistress of the house.

"Do you really fear me so much?"

Anne jumped—Brodick's voice came from the shadows. It was soft and silken as if he were speaking to a child.

"Or is it a game to prod me into doing what ye want and return ye to your father?"

Guilt slammed into her, making it hard to raise her head. The man deserved far better than the deception she was. But her pride demanded that she stop allowing him to think her a coward.

"I am not motivated by fear of your touch. Your insinuations angered me."

There was a soft step on the stone floor. The shadows grew until the earl was standing in front of her. He studied her, his gaze lingering on the soft waves of her hair.

"I did that true enough." He touched her hair, gently fingering a lock. A look of enjoyment passed over his face. It made her feel pretty, something she'd never experienced.

"For all yer demureness on the trail, there's a flame hidden inside ye." He sounded amused by her temper. Something she hadn't expected from any man. Even the lowest stable hand considered himself master of his own family.

"You cannot be happy to discover that."

He chuckled. "Ye think not?" She realized that the brooch holding his tartan was missing now, only his shirt covering his chest.

"Think once more. I told ye already that I have no taste for a coward."

A tingle of awareness went through her, as though she was proud of showing him that she would not submit meekly.

"I didn't take that to mean that you enjoy shrewish behavior."

His lips twitched up, a look of satisfaction taking over his features.

"There's a difference between passion and sourness."

He approved of her. She heard it in his voice. Her teeth worried her lower lip because she just couldn't help but bask in the glow of that praise. It meant even more because it came from a man she was growing to admire. Brodick wasn't a puffed-up shell with a title. He was a man who worked as hard as his people did. His attention dropped to her chest, lingering on her breasts behind the thin chemise. She was suddenly self-conscious and keenly aware that they were alone.

In her bedroom.

"You should not be here, my lord."

"Did yer father teach ye to tell everyone around ye what to do?" His voice was sharp, edged with impatience that thickened his brogue. "Ye do it often enough with me. I think it's time ye heard what I'm wanting."

"You want me in your bed. I have listened to you." She spoke too quickly, her emotions bleeding through to her voice. Brodick frowned.

"And ye want me to return ye to yer father." He placed a knee on the bed, judging her reaction. A ripple of sensation crossed her bare arms, raising gooseflesh along her limbs. His keen gaze followed it. "I notice ye don't ask to return to yer mother but instead to court. Is it any wonder that I question who is waiting for ye there?"

The collar of his shirt was open, displaying a deep vee of skin and brawn. He leaned in closer, joining her on the bed. The frame creaked as it took his weight. But he moved slowly as though he were attempting to lull her into a sense of submission. She did admit that it was mesmerizing having his large body invade her bed. It was something she'd heard about for so many years. Been warned to avoid, it had taken on almost a magical feeling. As if it could never truly happen except in her imagination. Excitement rippled through her when she smelled his skin. He was very real and so different from the few boys who had attempted to flirt with her at Warwickshire. Those boys had professed bravery in the face of Philipa's dictates but Brodick embodied that idea. She believed that he would never tremble with fear . . . never.

"Explain what drives ye to return to court."

"I did . . . I told you . . ." She shut her lips as he reached for her. Fascination took hold of her as her skin anticipated the contact between them.

She craved it.

Need blossomed inside her, spreading its petals wide to catch the warmth radiating from him. She lifted her face for his touch, sighing softly as his fingers smoothed over her cheek. A tiny sigh crossed her lips. Her eyelids fluttered, opening to see why he didn't touch her further. The suspicion tore through her and she lost the battle to deny him the solace of the truth.

"I truly want to see my father. No other. Only him."

She stared straight into his eyes as she spoke. He reached forward, stoking her face with a warm hand.

"Aye, I see that in yer eyes. Ye love him deeply."

"I do."

His thumb traced her lower lip. Sweet sensation filled her, traveling along her skin. It flowed down to her breasts, awakening the flesh so that she was keenly aware of it. Both nipples drew into hard points that brushed against the thin fabric of her chemise. Her heart thumped hard inside her chest, but outwardly, she felt amazingly calm.

"Which is why I willnae return ye, lass. I envy him that devotion and find myself longing for the chance to earn the same place in yer heart."

He kissed her, stopping the retort that bubbled from her

lips. He pushed the words back into her mouth as he cradled her in strong arms while laying her back onto the bed. His body trapped her there, but he caught some of his weight on his elbows as he teased her lower lip with the tip of his tongue. She shivered, a flood of sensation washing over her. The bed felt like a surreal place. A hidden paradise where they might frolic without earthy cares.

Never once had she imagined that an embrace could feel so good. His arms were hard, but his hold, soft. She squirmed, turning one way and then another but he controlled her with his body moving to remain in contact with her.

His scent filled her as his tongue thrust into her mouth, his fingertips turning her head so that their mouths could fit together tighter. His tongue filled her mouth, slipping and sliding along hers. He teased her until she returned his touch, tangling with his tongue.

Her hard nipples pressed against his chest and it delighted her. She was suddenly too warm for the chemise, the garment scratchy against her skin.

She was equally unhappy with his shirt, her fingers pulling on it as they searched for the skin she'd only glimpsed. He broke their kiss, trailing his lips across her cheek and along her jaw. Sweet delight flowed along with her racing blood and she arched her back to be closer to him. He kissed her neck, softly, tenderly, once and then twice. He cupped her nape, holding it still as he applied his teeth to the delicate skin. A mutter of pleasure left her mouth as she pulled on his shirt. The wide shoulders her eyes had admired felt so good in her grasp.

His legs were bare, his knee-high boots missing. With her wearing only the chemise, their legs slid against one another, heightening her enjoyment. His hands left her to press down on the bed beside her head. He raised his face to watch her.

Their lower bodies connected, the presence of his hard cock solid against her belly.

She shuddered, need raking its claws across her. Hidden between her thighs, her sex was hot and needy. The glow from the dying fire cast a ruby hue across her lover, bathing them in more heat.

"I like the way we talk without words quite a bit."

His voice was husky but also demanding. He sat back on his haunches, pulling his hands across her belly and over her thighs until he reached the bottom of her chemise. He watched her face as he pressed his hands onto her bare skin.

"Do ye feel that, lass? The passion is alive between us."

He moved up her body, pushing the fabric slowly upwards. She didn't care that it bared her to his stare; her skin was begging to be free. She had never longed to be naked but it took root in her soul as an absolute necessity. His hand smoothed over her hips, removing the barrier of her clothing. Higher still until her belly was clearly in sight. One thick leg pressed down on the bed between her thighs while he worked the chemise over her breasts.

"Ye're lovely indeed, lass. A vision."

She didn't get to see his expression because he was pulling the garment over her head and up her arms. But she heard the satisfaction in his tone.

"And ye would have sent me to a lonely bed." His gaze roamed down her length, hunger tightening his jaw until a muscle twitched along one side. "I think not."

He ripped his shirt up and over his head, baring his chest in one swift motion. A hard jerk on his belt and he threw it behind him. The folds of his kilt fell away from his lean waist, now that the belt was no longer holding it. He lowered his weight back onto her before the fabric revealed the cock she'd felt pressing against her.

"I think that I shall have ye."

He cupped her breasts, drawing a whimper from her as pleasure spiked through her. His thumbs brushed across her nipples, surprising her with how much she liked being touched.

"And I think that ye will enjoy being taken."

His mouth sealed out any further comments. A hard kiss taking command while his tongue thrust deeply. It was an invasion, a breaching of her defenses. Yet one she did not protest. Pleasure rose up from every point of contact. She was swept along by the powerful current, willing and eager to discover how much more delight there might be. She toyed with his tongue, teasing it with the tip of her own. Her hands sought out his shoulders, gliding along the sculpted ridges.

"That's it, lass, touch me."

His shoulders shook as she ran her hands along the hard ridges. His chest was coated in crisp hair that felt very male to her. He pressed a kiss against her neck as his hands gripped each soft breast. She'd never once noticed how sensitive the globes were. His hands sent sensations through her. They flowed down her body to her sex. But her nipples begged for him to keep his promise to taste them. He worked his way lower, kissing her neck and along her collarbones. His hands gently kneaded each mound as his mouth arrived over one. Her eyes grew round as her breath caught in her throat. Anticipation drew her as tight as a bow, her gaze fastened on his head.

"I've been wanting to discover what yer nipples taste like for too long."

"We only met two days ago."

His lips thinned with hunger as his thumb brushed across the tip of one hard nipple. "Aye, as I said—too long."

His hair hung down on either side of his head, brushing the side of her breast. A harsh gasp escaped her lips when he opened his mouth and closed the remaining distance. It was almost too hot. Sucking her nipple deep inside his mouth, the heat singeing the delicate skin. Her fingers made their way into his hair. She simply could not resist the urge to hold him in place. The sweetest pleasure filled her, covering her like warm sunshine.

He chuckled softly when she whimpered. It was a sound she'd never heard from herself. So needy, so hungry.

He raised his head and she moaned at the loss. He stared into her eyes, studying her for a long moment.

"Wife."

There was heavy possession in his voice. That single word more of a battle cry than anything the church sanctioned.

He released her breasts, sliding his fingers down and across her belly. The muscles quivered as he pressed her thighs wider, spreading her sex open. One large male hand hesitated for only a moment on the top of her mons before slipping into her sex.

"Brodick."

She sounded breathless but wasn't sure if it was from shock or excitement. Never once had she considered being touched between her thighs.

"I told ye that we Scots are practiced in the art of warming up our women. Believe me, ye aren't nearly warm enough to my way of thinking."

He stroked her sex, straight down the center with one finger. The little nub hidden at the top sent a jolt of pleasure into her belly when he touched it. A whimper rose from her as he lingered for a long moment on that spot, stroking it with a firm touch.

"Exactly the right spot to start a fire."

Her hips lifted towards his touch without her even thinking about it. She simply responded to the pleasure. Her nipples twisted tighter as she found it impossible to remain still. Her body twitched and pressed up towards his, seeking more. Fluid coated his fingers, making the skin wet. His fingers moved easily through the folds of her sex, toying with her clitoris.

Need consumed her. She reached for him, clawing at his shoulders, her hips bucking towards his hand. Pleasure tightened under his finger, twisting harder until she cried out for relief from it.

"Brodick . . ." She didn't recognize her own voice. It was strained and husky. Completely uncharacteristic for her.

But he withdrew his hand and she hit him, her hand smacking his skin. He laughed at her and thrust one thick finger deep into her body. Pleasure ripped up from the penetration, her bottom tilting to take him deeper.

"Do you like that, lass?"

"*Yes.*" It went far beyond wanting, she craved him inside her.

He sent a second finger into her sheath, working them in and out of her body. His knee rose to push her thighs up giving him more access to her sex.

"Then ye shall have me."

He withdrew his fingers, spreading her thighs wider with his hips. A rustle of fabric filtered up to her ears before she felt the first touch of his cock against her opening. He gripped her hips, shaking as he nudged his way into her. Just a mere inch at first and her body strained towards him, every muscle taut with need.

He kept her still, refusing to fill her further. His teeth were clenched as he withdrew. "Ye're too tight."

"I don't care." Her hands slapped against his shoulder again, the craving to move overwhelming. She could not contain it all inside her body, else she'd go insane.

"You started this inside me, so *finish* it."

He thrust forward but slowly. The muscle on the side of his jaw began to tic as his cock slid deeper inside her. Her sheath was too tight, protesting the invasion, but her hips lifted, welcoming more of his length. She dug her hands into the warm skin above her, gasping as her body adjusted. She wasn't sure if it was pain or not. Only that having him inside her quelled the raging need. She wanted him to thrust deep. Her body ached as he slid deeper but it also felt good to be full. A moan left her mouth as she arched towards him.

"That's it, lass, take me."

His voice was rough and demanding but it suited her mood. He lowered his body until he was pressed against her, his hands grasping the sides of her head. The crisp hair on his chest rubbed against her hard nipples as he caught his weight on his forearms, bracing above her shoulders. He gripped her hair, holding her head in place as his mouth captured hers in a hard kiss. His body moved at the same time, his back flexing. His cock left her only to thrust solidly back into her. This time her body burned as he filled her completely, pushing his entire length into her.

She bucked away from the pain. It was dull and burning. But his weight held her still, his cock fully lodged inside her sheath. Her fingers had curled into talons on his shoulders as she gasped, staring up into the canopy above her. Her lungs hurt because she forgot to breathe. Sucking in a deep breath, she felt the pain settle into an ache that didn't truly hurt overly much.

He pressed a tender kiss to her lips, coaxing her to open her mouth. His body flexed again, withdrawing his cock all the way to the tip before he sent it smoothly back inside her. His hands held her face steady as he kissed her, refusing to allow her to regain her senses by speaking.

He began thrusting in a steady motion, moving the bed gently as he lay over her, using his body to pin her beneath him. The hard length of his cock slid across the little clitoris at the top of her sex every time he moved. Ripples of delight rose up into her belly as the pain diminished. Her body returned to wanting him inside her. In spite of the ache, her passage felt good with his flesh stretching it wide. His lips trailed kisses across her cheek as she whimpered with new passion.

"Lift for me." His face returned to hover over hers. There was a hard glint in his eyes. "Wrap yer thighs around me."

She did it before thinking. The next thrust sent a harder bolt of pleasure up into her. Clasping him to her placed more pressure against her clitoris. Her hips rose to ensure that she took all of his length. Even her spine arched due to the ripples of delight running along it. Remaining still became impossible. She wanted to surge up toward his next thrust and hold him tightly inside her. Deep inside her. She felt like he wasn't lodged deep enough and strained toward him, trying to ensure that every last bit of his cock was sheathed inside her.

"More." She wasn't even sure what she craved only that she didn't have what she wanted yet.

He chuckled but it wasn't a nice sound. His body bucked, thrusting hard against her spread one.

"Aye, lass, I'll be happy to give ye all ye want and then some."

His brogue thickened, his words taking on an unearthly edge that fit the moment. She honestly didn't care if he was leading her to some pagan ritual that would steal her soul. Each downward plunge of his cock made her gasp with enjoyment.

She wanted more.

His pace increased. Each stroke gliding across her clitoris. A soft growl escaped his lips as she kept time with his motions, lifting to meet every thrust. Her wet sheath was taking his cock smoothly all the way to the base.

"That's the right of it, lass. Ride with me." He rose above

her, pressing his hands into the bed. His body became demanding, thrusting with hard purpose. Moving the bed as he took her, pressing his cock deeper with every plunge.

She rose to the challenge, lifting her hips for each thrust. Pleasure covered her like a thick fog, surrounding her. She could taste it because it was so thick, could feel it on every inch of her bare skin. Her breasts bounced as her lover thrust, a hard growl escaping his clenched teeth.

He dropped back down to cover her, his body moving in hard motions as he fucked her. His teeth grazed the side of her neck as pleasure began to tighten through her belly. There was an unexpected urgency to the sensation. Her hips bucked frantically to rise for his next downward motion. She clawed at his shoulders, her back arching up off the bed to press her against his body. Pleasure burst inside her, drawing a cry from her lips. It was so unexpected that she shivered violently, thrashing from side to side as it traveled along her spine to slam into her brain. It was all centered on the hard flesh stretching her passage. Her muscles attempting to grip it harder as she quivered in pure delight.

"That's the way." Her lover snarled his words, his body slamming into hers. She heard him gasp before his body went rigid. He thrust deep, burying himself to the hilt. There was a jerk from the hard flesh before she felt the hot spurt of his seed filling her. Her eyes flew open as he shivered, growling softly against her ear. His embrace was hard, holding her in place as his seed filled her.

Her entire body pulsed with satisfaction. She didn't think she'd ever been so at ease. Every muscle relaxed as ripples of pleasure moved over her.

Brodick's large body quivered too. Her fingers detected the tiny vibrations from where her hands were gripping his forearms. His chest rattled with a hollow breath before he lifted his head. His eyes glittered in a manner that drew her to stroke his shoulders. She couldn't truly explain the odd need to soothe him; only that it felt more intimate than anything she had ever experienced. He pressed a soft kiss against her mouth, lingering for only a moment.

He rolled off her in one fluid motion, withdrawing his cock to then lie beside her. She shivered, the separation striking her as harsh.

He slipped an arm under her, easing her up to rest her head on his chest. She tensed up, unsure of herself.

"Shhh."

He pressed her head onto his shoulder, making a few more soothing sounds as he settled her body alongside his. She knocked her knee against his as she tried to decide what to think. Every sense was overwhelmed, soaked in the pleasure he'd unleashed inside her. She lifted her head, trying to regain her poise by placing distance between them. Just a little so that she might think.

"There'll be none of that."

He sounded content, his voice almost lazy.

"None of what?"

He sighed but not softly, the sound was one of exasperation. "Lie down, lass."

He didn't wait for her to comply but sat up and turned her onto her side. He pressed her down onto the bed, taking a moment to grasp the heavy coverlet that had been folded at the foot of the bed. With one hand he dragged it up to cover her body. A moment later he pressed against her back, from head to toe his feet trapping hers.

"My lord—"

"When we're naked, ye'll call me Brodick."

Her next words got caught in her mouth as his cock pressed against her bottom. The thing was still hard, causing her to quiver. Brodick soothed her skin with strokes from his large hands, sliding his fingers along her thigh and over the curve of her hip. He nuzzled her neck, tucking the warm coverlet up to her collarbones.

"Ye may call me lover or a dozen other things, but not by my title. This is no place for rank or position. We're simply a man and woman sharing the delights of knowing each other."

"But we are not like others. Our union—"

"No more talking, lass. Ye spend too many hours thinking about things that no one truly understands. There is nothing wrong with enjoying something simply because ye like it. That's as old as time."

He bit her neck, a tiny, sharp nip that sent a little ripple of sensation down her body. Beneath the coverings, his hand cupped one breast, drawing a gasp from her.

"Surely you do not sleep here?" She didn't care if her voice sounded frantic, she was desperate to gain some small amount of distance from his hands. His touch drove her insane.

"My father has not yet been gone a full year. I never moved into his chamber, just as I didnae begin taking my supper on the dais. This chamber is better than the one I've been using. I had it furnished for ye. This bed was made for our children to be conceived in."

His arms tightened around her while he nuzzled against her neck drawing a deep breath in her hair. "I hope ye enjoy it as much as I am."

She did . . .

She wiggled as shock washed over her. It was the truth that she enjoyed the feel of his large body pressing against her.

"I warned ye once, Wife, keep me awake and ye'll need to entertain me." There was a hint of teasing in his voice now. His thumb brushed the nipple back and forth as his fingers cradled the soft mound. His cock thickened against her bottom, drawing a shaky breath from her. She tottered on the edge of bliss, not really wanting to think anymore. Especially not when her body felt so good.

Pandora's box . . .

"But no more entertaining tonight. I'd be a demanding brute if I pushed ye for more so soon after taking yer innocence."

She wasn't so sure that he'd taken anything. He had been bold, entering her chamber in spite of her refusal, but in those moments after he'd joined her, she'd offered as much as he had demanded. Her face burned as she recalled exactly how much she had wanted to be taken. She wriggled, trying to gain some space.

"So now you believe that I am not loose." Hurt edged her words. His embrace tightened, holding her against his body.

"Aye. It's nae an uncommon way of proving the issue."

There was no softness in his tone. But there was a ring of approval that she should have detested. Instead a small smile curved her lips because measuring up to his standards was something she did see the value of. Knowing that he was pleased stroked a portion of her heart, filling her with tender contentment. It was very tempting to lie back against him and savor the moment.

Oh, it was foolish to let the emotion wrap around her. But she couldn't stop it. Her eyelashes fluttered as she drifted off into slumber, warmer and more content than she could recall. A memory of her mother's face as she lay against her sire, filling her dreams. Sometime during the night, the face changed to Brodick's and she snuggled against him, holding onto his arm where it draped across her chest.

A warm hand stroked her shoulder. She muttered in her sleep. It felt quite good, that petting. She lifted her eyelids to discover who was being so motherly towards her.

Her mind snapped to attention when she looked into a man's eyes. For a second she was confused, stunned by the masculine face. His hair was tossed from the night and there wasn't a stitch on him. Nothing to shield his body. The early dawn light washed over his hard chest, down across his belly and along his thighs. He stood up, stretching his arms. Her eyes were glued to the sight of his magnificent body. The church would condemn her fascination with his earthly form, but her gaze roamed over him, touching the firm skin.

The sight was magnificent.

He turned, considering her with his midnight eyes. Even in the light of morning they seemed forged out of the night.

"I enjoy the look of ye tumbled in my bed quite a bit." His attention lowered to her breasts that were bare and uncovered. "Aye, I believe I'll take to waking up beside ye often."

She pulled the heavy bedcover over her nude body. He chuckled at her action. She expected him to tease her again but he bent down to retrieve his shirt where it lay on the floor. His kilt was draped over the foot of the bed and half onto the floor, the wide leather belt used for holding it around his waist lying a few feet from the bed. As he shrugged into the creamy linen shirt, she lowered her eyes to look at his cock. It stuck out from his body, the head slightly red. A deep chuckle jerked her attention back to his face. A grin decorated his lips.

"I'll have to see about making sure ye get a chance to look yer fill at me later." He shrugged his shoulders into the shirt. It slithered into place, the length of it falling to cover his cock.

"But nae now."

He scooped up his kilt. Using the end of the bed, he laid it in even pleats over the belt. His hands were confident at the task, telling her that he was not a man who expected service. She might even forget he was a titled man while watching him lean back over the bed. He grasped the ends of the belt and secured it around his lean waist. When he stood, the kilt fell perfectly around his thighs. His self reliance drew her interest. She found him likeable and that frightened her. Fear laced her thoughts as she contemplated a man she could see her heart growing fond of. If he'd been anything like Philipa, she'd have ignored him easily.

"Good morning, mistress."

Helen's voice bounced off the chamber walls. She led a string of maids in through the door, not stopping until she was leaning in among the bed curtains. The maid beamed. Helen reached for the heavy bed coverings and tugged them clean to the foot of the bed. Slumber evaporated instantly as Anne grabbed at the edge of the comforter. She flopped over onto her belly as graceless as a newly caught fish, her eyes rounding when the morning air brushed her bare bottom.

"No need to be shy, mistress." Helen was surprisingly strong, pulling the thick cover clear off the bed. A satisfied smile lit her face.

"Here now, out of bed with ye."

Helen didn't wait for Anne to overcome her modesty. She gently grasped a wrist, pulling her out of the bed. The row of maids all lowered themselves. There was a snap of fabric behind her. But she froze as she looked into Brodick's eyes. He stood watching her, his expression unreadable.

"There now." Helen held up the soiled sheet triumphantly. She showed its bloody stain proudly to the waiting maids. They all lowered themselves once more before turning to fetch her clothing. Brodick eyed it, satisfaction lifting his eyes. He had his boots on now and looked like the earl once more, the man she'd woken up with hidden behind a controlled expression.

"It will serve as a fine example to the castle folk to have this flying outside yer window." Helen inspected the sheet closely, nodding approval. "Aye, indeed it will. Too many of the young are tempted to dally outside of marriage."

Helen refused to give up the sheet, keeping a tight hold on it. She watched the maids bring forward Anne's clothing with a keen eye.

"The lot of ye take notice, the lass is nae having her monthly curse."

Every set of eyes flew to her bare thighs. Anne groaned softly, more embarrassed than she'd ever been in her life. Helen had no pity for her plight. The senior maid took an edge of the soiled sheet that was still clean and swiped it along her inner leg.

"You see? White as snow it is."

"Helen . . ."

The maid didn't look a bit contrite. She lifted her chin, satisfaction shining in her eyes.

"Just making sure that there is no question of yer honor." She aimed a hard stare at the frozen maids. "From any corner of the castle."

"Aye, ma'am."

"Ma'am."

"Indeed, mistress."

" 'Tis so, ma'am."

Helen nodded approval. The maids began to dress Anne taking care to lay each garment softly against her skin. Her unbound hair was lifted gently by one set of hands while another eased her doublet up her right arm. Brodick watched, seemingly interested in her dressing.

"We'll have some of yer clothing altered by tonight. Yer mother's housekeeper should be demoted. None of yer corsets are the correct length on the sides. Such an oversight is shameful."

A maid was closing the front of her doublet when a fist landed on the door.

"Open it." The earl spoke with firm authority that sent every maid to lowering herself instead of doing what he wanted.

"Now, Ginny."

Helen didn't lack command presence—the maid jumped to the ring of urgency in her voice. One of them pulled the door wide. Cullen and Druce stood there along with three other men.

"Thank ye for attending us, my lords." Brodick sounded more serious than an executioner. He pointed toward Helen.

The senior maid proudly pulled the sheet wide between her outstretched arms. Anne felt her face burn as the men all inspected the stain. They didn't say anything, only stared before their gazes drifted over her.

" 'Tis settled then."

Brodick nodded as he swept the room with a firm glance. He paused at each maid before eying the men. When they had all returned his nod he moved across the chamber to her.

"I do see the value in some traditions. Now the matter is proven truly." He stroked a hand across her cheek, tenderness flickering in his eyes. It vanished almost as quickly as his fingers finished stroking her face.

"Wife."

He strode from the chamber without another word. Her throat felt tight as if a hand was squeezing it. She had to force her next breath down to her lungs.

"Men. They bluster but don't know what to do when presented with solid evidence. Never ye fear, mistress, the lord is pleased with ye. He'll remember to say so later, once he knows that his men have been shown the proof of yer consummation."

"I shall hope they are satisfied."

Helen patted her shoulder. "I suppose ye dinnae ken the way it is in Scotland but knowing that the lord took ye to his bed will keep any trouble from arising among those that want to steal ye."

Anne stared at Helen but heard a few smothered sounds from the maids that sounded like laughter. "You must be mistaken. No one steals other humans."

One of the maids did laugh outright. She tried to catch herself but her cheeks turned ruby. "Beg pardon, mistress."

She didn't sound contrite. The other girls grinned at her as well. Helen sighed.

"Well now, ye might as well share with the mistress since ye all but spit it out. Vanora here was born on McAlister land. They don't like their daughters marring McJames men so her husband snuck her away by the harvest moon."

"I see." Anne stared at the girl but she winked, clearly content with her lot.

Ginny tried to take the sheet but Helen shook her head. She returned to smiling. She even hummed some springtime melody.

"Nay. I pulled the covers back, so the sheet is mine to hang from the window." She offered Anne a firm look. "There will be no gossip. I'll lay my hand on the altar and swear to yer purity myself. Every one of these maids comes from family that has served this house for generations. I selected them carefully."

Pride rang in her voice but it also shone from the faces of each girl. It was the same at Warwickshire. Even in the face of Philipa's sour personality, the staff was loyal. Their parents had served the Stanford nobles and the generations before them. It was an honor that even a surly mistress could not drive them away from. To argue against your place was to question God's will in putting you there.

The shutters were opened wide, fresh air sweeping into the chamber. It took the scent of candle wax away, leaving the first traces of spring. It also carried the smell of Brodick's skin away. She'd never noticed that men smelled attractive. Yet Brodick did. Lifting one hand, she found a trace of it lingering on her skin. Her passage was sore, marking where he'd been. It was a moment she'd been raised to think of as sinful, yet it felt very right. As though she had been made for him.

"I told ye that ye'd be lamenting sunrise." Helen smiled with the same sort of superiority her own mother had often aimed at her children when she knew that their youth was preventing them from understanding one of life's realities.

"I am going to fly this sheet. 'Tis a moment I've looked forward to."

Helen knotted one corner of the sheet through the shutter just above the thick iron hinge. She threaded the opposite corner through the shutter on the far side of the window, making sure it was tied tightly. She pushed the length of the sheet through the open window.

A few moments later the bells along the walls began to ring. First only the one nearest to them, but as it sent its sound into the morning, another rang out and then another until the sound echoed up and down the long length of walls.

She blushed but her heart swelled too. She hadn't shamed him.

Brodick was worthy of purity.

The emotion caught her off guard. It was so very tender that she covered her mouth with a hand. She liked him too much. In sooth, she enjoyed the duties of a wife far too much.

You should have no objections to being used . . .

Yet was it being used? Taken, aye but she had enjoyed it full well.

Her temper suddenly lit. Philipa had been left far behind her. With everything else that she needed to worry about, the woman's ill words were not among them.

"Come now, mistress, a good meal will help place strength in ye. Ye'll need it when the lord's babe begins to grow inside your womb."

The color drained from her face. Icy dread locked its grip around her heart.

His babe.

Bonnie had said she would have it.

"Och now, look at ye. Such worry in one so young." Helen laid a motherly arm around her shoulders, hugging her firmly.

"There's no need for losing yer color. Ye heard Agnes yerself. Ye're strong and sturdy. A babe will be no trouble at all."

Helen swept her out the door. The maids all followed while the bells quieted.

If only it were as simple to still the ringing of dread inside her head.

It was not.

Chapter Eight

S he did not suffer inactivity well.

Before noon, she was pacing for want of something to do. Every maid in the castle seemed intent on feeding her until she burst. The well-meaning girls and women bore trays to her, all of them carefully laid out to please not only the palate but the eyes as well. It was the women who were harder to send away with their dishes unsampled. Lady Mary was spoilt enough to slash others' effort without a care, yet Anne knew what it was to heat an iron on the coals. She herself had carefully smoothed the wrinkles from linen napery in preparation for it being laid on a tray for the head table. Extreme care had to be taken to ensure that no soot marred the fine fabric. She'd burned her fingers a few times when the cloth wrapping the handle of the iron slipped or was too thin.

She was not callous enough to reject such offerings but her stays were growing too tight to bear.

She froze as she turned to face yet another lowered head. Deception or not, she was finished acting contrary to her nature.

"I believe it's time for me to meet the cook."

The maid lowered herself. "I'll fetch her straight away, Mistress."

"Nay, no. I believe the woman should be busy, what with the noon meal so close to serving. I will follow you to the kitchen."

The girl looked unsure. Her teeth appeared, pressing into her lower lip. Anne refused to be swayed. Just the mention of going to the kitchen had started her thinking. Yes, she was done being idle. She could not be Mary, didn't know how to act as her half-sister. It was much better to be herself. At least that way, she would not be stumbling over mistakes every other hour of the day.

"What is your name?"

"Ginny, Mistress. I greeted ye this morning."

"I recall your face now. Do be kind and show me the way to the kitchen. It is time for work now that all of these wedding traditions have been seen to."

Ginny beamed at her, clearly approving of her work ethic. "We didn't know exactly what ye might be expecting."

The maid hesitated, her mouth closing as she stopped mid-thought.

"Because I'm English, you mean." It was a fact. The coming secession would change hundreds of years of battling between the two countries. Some questioned Elizabeth Tudor's decision not to marry, but Anne saw the benefit of it. Was not peace worth one woman remaining unwed? She had been one of the best monarchs in history, cultivating a richer economy. Who was to say Elizabeth hadn't decided long ago that remaining a spinster was a path to a better future for her people? The queen had often said she was married to her subjects. Anne could see the wisdom in it.

Anne followed Ginny. They walked through the circular eating hall she'd supped in last night. The tables were empty now, the floor swept clean. The scent of roasting meat drifted from the kitchen. In back of the tower was a building with a slopped roof. Five huge fireplaces were built along the outer

wall. There were also ovens between them, iron doors covering them. Long tables ran the length of the building, thick,
wooden tables that bore the marks of use. One end was
dusted with flour. Two women worked large lumps of dough
there, their chemises rolled up past their elbows. They looked
up, watching her enter, but never stopped kneading. But their
motions slowed down.

"This is Bythe. She's the head cook."

The woman was formidable. Age didn't mark her face but
confidence did. Bythe nodded respectfully. A strip of linen was
wound around her head. Only a tiny hint of her dark hair
peeked out at the edges. Her forehead was shinny with perspiration. The end of her nose was slightly red from leaning
into the fire pits. Her forearms were bare too. A large apron
was pinned to the wool of her bodice as well as being tied
around her waist. She wore a strip of tartan over one shoulder
that draped down her back. In fact all the women did. The
plaid was the same weave of colors the men wore in their kilts.

"Welcome, mistress."

Bythe was clearly uncertain as to what to do with her. Anne
offered her a calm smile before looking at the table closest to
her. Fresh fish lay on it, their scales still shiny with water. The
lenten season had begun and good Christians dined on fish.
Two large bowls stood ready for cleaning, a large knife lying
nearby. Several smaller bowls were neatly set out awaiting the
fish, holding spices of salt, rosemary, pepper and even nut-
meg.

"I see you are very confident in your position, Bythe."

The cook's expression flickered with a hint of relaxation.
Anne unbuttoned one sleeve at her wrist, folding the fabric
back along her forearm.

"Yet there is always work for another set of hands in any
kitchen."

The rest of the work slowed to nearly a standstill. Anne reached for the knife, hefting it in a firm hand. She grasped a slippery fish with the other, not a hint of hesitation in her. With a few skilled slices, she cleaned it, removed the bones carefully, inspecting the skeleton to make sure she had them all. She felt the weight of every set of eyes on her. But that was something she could thank Philipa for teaching her.

How to keep her back straight under pressure. She would not falter.

She finished the fish without looking away from her task even once. Laying the meat on a clean tray between cleaning bowls and the ones holding the spices, she reached for another fish.

"I see yer mother taught ye yer way around the kitchen, Mistress." Bythe took up another long knife. With a quick slice, another fish was well on its way to being ready for cooking. "Since I heard ye were at yer English court for some years, I'm pleasantly surprised to see ye so practiced."

Anne laid another fish on the tray. She didn't want to outright lie by claiming that she'd worked in the kitchens at court. Yet she had to find some answer.

"I was sent to the kitchens at Warwickshire when I turned eleven." That much was true.

Bythe nodded. "My mother worked her entire life at this table. I turned pastry on it when I still needed a stool to see over the top."

Work resumed around them but not the conversation. The others were listening, waiting to judge her character. She was their mistress, yet English. There were many who didn't think the two could coexist. More than one English bride had spent years in her chambers, remaining a stranger even as she bore the next generation. She did pity her half-sister that fate. With

Mary's vanity and spoilt nature, she would have been bitterly unhappy at Sterling.

I like it though.

It was another one of those unexpected thoughts. They were coming more often now. Maybe her mind was becoming soft. She'd heard about prison breaking first the personality of its victims and then the body.

She mustn't think about such a fate.

With a stiff back, she began spicing the fish. There was much to do and Anne dedicated her attention to the tasks. There was a sense of security in doing the things that she would have been doing if she were still at Warwickshire. She kept her mind away from the fact that she hadn't slept behind the kitchen.

But her body refused to forget that she'd spent the night with Brodick. Heat whispered over her skin. Need awakened from places that two days past she'd never noticed she might feel. Such as the skin on her thighs. Gooseflesh spread up her arms with the recollection of the way Brodick stroked it. His hands were large, the skin suffused with heat.

Her blood ran warmer, her heart beating faster. Even sore, her passage began to clamor for another taste of his hard flesh. She failed to understand how being impaled could feel so good.

Yet it had.

Her lust had truly opened Pandora's box because now she craved more. She could feel the insanity flowing along with her blood. It unleashed a desire to be stripped bare like Brodick had taken her. No clothing to separate them.

And just as any lunatic at Bedlam, she was cheerful in her insanity. Her lust was welcome because she knew what delights were to be gained by feeding it.

She would adore a babe.

That idea sobered her, washing her fever aside. It was the secret of her heart, the desire for a child. Living under Philipa had robbed her of that joy. She'd buried it deep down inside her to avoid the pain of watching her friends grow large and round with child.

Brodick wanted a child from her.

Temptation urged her to take the chance offered her. Conceive and let the details be damned.

It might be she that ended up cursed if she did. Setting her thoughts to remaining childless, Anne forced her cheerful ideas of a babe back down to where she'd buried them.

She would not find happiness here. Such a reward couldn't possibly result from so ill a deception.

Yet that did not stop her from lamenting.

"I have heard a most interesting rumor." Cullen was in full teasing form. Brodick rolled his eyes. He was more interested in finding his wife, but that only made him grimace. Enjoying her was one thing. No man needed to be drawn to a woman when there was work to be done.

Cullen smirked. "It seems yer wife spent the day in the kitchen."

"Doing what?"

"Ye sound mighty suspicious for a man who had his doubts about his bride's purity proven so recently."

"Dinnae play with me, Brother. Someday soon ye'll marry and I've a fine memory."

A hint of contriteness covered Cullen's face. "Och well, I forget that ye cannae stand for a wee bit o' teasing. Ye buckle like a moist reed."

"*Cullen . . .*"

His sibling grinned. "Ye'll know soon enough. She cooked

yer supper. I hope yer stomach is stronger than yer tolerance to jesting."

Brodick turned his attention to the table, fearing what he might see. Attending court didn't teach a woman how to turn a loaf of bread. But as mistress of the house, his wife could do whatever she pleased in the kitchen. None of the staff would argue with her, even if they knew she was incorrect.

"I have nae seen you so pale since Father caught ye with yer first woman."

His brother laughed at him, his voice echoing down the supper table. The food there looked wholesome and normal enough to his eye. But it was taste that mattered.

"You will nae be so smug if she laced supper with foxglove."

"Still so ready to tell me that you will not doubt me at every opportunity, my lord?"

He flushed, the soft voice reprimanding him better than any slap might have. He was being a brute, even if he had been verbally sparring with his brother.

"I meant that for my brother, nae you."

She paused, sweeping the men at the table with her gaze. Her lips set into a tight line.

"I see, my lord." Her voice was tight as she added his title.

His wife passed him. A large meat pie in her hands. Steam rose from it, spreading the scent of spices in the air. The men at the table watched them intently. His wife set the pie down. She cut into it with a knife, letting a cloud of steam loose.

"I suppose it is a good thing that I understand how you prefer to have matters settled between us." She dished up a hearty slice and presented it to him. Her gaze was steady, the plate unwavering. Challenge shone from her eyes, sending heat down his body. Need prickled along his skin, her stance sparking more lust to fill his cock. The organ twitched, swelling to stand up beneath his kilt. She lifted one eyebrow.

"I thought you said your words were for Cullen. Do you suspect me of foul play?"

The conversations near them died abruptly, his men casting worried looks at them. With a frown, she broke off a chunk of pie. She tossed it into her mouth without a thought, chewing and swallowing it quickly.

She deposited the plate on the table, her face turning red.

"I find I have no stomach for meals frosted with suspicions."

She lowered herself before turning in a huff and flurry of skirts. But she did it artfully as though she was accustomed to holding her displeasure inside.

He found that fact most unsettling of all.

A man should not be able to hurt her feelings.

Anne fought off tears while her feet moved quickly through the tables. Pain filled her. She hissed with frustration when she entered the hallway. She should not care. It made no sense. So what if the man had doubted her cooking? Let him and every one of his men go to bed with rumbling bellies.

Yet it chafed. His suspicions. She had given him her chastity to prove her worth. That gift she might only bestow on one man her entire life. Hurt filled her chest. She didn't go up the stairs. The chamber was filled with the memory of the night before and that drew more pain from the wound.

The turmoil gave her feet more speed. Walking through the entry doors of the tower, she moved into the bailey. There was much of Sterling that was still a mystery.

Moving across the courtyard, she paused near the stables. The horses snorted in their stalls. The musty smell of hay permeated the air. It was quarter moon now. Little light shone down from the night sky to pierce the night. Along the walls, fires were lit in iron torch cages. They were set along the castle fortifications every twenty feet. There was no lantern left near the stables for fear of fire. The horses were expensive. No one dare risk losing some of them to a mishap caused by the wind.

But enough light drifted down from the walls. Moving into the stable, she marveled at the number of horses. Hundreds of them stood quietly in the dark all in neat rows. Reaching up, she rubbed a velvet-covered muzzle.

"I didnae say I suspected ye of poisoning my table on purpose." Brodick's voice was low but she still heard the exasperation in it. "There be a difference."

"Yet you stood there afraid to touch the plate."

Her anger made little sense to her but she couldn't seem to contain it. It bubbled up, spilling out of her. She heard him snort. "What do you expect from me? Am I to sit idle during the day awaiting your return?" She turned on him, pointing a finger at his larger chest. "So that I might spread my thighs to be of service?"

"The idea has merit." His voice was deep with frustration. He grasped her wrist, tugging her forward. She tumbled into his chest. He locked her against him with a hard arm. "Since we appear to find more peace when we're fucking, I find that idea very appealing."

His brogue thickened. A hard hand slapped against her bottom, pushing her hips toward him. His hard cock pressed against her belly.

"That's what held my attention, Wife. I looked at ye and stiffened up like a fresh-faced lad."

His lips claimed her in a solid kiss. He demanded surrender but she twisted away from his lips. With a growl he followed her, one hand gripping the back of her head. He plundered her mouth, pressing her lips apart. A hard thrust from his tongue invaded her mouth, drawing a soft moan from her. Delight washed over her, the heat she'd tried to suppress all day igniting. His warm male skin smelled so good. Her hands spread, searching for the button that held his collar closed. She needed to touch him. Wanted to press against him.

"I spent half the day thinking about getting back between yer thighs."

He didn't sound very happy about it, either. But his confession pleased her, her nipples tingling behind her stays.

"I thought about you as well."

The words tumbled past her lips. There was no considering them. The grip on the back of her head softened.

"Och lass, we've more than our share of passion, that's for sure."

The hand on her bottom began stroking her. Heat moved through her passage in response, hot and heavy need settling inside her. The hard outline of his cock was a teasing torment to her. She shuddered as her clitoris pulsed, hungry for friction.

"Best ye ken, lass. I will never send ye back to yer father."

There was a hard edge to his voice. Fierce possession that somehow made her feel cherished. He picked her up, sweeping her up against his chest as if she were no more than a child.

"Ye're mine and I dinnae care if I have to remind ye of that over and over."

He carried her into an empty stall. There was new hay on the ground, smelling clean and fresh. Brodick knelt, lowering her to the floor as he followed her. The hay got caught in her hair as he pressed her back onto it, his lips finding hers and taking them in another long kiss. The tip of his tongue stroked over her lower lip before thrusting into her mouth to tease her tongue.

"Since ye were a maiden, ye've never been tumbled in the

hay afore." He rose above her on his elbows, a shadowy figure. "I feel the need to introduce ye to trysting."

"A tryst is between lovers." But it made her breathless. Excitement made her voice sultry.

"And ye nae think a husband might serve as a lover?" His fingers found the buttons of her doublet, working them loose. "I assure ye I'm up to the task."

She suddenly felt bold. Reaching down, she found the bulge of his cock. A harsh breath was his response as she stroked it through the pleats of his kilt.

"A statement that I must insist you prove."

She pushed at his wide shoulders, unsure if he would allow her to lead him. The night didn't let her see his expression. She pushed harder, lifting her own shoulders up. He dropped back as she sat up.

"I've heard a few tales of trysts and lovers' ways."

"I insist that ye confess every one of them to me."

With one hand, she loosened the button at his collar. She stroked her fingers down the center of his chest, easing between the edges of his open shirt.

"The church does command that a wife obey her husband." She stopped with her hand beneath his shirt, the crisp hair on his chest holding her attention.

"It does indeed."

His words were clipped. It was very arousing the way he laid so still when she knew he was much stronger than she. A fragile trust threaded its way between them, unleashing her curiosity.

"I heard that there is more than one type of kiss. A meeting of lips and male flesh that the French ladies use to beguile their lovers."

"Who told ye about that?"

She shrugged, trailing her fingers over his belt. There was no way to tell him that the servants knew absolutely everything in a large estate. When important nobles had visited Warwickshire, the nightly escapades provided many evenings of entertainment for the gossips. Just because she was a maiden did not mean she hadn't heard exactly how men and women coupled. She stopped over his cock, her hand resting on top of the hard bulge.

"I suppose I could put it out of my mind . . ."

A hard hand gripped her hair. He wound her thick braid around his hand. The hold drew her against his chest.

"Lift my kilt and try it, lass. I dare ye."

She stroked her fingers to the edge of his kilt, fingering the fabric. "Does that mean you're not afraid I might bewitch you? I hear many Puritans believe pleasure of the flesh to be the work of demons leading us sinners to eternal damnation."

He pressed her back against the hay. She gasped at the speed with which he rose up. There was a great deal of power in his body. It should have frightened her but she trusted him. That was often the difference between a lover and a husband. The lover you shared your body with. A husband you prayed might not be too much to bear.

"I suppose I'll just have to beguile ye first."

He pulled her skirts up, the night air bushing her thighs, making her shiver. But it wasn't with cold. Her heart raced, making her skin warm.

"Now, about that spreading yer thighs bit you mentioned earlier . . . I've a mind to sample that bit of wifely service."

Her breath caught. Brodick chuckled as he stroked one thigh. "There's something that we are going to have to practice, lass. Talking."

"One does not talk about intimacies."

He touched her slit. A single stroke that sent pleasure up

along her passage. His fingertips remained touching her clitoris, rubbing a slow circle over the top of it. The urge to lift
her hips took great amounts of self discipline to quell. She
was struck dumb by how good that touch felt. It didn't seem
possible that any single part of her body could feel so much
pleasure.

"Then how did ye learn about French kissing?"

She blushed in the dark. "That was talk shared between
women."

"Yet it was about sucking a man's cock between yer lips. Did
ye just overhear or were ye asking for advice on how to handle
me?"

"*Brodick*."

He chuckled, low and deep. The sound sent a shiver up her
body because it sounded so . . . hungry. He hovered over her
slit for a moment, teasing it with his fingertips. Sweet pleasure
flooded her with each tiny touch but soon it wasn't enough.
She felt empty, aching to be filled.

"You smell hot, Wife." He pushed her knees up. "Just the
way I like my lover to be."

A breathless whimper crossed her lips. His lips pressed a
kiss against her spread slit, the tip of his tongue flickering
across the sensitive bud at the top of her sex. There was too
much sensation. Pleasure, need, hunger all twisted inside her.
It was impossible to remain still. She arched toward his teasing tongue. Her hands curled into the hay, grasping handfuls
of it. He lapped her slit from the opening of her channel to the
top where her clitoris pulsed for friction.

"Sweet, verra sweet." He pulled the folds of her slit apart to
expose her clitoris further. He sucked it deep into his mouth,
pushing her to the brink of climax. But she didn't tumble off
the peak of arousal yet. He kept her there, her sheath begging
for penetration. One thick finger slid deep and she moaned.

"Now, there's a sound that I approve of ye making."

He pulled free and returned to her sheath with two fingers. He teased the opening before thrusting back in. His lips returned to her clitoris, sucking on the tender bud while his fingers worked in and out of her body.

"Brodick . . ."

"Aye, any more of yer sweet nectar and I'll spill myself like a green lad."

Her body pulsed, hungry and aching for fulfillment. She was poised on the edge of climax, so close, one hard thrust from his cock would send the hard pleasure shooting through her.

She was at his mercy once more.

That rubbed her temper. Jerking up, out of the hay, she pushed him onto his back. She wanted to be more than complacent. More than quietly going along with Philipa's plan. She wanted to take a lover.

He flopped back onto the hay, raising a thin cloud of dust. It smelled of spring, suiting her mood. Moving down his body, she boldly pushed his kilt up to expose his cock. The organ was stiff, swollen with the same need that burned inside her passage. Reaching for it, she clasped it, stroking the soft skin. It was very hard, making her long to lay back for his possession.

But not just yet.

"Go on, lass."

His voice was tight as though his control was stretched. She enjoyed that idea. Touching her tongue to the head, she tasted the skin. It was pleasant, filling her with a sense of control over him and his greater strength. A soft groan rose from his chest when she licked the slit. There was a drop of slightly salty fluid hidden there that her tongue carried away. Opening her mouth she sucked the entire head between her lips. His hips jerked, thrusting toward her head. His hand grasped her braid once more, a harsh sound coming from his lips. For long moments she flicked her tongue over the cock in her mouth. Little thrusts from his hips moved it in and out. She listened to his breathing turn ragged, the fingers in her hair tightening. Little zips of pain crossed her scalp, but they only added to the intensity of the moment. Her body was so alive with need that every sensation added to the inferno.

"Enough." He pulled her head away from his cock, the head leaving her lips with a small pop. "Ye've a wicked grasp of applying what ye hear to the practical act."

He sounded immensely pleased by that fact, too.

"I suppose it's a good thing you don't want a dim-witted wife."

He scoffed at her. "We were both born to the positions that required we marry well. I'm pleasantly surprised by who ye be without yer father's lands."

The hand in her hair pulled her back up his body, until they were face-to-face once again. Clasping her tightly against his chest, he rolled over, her thighs spreading for his hips. She whimpered when her skirts got in the way. She loathed the barrier, reaching down to yank the fabric out of the way herself.

"In fact, I dinnae care a wit if ye're poor as a beggar. I'm going to tumble ye good and hard."

He raised his kilt and the head of his cock pressed against the wet opening to her body.

"Ye'll be tender." He thrust forward, controlling his speed. His body shuddered with the effort. "Easy . . ."

He didn't sound as if he wanted to enter her softly. His voice had deepened and roughened. But pain rose from her sheath as it was stretched by his flesh again. It didn't last as long as last night, fading into a dull ache almost instantly. Her clitoris begged for friction.

"Take me, lover."

Her words were as bold as her needs. She heard his swift intake of breath before he pulled free. With a hard thrust he impaled her again, pushing his length deep into her body. Sweet enjoyment speared up into her belly, her back arching to make sure he was lodged completely.

"Aye, lass, that's exactly what I plan to do with ye."

His body jerked, setting up a fast rhythm of hard thrusts. Each one drove his cock deep before he pulled free for only a mere second. The skin of their thighs slapped together from the speed and force of his action. Her hips rose up off the hay to meet each downward motion. Each stroke drove more delight into her belly until she couldn't endure any more. Tension knotted around her sheath and the hard flesh stretching it. She reached for her lover as a cry left her lips. Savage enjoyment flooded her, ripping her away from any thoughts or concerns. There was only the pleasure and the hard body of her lover. He growled in her ear a moment before she felt a spurt of hot fluid hit her deep inside her passage. His cock jerked as it pumped his seed against the mouth of her womb. Her passage tightened around his length, milking every drop from it.

She was suddenly aware of their breathing. It sounded loud against the silence of the night. Perspiration dotted her skin and the night air was cool as it blew across her exposed legs. But her lover was warm. His body weight was caught on his elbows, his chest working like a bellows. Raising a hand, she placed it against his chest. Her fingertips caught the hard thumping of his heart.

A soft kiss touched her forehead.

"Did I hurt ye?" He kissed her cheek and then her lips before raising up to look at her face. "Did I?"

"Only when you looked at me with suspicion."

That fragile bond of trust was growing into a web. Surrounded by the night, she felt at ease confessing her feelings. He sighed.

"I was so busy fighting off the urge to tumble ye, I didn't give a damn about supper. I was trying nae to toss ye over my shoulder like a raiding barbarian."

"Your brother—"

"Was teasing me. So I shot him back a harsh answer."

Her lower lip trembled. She wanted to believe him. Her heart needed to believe that he trusted her. All of the tender emotions that had begun to grow deep inside her demanded that she embrace his words.

"Since ye nae have any siblings, ye dinnae ken how they can needle at each other. 'Tis a way of showing affection. I swear it."

He sat back on his haunches, gently closing her legs for her. A firm hand drew her skirts down to cover her legs, too. A shaft of pain went through her heart as she considered how true his words were. She often teased Bonnie, and her brothers were hellions when it came to taunting one another. Only their mother managed to quiet them.

He drew a stiff breath when she remained silent.

"I suppose I'll have to be patient with expecting ye to trust what I say."

She could hear how much he didn't like waiting for that to happen.

"Come on now, lass. I'd better get ye into a warm bed before ye catch a chill."

He pulled her to her feet, the hay falling off them both. A soft giggle escaped her lips, surprising her. She hadn't made such a carefree sound in years. Brodick picked a few larger pieces from her hair, brushing his hands down her skirt to dislodge what he could.

He clasped her hand in his, silencing her once more. She looked at their joined hands, oddly touched by the simple gesture.

"Helen will tear a strip off my back if ye take ill from lying down in the stable."

"Do you actually think women are so frail, or is it merely because I'm English?"

He turned to look at her. "Aye, I see ye're fine and strong. Maybe I'm a wee bit overprotective. I know many a lass who would have quarreled with sleeping on the trail."

He sounded pleased with her. Her heart latched onto that information, clutching it tightly.

"But we've a fine bed waiting for us tonight. As much as I enjoyed the hay, I believe we'll leave the stable to the horses and the maids."

She laughed at his suggestive comment. "You're a poor example, talking that way."

"What example? Did I nae get married? Have I nae followed ye out of the hall twice to do my husbandly duty?"

"*Brodick.*" She cast a look toward the wall. "Your men are listening."

He leaned close, his breath warm against her ear. "I hope they heard ye yelling with pleasure."

"Oh . . ." She slapped a hand in the center of his broad chest. The brute chuckled at her temper, tugging her along behind him.

"Come, Wife. Let us to bed."

He raised his voice so that it bounced off the walls. Her face flamed scarlet with his amusement ringing in her ears. Yet there was also pride filling her. She could not deny that it pleased her to know that he wanted everyone to know that he enjoyed having her in his bed.

Many noble brides were not so desired.

If that meant she was guilty of the sin of vanity, so be it.

He took her across the courtyard, several of the men on the walls peering down at them. Brodick held her hand fast, even when she wiggled her fingers. Night surrounded them. Even in the tower there was meager light. Few candles were lit along the walls inside. It was quiet, too, no one in sight. Brodick led her up the stairs, his boots making no sound on the stone steps. For so large a man, he moved well. It spoke volumes about him. His father had clearly seen to his training. No man learned the art of carrying his weight without tutoring. Boys began their tutelage at five, the same time daughters began to follow their mothers to work. Lady Mary had been instructed in dance, movement and royal service for years before being placed at court.

Brodick pulled her into the chamber they'd shared the night before. Changes had taken place during the day. Three ornate tapestries covered the walls near the fire. There was also a matching set of candlestick holders on a newly arrived vanity table. Made of silver and carved with artful designs, they held lit candles that filled the chamber with yellow light.

On the table was a mirror. Anne gaped at the costly item. She couldn't recall the last time she'd snuck a peek in Philipa's. Such an item was worth more than the mare she'd ridden to Sterling. The candle flame flickered off the polished surface of the mirror in a pagan dance that mesmerized. This was a highly prized possession even for an earl's house. She reached out, stroking only the silver frame that held the polished glass. Her reflection joined the flame. Anne stared in wonder at her face. Her lips were slightly swollen, far sultrier than she'd ever considered herself. She knew her hair was brown but in the mirror it shimmered with copper highlights, tiny wisps of it loosened from her braid by Brodick's hands framing her face. Her skin was creamy and smooth like fresh cream in the spring when the cows were eating lots of greenery.

"You've met with Helen's approval for certain." Brodick appeared behind her. "As well as my own."

He wrapped his arms around her. The embrace was warm and secure, such as she couldn't recall sampling from anyone save her mother. A steady reminder of how strong he was. She felt the thumping of his heart against her back. His lips twitched at the corners as he watched her in the mirror. He moved a hand up from her waist and over the swell of her breasts. Even buffeted by her doublet and stays, she shivered, her skin humming with approval. His fingers rubbed a small circle on the soft portion of her upper breasts.

"I'm glad to see that ye like yer bridal gift."

"Gift?" Her breath caught as he moved his hand to her bare throat. She felt so vulnerable, the column of her neck fragile compared to the strength she knew he had in his hand.

"Aye. The mirror is a present from me. A good friend of mine brought it back from his recent voyage to France."

"That was very . . . very kind."

He leaned down and she watched, fascinated, as he kissed her neck. Seeing it was incredibly arousing. She could see his lips compressing against the smooth surface of her throat. At that same moment, her skin rippled with the warm sensation of his kiss.

"I can think of a few things to do with it myself."

His hand cupped her jaw, lifting it. With a twist of his fingers he opened the first button and then the second. A tiny gasp crossed her lips as he set his fingers between the open edges of the garment to touch her bare skin.

"Things I nae considered a mirror being useful for, as a matter of fact. It may have been well worth the gold I traded for it."

The next button separated and several more. She followed his fingers devotedly, excitement rising inside her with each little pop. He used both hands to spread the edges open. The mirror reflected her stays and the swells of her breasts.

"Now that's something verra pretty to gaze at."

He pulled her doublet over her shoulders and down her arms. There was a brief moment when he stepped back from her to free the garment from her wrists. She shivered at the loss of contact, sighing when he returned to press up against her from head to toe. Her attention was drawn to the differences between their genders. His wider shoulders that appeared on either side of her own. His face was harder, his jaw more firm with less curves than her own. Her eyes were framed by longer lashes that looked somewhat coquettish.

"We do make an interesting view. I like it much better now that yer sweet skin is in sight."

"This must be wrong."

His fingers trailed up the center of her stays and she stared at them intently.

"Why is that?"

His voice had deepened to that tone he used when he was becoming aroused. Her gaze dipped to the kilt shielding his cock from her sight. Was he growing stiff behind the wool?

Her face flooded with heat, her eyelashes fluttering. His eyes glittered as they noticed the telltale movement. With a shaky breath, she tried to leave. His arms tightened to keep her in place. His head tilted and she watched him open his lips. He closed them gently around the lobe of her ear, sucking it into his mouth.

"*Brodick . . .*"

"Aye, Wife?" He locked stares with her in the reflection. "What is wrong with enjoying yer gift? I bought it to give ye pleasure. Do ye deny that ye're quivering with enjoyment?"

Her lips rounded with a little sound of confusion, all other words failing her. He chuckled near her ear, his chest shaking against her back. It was decadent. All of the sensations and sights combining into a mixture that intoxicated her senses. His fingers reached the tie holding the front of her stays closed. With a quick jerk he pulled it loose. Hooking the first crossing of laces with a crooked finger, he tugged the lace out of the eyelets. Her breasts felt heavier, almost swollen. He hooked the next crossing of laces and then the next. The stays lost their supporting hold on her, the stiff garment falling open now that it wasn't held in place by the strong cord.

"I think there is something very right about this moment."

He pulled her corset free, dropping it carelessly onto the floor. Her chemise was thin, made of fine cotton, the darkness of her nipples showing through it. Another gasp left her lips. This time Brodick echoed the sound with a swift intake of his own breath. His hands hovered over her breasts, only two fingertips pressing against her chemise to stroke her nipples. A deep shudder sent gooseflesh down her arms. She could actually see the tiny bumps decorating her forearms. Behind the fabric, her nipples drew taut, the hard tips visible in the mirror.

"Now there's a sight I'm sure I dinnae want to miss. Yer nipples are very pretty."

Were they? She didn't know. Moving her gaze to his face, she witnessed the hard hunger drawing his features tight. Her waistband popped open, making her jump.

"I could get used to maiding ye with my own hands."

"Wait." Her skirts puddled around her ankles and shins before she spoke. The small padded roll around her hips didn't last very long either. Brodick had untied it without hesitation. "We already . . . um . . ."

"Fucked? I remember it very well." Amusement coated his voice.

"Why are you toying with me?"

Her chemise billowed now, falling around her body loosely. The flicker of the candle flame illuminated the curves of her body, causing her to look like some pagan offering. Heat moved through her passage, slow and deep. It wasn't the white-hot flash of need that had assaulted her in the stable; this time it was centered in her womb.

"Who told you that a man and woman could only share intimacies once a night?" He set his hands on her hips, trapping her chemise there. The action drew the fabric tight across her breasts, showing off her hard nipples.

"Now I want to seduce ye."

His hands smoothed over her hips, moving down her thighs to the edge of the undergarment. When his hands slid onto her bare skin, sensation ripped into her. He curled his fingers into talons, pressing each fingertip into her legs and raking his hands back up her thighs. The chemise rose and she stared in fascination as her thighs became visible. Higher, and the soft hair on her sex was revealed. Breathing became difficult as her belly was exposed. Her own hands gripped his kilt while he drew his fingertip along the sides of her breasts.

She lost the vision in the mirror as he drew the fabric over her head. Her eyelids fluttered, a soft moan crossing her lips when she gazed into the mirror again. The flickering flame illuminated her bare body. Her breasts were small, round globes that hung like tear drops, slightly fuller towards the bottom. Each one was set with a small pink nipple, the tips hard buttons.

"You're a vision, lass. Like a siren from the Greek voyages. I'd follow ye to the rocks."

"You shouldn't say such things."

He didn't return his hands to her. He reached up to untie his sword. The dark handle was still visible above his right shoulder. The wide leather strap that held the scabbard along his back was shiny in the candlelight. He untied it with a quick, practiced motion. He set the sword down, leaning it against the wall directly next to the table. His kilt brushed against the back of her thighs when he moved back next to her.

"And ye, sweet wife, shouldnae be so quick to place borders around our union. Our marriage is a tool for sweeping aside outdated ideas."

His hand hovered over his belt buckle. Her gaze centered on the reflection, her breath stilling in her throat.

"Since it excites ye and me, what is wrong with enjoying our mirror?"

"I don't know."

And she didn't care. His fingers turned slightly white as he gripped the end of the leather belt. With a jerk he pulled it back enough to allow the twin prongs to spring free of the holes in the thick leather. Her gaze became fixated on his kilt. She wanted to know if his cock was hard.

Could the idea of lying with her actually raise him a second time in as many hours?

A wicked idea for certain, but heat flowed into her passage, awakening her clitoris. His grip released and the belt fell. She felt the slither of the fabric dropping along her bare legs until her stockings interrupted. His shirt didn't allow her to see his cock.

A soft chuckle shook her back. "Dinnae look so disappointed, lass. Patience is a virtue."

She scoffed at him. "Your teasing is misplaced."

"Och now, is it?"

She pursed her lips and shrugged. "I could be as cold as a newly netted fish. Unresponsive and very uninterested in seeing anything you might have behind your kilt." Reaching back, she pressed his shirt tail against his crotch. The fabric folded around the erect form of his sex, her hands gently fingering it for only a moment. His cheek jerked as his eyes narrowed, the mirror showing her his response clearly.

"Just think, my lord. I might lie upon your bed squeezing my eyes shut as stiff as an effigy."

Anne turned, retaining her grip on his cock. Watching had lost its appeal. Need was whirling around deep inside her belly. She wanted to touch and be touched. But she was also feeling bold, as though she needed to be as confident with the subject of intimacy as he was. She wanted to tease him with the same ease that he toyed with her, not shiver like an ignorant virgin.

"Ye certainly tried to avoid me well enough." A hint of frustration laced his tone. Working her fingers over his cock again, Anne shrugged.

"Really? You believe so?"

He grunted. "I have a good memory."

Anne walked past him, careful to step over of her skirts. She felt his eyes on her bare bottom, her clitoris begging for a stroke from his fingers. The side bed curtains were drawn, the interior of the bed glowing red from the coals in the fireplace. Casting a look over her shoulder, she placed a knee on the bed.

"Be careful what you suggest. I might decide to repent my lustful infatuation."

The bed ropes groaned when she crawled up onto the ticking.

"I'd have to take ye in hand and warm you up . . . again."

He was following her, slowly stalking. He paused near a stool, propping one foot onto it. With a pull and tug, his boot dropped to the floor. The head of his cock pushed against the creamy shirt tail when he moved. A smug look decorated his face because he watched her looking at his crotch. Anne didn't lower her eyes. She stared straight into his gaze, refusing to consider whether it was right to look at his sex.

Watching in the mirror had been very pleasing and she wasn't a liar.

His second boot hit the floor. "Lie back."

"All the way?"

"Aye."

She scooted back while he gripped the hem of his shirt and drew it over his head. There was no teasing about it. Brodick threw his remaining garment across the room. With him completely bare, she lost a great deal of her bravado. He was magnificent, his body honed into tight ridges of muscle. On an animal she would have been impressed; in this man she quivered because his strength would soon be working between her thighs. The idea was as intoxicating as the reflection had been.

"Now spread yer legs."

Her thighs pressed tight instead.

"Do it." Command colored his words. His eyes narrowing with expectation. "Part yer thighs. I want to see if yer slit is glistening with sweet dew."

It was . . .

The folds of her slit were already slick. Her attention moved to his cock, the staff thick and engorged.

"Unless ye be too timid."

She forced her hesitating knees to part. He didn't chuckle, didn't mock her for the slightly nervous way she complied, spreading her legs so that he could see her sex.

"Wider. Much wider."

A ripple of excitement went through her. The folds protecting the opening to her body separated, exposing her completely.

"Now lie back and close yer eyes. No peeking. Wait for me to touch ye."

His voice was rough. It suited the sharply defined muscles running over his limbs and body. Everything about him felt and looked hard.

And she was soft.

Her body fashioned to be opposite to his. The bed ropes creaked once more as she lay back. Closing her eyes raised a soft moan from her chest. Every inch of her skin suddenly became more aware. She could hear her own heart beating faster, feel her blood accelerating. Goosebumps rose along her arms and down her torso. The tiny bumps covered the mounds of her breasts. Through her eyelids she detected only the flicker of the dancing candle flame.

A moment later it died.

Her heart increased its pace yet again. The folds of her sex turning hot as blood rushed through the delicate tissues. Without her sight, time moved slowly as she waited for a tiny sound to tell her where Brodick was. The bed was still, her ears failing to hear anything.

That left her waiting.

Anticipation was a torment. Her clitoris throbbed with demand. Her passage begged to be filled. A single stroke down the center of her slit drew a cry from her lips.

A hard hand pressed her back down.

"Interesting, isn't it? The way the flesh heightens its awareness when ye don't have yer sight."

"Indeed." The single word was an effort to force past her lips. Her breathing was uneven, most of her attention needed to keep her eyes closed. She was rapidly losing the ability to conquer her impulses. Signals raced from her skin to her spine and up into her brain so quickly she couldn't make sense of it all. Couldn't understand what she wanted anymore. Part of her wanted to open her eyes to restore her balance. A hard shudder shook her, the spasm pressing another sound past her lips and this one sounded more like a wail.

"Enough, lass."

The bed rocked as she was caught up against his body. Hard arms drew her into his embrace, his skin caressing hers. It was sweet balm to her quivering flesh. Reaching for him, she held tight as he rolled her beneath his large body.

"Enough play for tonight. I just want to rock ye to sleep."

Her thighs clasped his hips and he cupped the back of her head. His lips sought hers, teasing them with a warm kiss. It was a slow meshing of their mouths, his tongue soothing the dry surface of her lips. His cock pressed against the opening to her body, sliding smoothly into her sheath. There was no protest from her body this time, his cock lodging deep with the first penetration. His tongue delved deep at the same time, filling her mouth.

He moved between her thighs, rocking her with a gentle rhythm. His cock departing and returning slowly. Each breath drew his scent into her senses. Every downward motion pressed his chest against her breasts. The soft globes gave way to his harder torso. Pleasure streamed along her body, first from where he rode her and then back to tighten around his hard flesh. She was keenly aware of the entire length of his cock. It slid against her clitoris, pressing down on the sensitive nub until the head knocked against the mouth of her womb.

She broke their kiss, gasping for breath. Her body was twisting tighter and tighter again. It was far too much to hold inside. Her lips remained open as she panted and wailed. It was a thin sound she didn't recognize. Pleasure washed over her and she willingly went with the current.

"Aye, lass. That's the way of it."

The speed of his thrusting increased, his hips working harder. His embrace tightened as she heard his breathing turn harsh.

"Look at me."

Her eyelids felt too heavy to move.

"*Open your eyes.*"

His words were hard. Her eyelashes fluttered to obey. Hard hunger met her stare. It was far more primal than she'd ever seen on a human. His eyes glittered with determination as he thrust harder against her spread body.

"Dinnae ever leave me. I'll come for ye. Ye have my word on it."

He gritted his teeth as she felt his seed spurt deep inside her passage. A harsh growl made it past his teeth as he pressed against her to empty all of his offering into her. His shoulders quivered a moment and he drew in several long breaths.

"Ye're mine."

He rolled over onto his back, clasping her against his chest. His words echoing inside her head, both endearing and frightening. He stroked her back with a warm hand as she felt his body shudder softly. It was almost too slight to feel, just a mere whisper of vulnerability in his hard body.

Yet she felt it.

Laying a hand on his chest, she threaded her fingers into the crisp hair. Somewhere inside his honed exterior was the same doubt that plagued her. It was an unspoken thing, but one that gave her peace. With a sigh, she allowed sleep to lead her away. Back to that place where she'd slept last night, where her lover cradled her against his warm body, his heartbeat filling her head.

It was perfection on earth.

* * *

The bells on the walls shattered their bliss.

It was soft at first, only invading her slumber like a memory. But more bells rang, bringing the volume up. The chest her head was pillowed on jerked and sat up.

The chamber was much darker now, the candles extinguished. Yet the ringing of the bells was loud.

"What is it?"

"Trouble."

There was a soft growl in his voice. He left the bed, grabbing a boot first. His hands made quick work of lacing it closed and he pushed the second one onto his foot.

The clanging of the brass bells drove every bit of sleep from her mind. Whatever befell the castle, she would share it. In the eyes of Brodick's enemies, she was his wife and a possible target to extract vengeance from. Crawling over the heavy coverlet, she stood up, trying to find their clothing in the dim light. His shirt was a soft hump on the floor. Picking it up, she shook it and turned it right side out. She turned and took it toward him, her heart moving faster as the bells continued to ring.

Brodick looked surprised. He was already pleating his kilt across the foot of the bed, his wide leather belt in place. Stretching up, she placed the shirt over his head. She didn't worry about her own nudity; getting the men to the walls was the first priority. He lifted his arms and put them through the sleeves of the garment. Her fingers were already closing the button at the collar.

"Thank ye, lass." He sounded surprised but pleasantly so. A soft ripple of emotion went through her as she witnessed the way he watched her maid him.

The bells droned on, instilling urgency in her. There was no time to dwell on the intimacy of the moment. He lay down across his pleated kilt to secure the buckle. When he rose,

Anne offered him his sword. The weight of the weapon made her hands tremble. Too many wives performed their last duty to their spouses by handing them their swords. She might be sending him to his death. There was no way to know what set the bells to ringing.

It was a sure thing that it was not good news in the dead of the night.

But she held her worries inside. That, too, was a wife's duty. Brodick clasped the sword in one large hand.

"Get dressed and join the women in the lower keep until ye're told otherwise."

"Aye." She turned to begin looking for her clothing. An arm snaked around her waist, pulling her back against the body of her lover.

"But kiss me good-bye first."

"Aye, my lord."

That was a duty she performed most happily. Reaching up, she placed her hands against his shoulders, his mouth claiming hers in a hard kiss. There was no time to linger, only a mere moment to steal one last press of lips before he set her away from him.

"Hurry, lass."

He left her and she was suddenly cold. The chill cut all the way to her heart. Moving around in the dark, she pulled her chemise from the floor. The bells stopped, leaving an eerie silence. In the dark, the lace that had secured her stays was nowhere to be found. Half dressed, Anne dropped to her knees to feel across the floor for it. She discovered it hidden on the pattern of one of the newly arrived carpets. Standing back up, she moved in front of the fireplace to use the meager light from the coals to thread the lace through the eyelets. It was slow work.

Many slept in their corsets because the garments were not

quickly donned. Tonight, it felt like an eternity before she tugged the lace tight to secure her breasts. Struggling into her doublet, she worried that too much time had passed. She didn't know her way around Sterling. Her hopes lay in following the other inhabitants to the keep that would be protected down to the last man. Scotland was more violent than England. Yet even Warwickshire feared encroaching raiders. Any castle near the coast kept its walls manned since the Spanish had launched its Grand Armada with the intention to reclaim England for the Catholic faith.

Brodick had left the door open. There was no sound on the steps and none rising from the floor below. The darkness was thick. Anne hesitated. Wandering the dark corridors alone might be more hazardous than remaining in her room. Yet cowering behind her door was certain to drive her insane before dawn. The double doors that led to the courtyard were open, the light from the wall fires coloring it faintly.

Any light was a beacon. Her chamber and the hallway that led to the next tower were nothing but black caverns. Walking toward the open doors, she peered out into the courtyard. It was full of men and horses. Younger boys, their arms laden with armor, wove through the mass. White clouds rose from the horses' mouths and the men alike. Every man had a sword strapped to his back. In England, her father's men held their weapons on their hips.

There was the sound of leather tightening and horses being bridled. The men on the walls held their bows ready, an arrow slotted. Brodick was already in the saddle, a thick breast plate secured around his body. Anne pressed back against the wall. The shadow hid her there. Defending his home was the blunt reality of their uncertain times. Brodick needed his wits about him, not the distraction of thinking about her.

"Mount!"

His voice filled the courtyard. There was a flurry of motion as the men gained their saddles, the fires from the walls dancing over them. The huge doors were opened with a loud groaning of chain. Men and horses surged through the opening in a force that held her spellbound. Each man wearing the same patterned kilt with Brodick leading them.

The pounding of hooves fairly shook the ground. Looking through the opening, she saw the signal fires burning in the valley below the castle. The stream of men heading toward the bright point of light left the castle quiet.

It was an eerie kind of silence. Younger lads, still too slight to handle the broadswords, were left to pick up anything left in the courtyard. Only the archers remained on the walls, their attention turned outwards. A loud cracking sound made her shiver as the gate was closed with the huge wheels used to wind the chains. It slammed shut and men pushed heavy bars through wide iron locks to reinforce the door.

There was nothing to do but wait.

And pray.

Half of the men returned at dawn.

Anne ran with the rest of the inhabitants to search their faces but Brodick was not among them.

"Give a hand with the wounded."

There was a flurry of action as several men were helped from their horses. The morning sun lit the blood on them. But their mood was jovial. Relief settled over most of the women. Anne didn't breathe easy just yet. Without Brodick she felt alone. It was a selfish way to think yet she could not dislodge it from her mind. For some unknown reason she felt shunned by those around her, the looks cast her way far more cold than yesterday.

It made no rational sense but persisted as the morning wore on.

She was relieved of her concerns as the men filled the tables to break their fast. Every pair of hands was needed to carry food to them, fill tankards and make sure that they were rewarded for placing themselves in harm's way.

Ginny stopped when most of the meal had passed away. The younger girl gazed at her suspiciously, clearly considering if she wanted to speak with Anne. She finally stepped closer.

"Helen's daughter was laboring last eve. She went down to Perth to be with her, so Helen will nae be back until the raiding McQuade have been driven back to their dens."

"I see."

Ginny didn't remain to offer any more information. The girl turned her back abruptly without even a nod of respect. The other maids followed suit, ignoring her with cutting glances.

Emotion thickened in her throat, choking her. After so warm a welcome, it was even harsher to be shunned. Without the lord around, his staff saw no point in treating her with kindness. It was not an uncommon fate for brides that were married off into other countries. The lord might order his people to lower their heads but no man held the power to force any servant to like a foreigner.

For herself, she had no liking for false allegiance. Better to know the true feeling of the household staff than live in ignorance.

Yet it hurts.

Anne left the hall, not knowing where to take herself. Once more she was completely on her own. The despair that had imprisoned her when Philipa unveiled her scheme returned. It felt stronger now that she had escaped it for a time. Much more intense since the tender moments in Brodick's embrace.

He'll plant a child in you and return to his Scottish warring ways . . .

Philipa's words slashed through the fragile happiness she'd enjoyed at Sterling. She walked past the steps that led to her chamber, their bed a place of torment now. Helen had hidden the true nature of the castle folk with her seniority. Now there was nothing to make them accept her.

She didn't want dishonesty, anyway. Lifting her chin, she moved away from the tower her chamber was in to explore the next section of hallway. Above her was the wall where the archers were poised. Long fingers of sunlight stretched across the floor every five feet. The shutters were open, allowing the morning breeze to sweep inside.

A soft voice touched her ears. It was a woman singing softly. A doorway led to a large room where a young girl sat at a spinning wheel. Her foot worked the pedal as her fingers pulled on the raw wool in her hands. It was a fluffy ball that she skillfully fed into the twisting action produced by the wheel. A large stack of carded wool sat near her and she reached for some of it, her foot pausing until she had mixed it with the wool in her hands. A spindle was winding the new thread on top of the wheel.

"Who's there?"

She didn't look at her. In fact the girl didn't really look at anything. Her eyes were strangely unfocused.

"I could use a pair of eyes if ye've a bit o'time to share."

The girl was clearly blind but her hands were still clever and skilled at the art of weaving.

"How may I help you?"

The foot on the pedal paused. The smile fading from the girl's face. Anne felt her shoulders resume carrying their heavy burden. But the girl suddenly brightened back to the cheerful state she'd been in before hearing Anne's unmistakable English accent.

"Good morrow, Mistress. I be Enys."

"Good day. How may I help?"

Enys paused to reach for more wool. "I didnae ken it was you, Mistress, when I asked."

Her voice was still kind, lacking the chill that Ginny's had adopted. It was most welcome, whatever the reason.

"I would be most happy to assist you. Shall I card for you?" Anne moved into the room. The wooden cards were sitting near another stool with a mound of washed raw wool. Each card had thin metal teeth that were used to straighten out the wool hairs. Only after raw wool had been brushed back and forth on the cards several times was it ready for spinning.

"I need the bobbin changed and I don't know where Tully set the empty ones. The room is rather large to go searching it with my hands."

Enys added a smile to her comment, her foot steadily working the pedal. The foot-long wooden bobbin at the front of the wheel was getting full.

"I should be happy to lend a hand. It has never been my way to be lazy."

Enys nodded her head. "I'm most appreciative. Since losing my sight, I find my pride suffering when I'm reduced to asking for help finding things."

Anne searched the room, finding a crate of empty bobbins. "You weren't born blind?"

"Nay, and I think that's more of a torment. Knowing what I miss. My memories are as clear as the daylight used to be."

Enys sighed, a look of longing passing over her face. She tilted her head when Anne pulled one of the bobbins free and the others clicked against one another. Her foot stopped and she allowed the wheel to stop turning.

"I was in the yard and not minding the horses. One kicked out, planting his hooves in the center of my head. To hear it told, I flew like a bird across the yard. When I woke up, my sight was gone." She snipped the new thread with a pair of small shears hanging from a lace tied to her skirts. With a confident hand she removed the full bobbin, holding it out toward Anne.

"You appear to use your hearing very effectively for one not born afflicted."

They traded bobbins, Enys quickly attaching the new one to the end of her thread. The bobbin in her hand held fine work. The spinning was even and the thread thin, both difficult tasks for someone without sight.

"You do very good work."

Enys beamed. "Thank you. I do enjoy knowing that I'm of use. My mother despaired when my sight didnae return." She grimaced. "But the man I was set to marry took my cousin instead."

"Obviously he hasn't seen your skill with the wheel."

Merchants paid well for even, smooth thread. To weave good cloth you first needed the thread. In London, young girls who showed such skill were coveted as brides. They needed no dowry, only their skill. It was quite the modern thing now for some women to marry with the only thing changing hands between their families the skill they had. The middle class flourished, too, some families amassing wealth that equaled that of the nobles.

Taking a seat on the stool, Anne reached for the cards. The room was a welcoming refuge from the chilly glances in the eating hall. Enys tilted her head once more when Anne drew the metal teeth past one another. She seemed unsure what to say as the mistress of the house joined her in common chores.

"Do not worry; marriage comes along to us all."

"Ye sound as though yers took ye a wee bit by surprise."

Anne sighed, pulling wool with smooth motions of her arms. "Yes, it did."

But she did not lament it. That was rooted deep inside her now. It was startling to notice just how greatly one week had changed her. The girl who greeted Philipa each morning was foreign to her now. Enys began singing again, a sweet tune of springtime. Anne found her foot keeping time with the melody while her arms worked the cards.

In the wilds of Scotland

"Damn raids. I've had a belly full o' them." Brodick cussed under his breath.

"More like yer wife has a full belly with the way ye tumbled her in the stable."

Brodick rounded on his brother. Cullen dropped his jesting when he looked at his brother's face. He kicked at the ground.

"Och now. Why do ye have to go soft for a woman? That's sure to ruin half my fun," Cullen huffed, propping his hands onto his hips. "What am I going to do now? I thought ye were only getting married, no losing yer heart to a lass."

"I'm nae gone soft."

"Aye, ye be." His brother added a Gaelic word under his breath. "Ready to lay me low for mentioning what ye didnae mind shouting out to half the garrison last eve. If that is nae soft, I dinnae know what is."

Brodick felt his anger deflate. Cullen had the right of it. He had raised his voice, happy to ensure that everyone knew what they'd been about. The true reason for his foul temper was frustration. Looking back over the burnt-out shells of three homes, he cussed. Druce turned to look at him, a frown marring his face.

"They are hiding in the canyons, no doubt."

"No doubt." Which meant he and his men were set on a merry chase that might not end soon. But it was a sure wager that they could not return to Sterling. There would be another few homes destroyed by tomorrow if they didn't chase the guilty down. It was the duty of the lord to protect his people. Every man riding with him served his time in trade for the protection his family received. As the English queen grew nearer to dying, the neighboring clans became bolder. He had to defend his land with hard steel.

He was the McJames.

'Twas his duty and one he shouldered with honor. In spite of his frustration, he mounted his horse to take up the task with renewed faith. The reason was simple; he had a sweet wife who needed the strength of his sword. She was a McJames now and he would not return to her bed until his lands were safe for her and every other McJames soul.

"Let's run these villains to ground, men!"

A cheer broke the evening chill. His men mounted, determination shining in their eyes. Gaining his own saddle, he led them forward.

Chapter Nine

Sterling

Spring arrived in full glory. Winter lost its grip on the land and with it the people of Sterling became busy. Planting season began. Every set of available hands was pressed into service. The spinning room was empty save for Enys now that there was good weather.

Days turned into weeks without the return of the earl. Anne spent the time working alongside Enys, grateful to escape the rest of the castle. Helen remained in Perth while her daughter was in childbed.

Anne missed her sorely.

Be truthful . . . you miss Brodick.

There was a wicked streak in her nature, to be sure. It was boldly filling her dreams with heated memories of the nights she'd shared with her lover. She saw his face, heard his voice and even sometimes felt his hands on her body, her slumber shattering as she sat up in bed, burning for fulfillment only to notice that she was alone.

That had to be sinful.

The shadows lengthened as another day ended with no return. Anne drew a deep breath into her lungs to steady her nerves. She had grown to loathe the night. Eating in the hall had become so stressful, she avoided it, scavenging what she could once most of the men had finished their meals. The maids had only grown more cutting in their looks since no one checked their behavior. As mistress she should have.

Yet she lacked the heart to impose her will on them. She was a sham. Maybe they even sensed her guilt. Nobles were set above others by divine will. There was great disagreement just where blue-blooded bastards belonged in that heavenly ordered precedence. Was she beneath even the lowest beggar or above the maids giving her those frozen glares?

She did not know, so she did nothing, slipping away to work in the spinning room on some days. On the others she applied a needle to the clothing Mary had sent along with her. All of it had arrived back in her chamber without the alterations.

The quiet work suited her mood.

But the hours alone only encouraged her mind to think of Brodick. Telling herself to banish such ideas didn't stop his face from rising as she plied a needle. Loneliness settled around like a dark cloak. After a fortnight, it became comfortable. She spent long hours thinking about her family. Bonnie would be fifteen this summer; plenty old enough for that horrible marriage Philipa had threatened. Anne shuddered, nausea twisting her stomach. Bonnie was a ray of summer sunshine. Thinking about such an ill fate made her want to retch.

The fire had long since gone cold and no one came to rebuild it. Anne left the coals, putting her surcoat on to stay warm. She had never had a fire laid simply for her own pleasure at Warwickshire. Since she was destined to return there, she should not become accustomed to the comforts she would have to leave behind.

She was much more worried about what Brodick would do when he discovered she was not the heiress bride he'd come south to fetch. A lump formed in her throat. Tears stung her eyes and she had to turn her back on the bed.

He would be furious.

Every moment of tenderness they'd shared would be dust once he knew the truth. She dreaded the moment. Yet found no way to avoid it. Unlike Philipa, Anne did not agree that Brodick would not notice the difference between her and Mary. The only thing that was in question was just which of them would be in the room when he unearthed the conspiracy.

The nausea persisted, making the idea of food repulsive. More weeks passed. Many days went by without her speaking to a single soul. It was as if she were a ghost, moving through the castle, yet unseen by the rest of the inhabitants.

Philipa's insistence that she work as a servant came to be a blessing as the staff of Sterling ignored her. Anne knew her way about everyday work. In sooth, remaining busy was a kindness. At least while she was washing her bed linens and clothing, her mind had something to mull over that was not the possible fate of her family.

Was her mother still alive?

That question haunted her. Philipa hated Ivy. After years of hate poisoning Philipa's soul, she was now black with rot. Having found the courage to force Anne to leave with Brodick, it was very possible the mistress of Warwickshire had turned Ivy Copper out. It might have been done the moment Anne disappeared from sight. She had no way of discovering the truth. At Sterling she was even more cut off from her father.

It was a muddle that even the clear spring weather could not melt away. The sun warmed her face as she hauled water from the river to wash her laundry and still she felt chilled and shaky. Her belly remained queasy, a tight knot that despised all but a few bits of nibbled bread. Even that bland fare often turned her green.

She fell into a routine. Rising with the sun and sleeping as soon as it set. The candles in her chamber had long since burned low. She couldn't think of a good reason to burn another one since she only had her own needs to see to. It would be a waste of a good resource. A habit she didn't need to foster in herself. Who knew where she might find herself come next spring and under what circumstances.

Brodick would turn her out when he discovered the ruse. Tears stung her eyes and she wiped them away. Crying was foolish.

Still she could not stop the flood of regret that hit her. He was a fine man who treated his wife kindly, far more tenderly than many. Even with his staff being so cold to her, there was much about her life at Sterling to covet. If it were her home, she would take the staff in hand. But she remained an outcast because she knew that she was not the true mistress of the house.

She was the lord's leman at best, and even that would end when Brodick became wise to Philipa's game.

With no fire, she often slept in the surcoat, its sturdy fabric a welcome comfort in the chamber. Once huddled beneath the coverlet, she was quite warm. If only her heart could be thawed by the fabric.

That would surely be too much to hope for.

Home

Brodick didn't care if Cullen teased him. He was happy to be headed home. It wasn't the first month he'd spent on the trail. A harsh truth that it wouldn't be his last either. But tonight, he was following the moon back to Sterling. It set his heart to pounding and his mind to thinking about his sweet wife.

He caught Cullen staring at him.

"No teasing remark, Brother? Are ye sure yer nae feeling fevered?"

His brother didn't grin. Instead he looked serious and older than his years.

"I'm contemplating the fact that I'm envious of ye."

Druce reined in beside them. "Did I hear ye right? Was that actually wee Cullen admitting he can see the worth in marrying?"

Cullen glared at their cousin. "I always knew the value of the dowry but I didnae grasp the worth o' having someone waiting on my return. That's what I envy. Laugh if ye want, but ye've no one praying for yer skin, either."

Druce frowned. "Maybe, I admit I'm beginning to see the benefits o' such a thing. Possibly."

Had she really prayed for him?

Only his mother had ever done that. His face heated just a wee bit as another part of him was far more interested in knowing if she'd dreamed about him. Late at night, when the fire was low and her bed empty. He'd thought about her every night on the trail, his back feeling the rocks more than he had in years.

"Well, I'd be most appreciative if one of ye would catch that daughter of McQuade's and marry her. That way I'd nae have to chase his raiding clansmen across my land."

"Bronwyn McQuade?"

Druce and Cullen both scowled as they spoke the name. Cullen shook his head in denial. "Yer harsh, Brother. Bronwyn is a shrew, more sour than Medusa."

Druce chuckled. "I hear her pretty face is the lure she wiggles in front o' men before unleashing her hellcat temper."

"None o' us have ever even been in the same room with the lass. Could be 'tis nothing more than a fable."

"And I've no plans to change that, man." Druce looked set in his opinion. "I want a sweet lass waiting for me, nae a battle of epic proportions every night."

Brodick shrugged. "There were many who warned me against my bride. Told me the English bred weak women with tempers like the insane." The top of the first tower of Sterling came into sight. "I'm humbly thankful that I've been shown otherwise."

Brodick spurred his horse forward. Cullen and Druce watched him gallop towards his home.

" 'Tis more enthusiasm than any man so newly wed should have." Cullen didn't sound as confident as he'd like. Envy was still riding him hard.

"Well now, I suppose maybe we're the unlucky sods for nae having someone to make us that impatient."

Cullen slid his cousin a raised eyebrow. "Does that mean yer taking another bit of thinking over Bronwyn McQuade?"

"Nae." Druce said it too loudly.

Cullen smirked. "Nae? It sounds like ye might be thinking o' it."

Druce snickered, his voice low and mocking. "You first, laddie. I want to make sure she's fed before I go too close to her claws."

"Och well, nae every man has the amount o' courage I'm blessed with."

A couple of retainers laughed at Druce's expense. He pointed a finger at Cullen. "I cannae wait to see ye tame her. Ye won't be the first man she's sent howling from her with his tail between his legs."

Cullen frowned as more heads turned to listen in on their conversation. Druce smiled, enjoying his discomfort.

"Unless ye've lost some o' that great courage, cousin."

Chuckles surrounded him, raising his temper. "We'll see."

"Will we? I cannae wait." Druce smirked. "Truly I cannae."

"Ye will." Cullen kneed his horse forward. The snickering behind him sent his temper to boiling. He didn't care if he'd started it, the idea that any lass might be so hard to handle didn't sit well with him. His brother was right. Marrying up with Bronwyn would settle a great many scores. His aching back found it a fine idea. Besides, beneath his teasing exterior was a son who had been raised with the same sense of duty that Brodick had. Marrying for the benefit of the McJames people was his future. 'Twas not just any bride he needed. Bronwyn McQuade was, in fact, a fine choice to be contemplating.

Now if he could only manage a way to getting close enough to the lass without getting his neck stretched on a rope by her father and brothers. That was the real trick. Not taming her.

There wasn't a lass alive that was too strong to resist his charm. It might be a wee bit of fun to pursue the stubborn lass just to see how fast she succumbed to his touch.

The bells didn't ring upon his return.

Brodick had ordered that custom stopped when his father died. He didn't feel worthy of the bells announcing his return until he proved his worth as the new Lord of Sterling. 'Twas not something that could be done in the three short years he'd held his title. He rode through the open gate with pride tonight. All the discomforts of the last five weeks dissipated as he looked over the peace of the courtyard. Men walked the walls, the fires were burning evenly and all of its inhabitants slept in ease.

That was the duty of the McJames.

The sword on his back was never too heavy. But he was glad to be home again. Swinging his leg off the back of his horse, he gave the animal a firm pat before letting a stable lad take the reins. The youth looked stunned for a moment, hesitating because Brodick normally cared for his own steed.

"Do a good job of rubbing him down, lad, and I'll see a reward to ye."

A smile parted the boy's face. "I'll be like his mother."

Men began spilling through the open gate, their voices cheerful. Lights began to flicker in the tower as wives and families roused. He looked up toward the chamber his wife slept in but saw no hint of light in the window.

That didn't discourage him.

All it did was unleash a wicked desire to wake her up.

He stopped halfway up the steps. Inside he caught a whiff of sweet lavender from the candles. A deeper breath gave him a hint of what his body smelled like. Turning around he moved toward the bathing room. The erection standing at attention behind his kilt would just have to wait until he removed the stench of horse and sweat.

His wife had a pretty nose that he had no desire to see wrinkled.

The kitchen was already lit up, Bythe and her helpers smiling with welcome. Several retainers had made their way to their families, joy spilling into the darker corridors.

"Bythe, I've need o' a bath and I dinnae care if it's cold as a spinster."

"Aye, my lord. It will be chilly, the fires are low." She wrung her hands, looking about nervously.

"No matter, 'tis no reason to fret. Send the water."

One of the maids scurried into the bath room with a candle. She touched the flame to the wicks of the candles mounted on the walls, bringing them to life. With a hasty lowering of her head, she departed. Water began splashing down the trough and into the tub. It gurgled, making a happy sound, and Brodick shed his clothing, grateful to be back in civilized surroundings. He was thirty-four years old and happy to relinquish the desire to ride through the night to the younger men who still considered it gallant.

He preferred his home.

Sitting down in the tub, he reached for the soap. It was a common bar, milled on his own land without any feminine perfume scents added. There was only a scent of beeswax. He applied it to his skin with brisk strokes, his thoughts centered on completing his task so he might get on with what he was truly craving.

His bed with his wife in it.

He was slightly disappointed that she had not come down to greet him, but shrugged it off. Her chamber was above floors and she was most likely still slumbering away, unaware that he'd returned. He suddenly understood why his father had the bells rung when he entered the courtyard.

It suddenly seemed like a fine tradition.

"Toweling, my lord."

Ginny spoke from the doorway, her head looking at the floor. She kept her sight on the hem of her skirt as she entered and left the neat linen on a stool.

"If my wife awakes, send her to me."

The maid swallowed roughly. Brodick froze, turning his attention to the girl, but she was scurrying out of the room as if he were Satan. He frowned, but dismissed the maid. The only woman he had to struggle to understand was his wife.

Now that was a task he was looking forward to.

His wife's chamber was too cold. Brodick frowned, his wet hair feeling the chill when he entered it. There wasn't a speck of light from anywhere inside the chamber. His suspicions rose as he cast a look at the fireplace. There was nothing there;

even the scent of smoke was missing from the room telling him that a fire had not been burning for many days, possibly weeks. The curtains on the windows were open as well. They should have been drawn at night to keep the fire heat from seeping past the glass. But having them open allowed moonlight and light from the walls to penetrate into the dark room. He'd expect such if a room was unoccupied.

Icy fingers closed around his heart. It was the sort of feeling he'd only experienced a few times in his life. Dread choked him as he moved toward the bed, trying to see through the blackness. The bed curtains were drawn all the way around the bed, only a mere few inches open at the foot of the bed. Inside, there was naught but darkness.

Had she fled back to her father?

Jerking one curtain aside, he reached into the bed and found a small lump. His breath expelled from his lungs in a rush of relief. His knees actually wobbled and he sat down heavily on the foot of the bed. His wife moved, stirring as her bed was rocked.

"What does the mistress require?"

His wife looked at the bed curtains, confusion marring her face. Her words didn't make sense.

"Don't ye mean the queen? When I attended yer English court, I dinnae recall her ladies calling her mistress."

"My lord?"

Anne stared at the large shape and trembled. Joy rushed through her. She reached out to touch him, needing the reassurance of feeling his warm skin. It felt as if it had been forever since he left.

"I believe I instructed ye to call me Brodick when in our bed."

He moved before her fingers made contact with him. The bed rocked, sending the curtains swaying like they were on a ship at sea. His large form looked huge in the darkness but his voice had been tender and welcoming. She sighed when his arms wrapped around her, hauling her up against him in a solid embrace that made her shiver.

She had dreamed of his arms around her.

"Brodick." She lightly stroked his shoulders, shaking with happiness. He groaned softly.

"Say that again."

Tracing a path up his neck she toyed with the locks of his hair. It was wet and curling.

"Welcome home, Brodick"

His mouth sought hers, taking a firm kiss. She slid her hands back to his shoulders. His lips pressed hers open, lingering over her mouth like a fine whiskey. He didn't rush but tasted her gently.

"What are you sleeping in?"

Her fingers tried to hold him close but he pulled away to look at her.

"Are ye wearing that surcoat in bed?" His hands ran over her shoulders, trying to discover exactly what she was covered in.

"It keeps me warm when you are away."

His hands stopped investigating her clothing. He framed her face gently, leaning back close until she felt his breath on her moist lips.

"Ah lass, ye'll turn my head with flattery like that." He opened the surcoat, working the buttons quickly, even in the dark. He pushed the garment over her shoulders, lifting her up to get at the tail of her chemise.

"Ye've no need o' it now. I promise to keep ye very warm."

His kiss blocked out whatever she might have thought to reply. His large body pressed her back into the bed. Anne reached for him, frantic to be touched. The solitude of the last month felt like an eternity. Brodick was warm and solid. Everything she craved.

She kissed him back. Her tongue boldly seeking his, his tongue tangling deep inside her mouth, stroking and gliding against hers. Her hands twisted in his hair, combing through the wet strands. Even that touch flooded her with sweet sensation. Each breath she drew brought his scent deep into her lungs, further confirming that she was no longer alone.

She wasn't cold either.

Her blood began heating, melting away the chill that had encased her. The skin that had felt nothing but cold for so long suddenly flickered with heat so intense it was like fever. Her feet slid along his calves, their legs entwining. The flow of heat entered her belly, swirling into her passage. One warm hand cupped a breast, firmly grasping it.

"I've missed ye." Husky and needy, his voice was pure delight. His thumb brushed over the puckered point of her nipple. A soft grunt left his lips.

"I think ye've missed me, too."

"I have."

He leaned down, boldly sucking her nipple into his mouth. The tip of his tongue lashing against it over and over again. A soft moan escaped her lips, her body falling back onto the bed to offer her breast to his lips. He plumped it in his hand, pushing the nipple up further. With a soft pop he pulled his lips free, his breath blowing across the wet skin. Goose bumps spread over the delicate skin as she shivered.

"Say my name, lass. I've longed to hear it in my dreams."

She'd say anything as long as he'd resume sucking her nipple.

"Brodick."

His breath roughened. "Again."

The fingers on her breast released the globe to trail down the center of her body.

"Welcome home, Brodick."

"Aye, ye're that, a welcoming thing to find waiting in my bed."

His fingers found the curls at the top of her sex. Her back arched, sensation drawing her muscles tight with anticipation.

"I wonder though. Just how welcoming ye're feeling."

One large finger parted her slit, sliding across her clitoris. A soft gasp crossed her lips as sensation jolted through her. It was wild and strong, spiking up into her passage, her sheath becoming needy and demanding.

"Warm, aye, but still not as hot as I know ye can be."

He was teasing her but she did not care. His finger stroked her clitoris, rubbing the little point of pleasure with slow circular motions. Heat raged inside her, growing hotter with each second. Her thighs parted further, the folds of her slit opening. He ran his finger down the plump lips to the opening of her body, gently teasing it all the way around before dipping into her sheath just a tiny amount. A harsh cry left her lips as the muscles of her passage tried to clasp that fingertip. She felt so empty it hurt.

"Now that's much hotter. I must have found the right coals to stoke." His finger penetrated deeply, gently sliding over the needy walls of her sheath. Her hips bucked, lifting towards him. Her body was slick, taking his finger easily.

"A man could nae ask for a warmer welcome than that."

His teasing was driving her insane. He felt too far away. She wanted to feel his body pressing down on top of hers, every bit of her skin in contact with his.

"Come to me, lover."

Her voice sounded foreign, sultry. Holding her arms open, she waited for him to answer her.

"*Aye.*"

Demand edged his voice. His finger left her body before he rolled over her. She clasped her thighs around his hips, spreading wide for him. His elbow took most of his weight, pressing against the mattress near her head.

"Aye, indeed."

He pressed his cock into her, stretching her body with his girth. She arched towards him, moaning with enjoyment. Her sheath gripped his hard flesh, enjoying the nips of near pain that ran through her because of his absence. Her clitoris began throbbing in earnest, begging for friction.

"Verra warm and welcoming."

His words didn't shock her tonight. They fanned the flames higher, sending more heat racing towards her passage. He moved, withdrawing to the tip of his cock. She echoed his motion, lifting her bottom when he began thrusting back into her.

A harsh cry left her lips as his length rubbed along her swollen clitoris. Her body shuddered, sweat popping out on her skin. She was too needy. Felt too hot. Her body was greedy and starving for his. She gripped his thick biceps, her fingers curling into the firm muscles.

"Aye, lass, hold on to me. I'll nae leave you wanting."

His body made good on that promise, riding her with a steady, pounding rhythm that shook the bed. Her cries filled the bed curtains, pleasure flooding her. The hard flesh riding her sent delight through her entire body. Her lover hissed through his teeth, growling as he moved faster, sinking his cock deeper into her with each hard thrust. Her pleasure began to tighten around his length as she felt him swell larger. He bucked and she gasped, her lungs freezing.

"That's it, *milk me*."

He snarled as his body thrashed, bearing down on hers, burying his cock with a savage grunt. Pleasure burst through her and it continued while his seed spurted against the mouth of her womb. Time froze, unmoving as she heard only one heartbeat and then waited for the next one.

When it came, she fell back onto the bed, her muscles spent. Satisfaction rippled along her limbs while Brodick rolled off her. He captured her body, pulling her against his chest.

"I've a good mind to ride out every day for the rest of our lives just so I can be welcomed back."

His hand smoothed her hair, gripping the braid she'd secured it into before lying down.

"I dinnae like your hair plaited."

"Yes, my lord." Anne drew his title out, fatigue taking away her worries. While the dark hid the rest of the world, she could enjoy being his lover. For now he wanted her.

She didn't have the will to deny him.

There was no fire in the chamber.

Brodick knelt in front of the fireplace, a hand held over the cold ashes. A deep frown marred his features. Pink colored the horizon, dawn visible through the open curtains.

There hadn't been one laid in the chamber for at least a week.

He knew it. His gaze cut toward the bed, suspicion darkening his eyes. Anne was still sleeping, curled up in the bedding. Her feet tangled in the fabric to hold it close to her.

He looked at one candelabra and then walked to the next. It held a single inch of remaining candle. Fury filled him as he looked around the chamber to find other tasks that had been left undone while he was away. His temper flared into a full blaze and he did nothing to check it. The slim form of his wife lying in the bed only added more fuel to his anger.

His wife would never go without . . . not while he drew breath.

She stirred, reaching out for him. A lump formed in his throat as she frowned when her fingers found nothing but cool sheets. Her eyelids fluttered and she looked for him, searching the bed while a worried look took control of her face.

It was the most haunting expression he'd ever seen. That look of longing . . . for him. The lack of comforts in the chamber became personal as he watched her shake the remains of slumber away to look for him. It was the thing he'd coveted when seeking a wife but the reality was far more precious than he'd imagined.

She was reaching for him.

Gone.

Anne tried to keep a whimper behind her lips but failed. She sat up and looked across the chamber to find Brodick watching her. Relief pulsed through her and there was no hiding the smile that turned her lips up.

Brodick frowned at her.

"Why are there no candles?"

Anne looked away from his keen stare. She didn't want to sully the name of his household. She'd hoped that he'd leave at dawn giving the servants a chance to right the chamber.

It would seem that no one at Sterling was lucky this morning.

"It is nothing to worry about."

Stepping from the bed, she hurried into her clothing, fighting off a queasy stomach. Worry was filling her belly with nausea so thick, she had trouble keeping it down. She reached for some of the bread left on the vanity without thinking about it. Moving the cloth she'd wrapped it in aside, she pulled off a piece, desperate to calm her belly.

"Have ye been supping here as well? On naught but stale bread? Little wonder yer face is thin." He sounded deadly now. "Where's Helen? I've a few questions for her."

Anne lifted a hand to feel her face. Her cheekbones were more pronounced.

"Aye, madam, you've lost a stone if I'm nae mistaken." He moved toward the door and pulled it open.

"Helen!"

His voice bounced around the lower tower.

"She is not here. Her daughter gave birth the night you left. You mustn't be cross. Family is very important. I do not begrudge her the time."

Brodick turned a hard glare on her. "Then where is Ginny? There's maids a plenty in Sterling. Helen would nae have left without assigning the duty to another. She's served at Sterling for too many years for such a lapse."

"I do not need pampering."

"Pampering?" Anger flickered in his eyes. "Nae even the stable lads endure without warmth and light in this castle. Did ye tell Ginny to leave ye without?"

Brodick didn't wait for her answer. She was still closing her doublet when he shook his head in disapproval.

"I dinnae care, she should never have listened to ye if ye did command her to do such a foolhardy thing. 'Tis nae warm enough at this time o' year to be without a fire on the second floor. Ginny knows Sterling better than ye. There be nae reason for such an oversight. Ye were shivering last night."

He was out the door before she knew his intention. Pushing her body after him, she frantically tried to think of a way to dissuade his anger. Yelling at his people would not endear her to them. She refused to be like Philipa receiving false respect while the gossips griped about her in the kitchen.

"My lord, it takes time for acceptance to grow. You must not be cross."

He stopped on the main floor of the tower, turning to look at her, aghast by her words.

"What? There is no question of acceptance. Yer my wife." He paused for a moment, trying to regain his composure. His temper looked frayed. "Tis nae that I do not value yer opinion, but this be a matter of yer health, madam. I'll nae be told to ignore it. I'd be cross if I discovered the young lads in the smithy enduring such. Discovering my wife huddled in a surcoat in her own bed is cause for far more."

"Yet I have told you that I am not frail and I am English. The surcoat kept me warm, I was not without comforts. Do understand there are a great many years of distrust between our people."

He stiffened as though fighting to regain his composure and not shout. A muscle on the side of his jaw ticked.

"I'm nae the one to be understanding, and ye, my sweet wife, will nae shelter anyone who's behaved shamefully while I'm away protecting this castle."

He captured her hand. This grip was very different from the one he'd used to pull her out of the stable. Her hand was a caged prisoner in his larger one. He tugged her along with him, her feet hurrying to keep pace with his longer strides. At the entrance to the eating hall, his cousin Druce stood watching them approach, a frown on his lips.

"My lord, there are many other matters that are more important."

Brodick froze, his shoulders stiffening. His head turned to catch his cousin in his sights.

"Hold onto my wife, Cousin. I've a few issues to sort out with my staff."

"Brodick . . ."

He pressed her into his cousin's embrace, a hard look on his face. It was the sort of anger that she'd known he would have in him if he was ever crossed. That thing that she feared would be cast unto her when he discovered her true identity.

"Yer too kind, Wife, for yer own good. I'll nae tolerate such from any member of this house. Nor will I have ye use my name to wheedle me into bending when I have good reason to quarrel."

"Tolerance is a virtue that brings many rewards."

Brodick shot a stern look at Druce. "Hold her here. I'll deal with her when I've finished with my staff."

Brodick didn't wait for a response as he turned in a tightly contained motion of lean strength. Fury radiated from him as he shouted for Ginny.

Anne stepped after him only to have Druce grip her upper arms. She turned an incredulous look on him, having to look up to see the man.

"Release me, sir."

"Now dinnae go getting all flustered. Ye heard the man." The large Scot gave her a stern look but she found that it didn't impact her in the same manner Brodick's displeasure did. All Druce stirred in her was temper.

"I said, release me."

Druce pressed his lips into a tight line. "Nae. Yer to stay right here and dinnae make me sit on ye. I dinnae need to fight with my cousin because he thinks I've handled ye roughly."

Anne growled for the first time in her life. Every bit of self discipline deserted her as she heard a crash from inside the eating hall. She rounded on Druce in a ball of fury.

"I am not going to stand here arguing with you while Brodick sets down what is best for me. I'll be the judge of what I need."

It was a bold statement. Druce frowned, clearly thinking her daft.

"The man is yer husband."

"Very newly so. He does not know my strengths and he never will if I allow him to whip every maid for not lavishing me with comforts. I assure you, I can endure as well as every one of them."

Anne gave a hard shrug, but Druce stubbornly retained his hold on her arms.

"I am warning you, sir. Release me now."

"Nae."

Her eyes narrowed dangerously.

Brodick held onto his control but it was not easy. Ginny offered him a stubborn, defiant look that wasn't sorry a bit. The maids lined up beside her, clearly supporting her behavior. He'd known to expect it but was still stunned by the open animosity shining on their faces. If his bride were a mean-spirited woman, he might understand. He aimed his first comment to the cook, who was also staring straight at him without reservations.

"I'd never suspect ye to be so hard-hearted. Ye've daughters of yer own who'll be marrying soon."

Bythe flinched, not because he shouted, but because his voice was so soft. Most of the maids shifted, faltering in their determination to remain unmoved. A few even cast their eyes at the floor.

"The lot of ye should consider what it must be like to marry so far from home with nae a single familiar face in sight. She didnae even bring a maid but I'm thinking that was a miscalculation on my part. I thought that surely Sterling staff were worthy of taking care of its mistress without an English maid being set above ye all."

More than one face turned pale. Brodick had no pity for them. "Ye'll be telling me the reason behind such disrespect. Was my wife . . . difficult?"

Some of the younger girls looked toward Bythe and Ginny for leadership. The two senior women held their tongues.

"I'll discover the truth of this matter and I will know it today." Scanning the line of uniformed girls who all drew pay from his coffers, he pointed at one.

"Mogen, tell me what prompted there to be no service. If 'twas by my wife's dictate, say so."

"That will solve nothing, my lord."

His wife strode into the kitchen, stiff pride shining in her eyes.

"I told you to keep her in hand." Brodick glared at his cousin, wondering just when his life had turned inside out.

Druce scowled at the sweet smile Brodrick's wife cast toward him. He lifted his finger and pointed at her.

"She bit me."

"Christ in heaven! Is there no one left in this castle who recalls I'm the lord here?"

"Berating your staff will not change how they truly feel, my lord."

Brodick stared at her, a crease appearing in the middle of his forehead. "And what do ye mean by that?" He kept his voice tightly controlled but she heard his frustration straining against his control.

"I might have dressed them down myself, if that was the answer."

His expression became guarded. "So why didn't ye?"

Opening her hands, Anne shook her head. "It is not my way to order others to like me, my lord. I prefer to be judged by and on my own merits. Be it to the good or ill. I do assure you that I am strong enough to survive without a fire or candles. The spring sun is warm and bright and I am not so dim-witted as to not fetch my own surcoat when night falls."

He stared at her again, admiration crossing his eyes. Seeing it on his face humbled her, but it also stiffened her resolve.

"It is not necessary to worry about me so greatly. As Agnes told you, I am healthy."

Brodick swung around to fix Bythe with his attention once more.

"Explain yer dislike, woman."

The cook stiffened, her eyes narrowing. "Ye said she tried to poison ye. Right at the table. Plenty heard it. Wife or no wife, ye be my lord and my loyalty is to ye."

"Are ye daft?" Druce sounded ready to drag the cook to Bedlam himself. "She may be English but I've nae seen evidence of a sinister bone in her body."

"She bit you."

Druce shook his head before he laughed. The sound was loud, shaking the copper lids hanging on the wall between the ovens.

"That's nae sinister. It makes me cousin a damn lucky man, to have that fire in the lass as he does."

There was a touch of heat in Druce's voice that made Anne stare at him. The large Scot sent her a smug look that drew a snort from Brodick. Druce shrugged at his cousin.

"Can't blame a man for noticing. Seeing as how ye put her into me arms yerself."

"Now don't you start telling me what I can't be taking offense at. I've got enough o' that at the moment."

Brodick turned his attention back to Anne. His jaw was tight as he battled the urge to deal with the maids the way he wanted to. Anne wanted none of it.

"Be at peace, my lord. There are some things that should never be ordered. I prefer to earn my loyalty. A few weeks is nothing compared to the true value of knowing that each bit of respect shown to me is truly meant."

There was more than one gasp from the row of maids. Bythe looked confused.

"Ye said it in front of all, my lord, refusing to eat. I heard the tale from twenty different men and women."

"She didnae try to poison me but it is possible the woman means to drive me mad." He shook his head but raised a dark eyebrow. "She was cooking under yer own nose. Are ye telling me that ye dinnae know what's going on in this kitchen?" He pointed to the ring of keys attached to the cook's belt. "Are ye so careless with those that anyone might get into the herbs without yer permission?"

Bythe covered her lips with a hand that shook. Brodick scanned the rest of the maids.

"Did it nae cross any one of yer minds that there would have been witnesses a plenty to such a deed? Or am I to assume that such harmful herbs are kept unlocked?"

Blythe's face turned red, one hand covering the ring of keys hanging from her belt. Being the cook meant she was charged with the costly herbs that served as flavoring and as ease for ailments. No one took such costly, hard to come by things without her unlocking the small drawer they were kept in. The keys were the symbol of her position at Sterling; they never left her sight. Her mouth opened but no words made it past her horrified lips. Anne turned her back on it all. More certain than ever that her guilt showed.

She was not worthy of Brodick's defense. It was a solid truth that she was doing something harmful to him. Stealing the dowry that he had invested so much effort into securing with her father. Two years of work that she would not bring him the reward of. She was convinced that God was working through the staff to force her to confess.

Her stomach heaved, the guilt making her sick. Anne ran from the eating area before she lost everything in her belly.

*   *   *

"The mistress has been very kind to me."

Brodick turned to stare at the single voice raised in praise of his wife. Coming through the doorway, young Enys used her hands to feel her way.

"Why do ye say that?"

Enys tilted her head towards him, lowering her head as if she could see him looking at her.

"The mistress has spent many days helping me spin. She does the things I don't have the sight for and she's a good carder. One who doesn't quit when the hours grow long."

He was suddenly tired, more fatigued than he could ever recall being. The wall of hatred between Scotland and England looked near impossible to scale. His wife had been sitting in the spinning room instead of taking control of Sterling. Yet she had not been lazy. He didn't know what to make of it.

He might be lord of the castle and of the land but it didn't seem to lend him any weight in this battle. That angered him. But it was not the sort of emotion that had sent him into the kitchen, ready to thrash a few maids.

It was a deep rage against injustice toward his wife. He wanted to spare her the ill will between their countries. The hope to unite that had seen him negotiating with her father was struggling to survive amidst the animosity. The woman he'd looked forward to returning home to was worth more than quick judgment.

"No one of us chooses our parents. I'm disappointed in the lot of ye. Sterling has nae ever been such an unjust place as I find it today."

He left. Druce followed him, the other man looking as confused as he felt.

"What man ever understood the way a woman thinks?"

Brodick wasn't able to shrug off the problem so simply.

"Why would she sit in the spinning room instead of taking her place as mistress of Sterling?"

Druce frowned. "Are ye sure ye want to become suspicious of her again, Cousin? That didnae do so well for ye before."

"It doesnae make sense."

And even if Druce was right, there was no stopping the suspicions that clouded his thinking. Mary was hiding something. He was sure of it.

Chapter Ten

"The lord asks ye to come down to the inner yard to go riding with him."

The maid lowered her head before quitting the room.

Anne sighed. Respect meant nothing when it was forced. She knew it so well that the sight of the maids scurrying to attend her made her ill. Tears stung her eyes because it was so distressing, but weeping would not help her.

Maybe confessing would . . .

She was tempted. But she was frightened, too. Brodick would put her from him. She knew it in her heart and it made her ache. He had the right. There was no doubt about it but she wanted to delay the moment when he'd stop looking at her so tenderly.

Stop touching her so intimately . . .

Anne had to blink rapidly to banish the tears before the two maids helping her dress noticed them. There wasn't enough for them to do, but they picked at her hair and clothing, finding things to straighten. She didn't have the heart to be ill tempered with them.

Even feeling her guilt so keenly, she could not stop herself from wanting to join Brodick. Her lust had truly destroyed her, exactly as the church preached. Having listened to the song of Satan, she was now a disciple unwilling to mend her ways.

One last time and then she would confess.

But she would lie with her lover a final time first.

A smile brightened her lips as she turned and hurried down to the courtyard. She was suddenly happy. Full of such bright joy that she felt as though she might burst with it.

The reason was simple. Brodick awaited her. The earl and master of Sterling had thought to send for her to ride with him. They would end up trysting and that made her move faster. Even if she had come to him by deception, he wanted her. He hadn't plowed her and left her bed for that of a mistress. She would savor it. Soak it up while the spring sun warmed the earth.

It was the only thing she'd have once the bitter truth was known.

Brodick was a magnificent sight.

Strong and perfect.

Anne paused on the steps, smiling at the way he waited for her. He wasn't in the saddle but stood waiting by the mare she'd ridden to Sterling extending a hand to her when she appeared, to help her into the saddle himself.

"I believe it's time I showed you a bit o' McJames lands."

He lifted her as though she were a child, placing her atop the mare and handing her the reins.

"Thank you, my lord."

He frowned at her, wrinkling his nose like a boy.

"I could not use your name in front of everyone."

He mounted his steed and cast a look over the curious eyes watching them. There was a hint of smug satisfaction in his midnight eyes. He cut a firm glance back toward her.

"Do it."

Anne suddenly understood and it reduced her to wanting to weep once more. He was making a public display of affection, dealing with the staff without ordering them to like her. It was clever and so touching she had to look down to hide the sparkle of tears in her eyes.

"You're too kind, Brodick."

" 'Tis nae something that should be absent from a marriage, lass." A warm hand reached across the space between them to cup her chin. "Just because ours is a noble union, that doesnae mean it must be unhappy."

He smiled and tossed his head. "Come with me, lass. The day is fresh and 'tis time I introduced ye to a bit of Scotland. 'Tis a bonny land."

Brodick gave his steed his freedom. As they cleared the gate, the pair of horses took to the road with zeal. In just moments the castle fell behind them, leaving her alone with her lover.

The sun was warm on her cheeks, spring finally dominating over winter. The mare felt it, too. She charged forward, her muscles flowing. They crested a hill and Anne gave the powerful animal her freedom. A valley lay below them, rich and green with new crops. Time and cares blew past her as fast as the ground beneath the pounding hooves of the horse.

Anne did not stay her but leaned over her neck, becoming one with the animal.

Brodick reached over and pulled the reins. The mare started, frustrated at having her run cut short. She pranced in a nervous circle but her husband held firmly.

"McQuade land begins over that river." There was a serious note in his voice that drove Anne's light mood away. His eyes scanned the ridge above them, searching it thoroughly.

"You do not get on well with your neighbors?"

Philipa's words about Scots raiding one another surfaced. The last two months had nearly driven all thoughts of her away.

"The old lord is nae friend of the McJames." Brodick shrugged. "He holds an old grudge against my father and in turn me. 'Twas his men I was chasing for the last month and a half."

"I see." She really wasn't sure what to make of Brodick's words; he'd told her little.

"You cannae ever cross the river, lass. Stay away from it." His eyes swept the area once more. His hand was still in command of her reins and he tugged on the mare, turning both horses around.

"Even then, the McQuades cross onto my land as bold as be. You should nae be riding alone at all. My men know to stop ye if ye stray onto unsafe ground. I'll be instructing the captain to nae allow ye outside the walls without good escort."

Clearly he considered the matter closed. Anne frowned, his tone rubbing her pride. He noticed the disgruntled expression.

"Dinnae be vexed with me for protecting ye."

" 'Twas more that I do not appreciate you taking up my reins, as if I can not heed a warning. Or understand the wisdom in not questioning why you tell me to do something as understandable as remaining inside your borders."

He scoffed at her but released control of the mare. "Ye dinnae ken, lass. McQuade would extract payment from ye for the wrong he thinks my father did him. Scotsmen can hold a grudge for a very long time. His men still burn down the farms of my people without a care for the loss it inflicts on them."

"And what was the grievance?"

Brodick frowned, his lips set in a hard line of refusal. He shook his head, denying her question.

"If he's angry enough to act out revenge on me, shouldn't I at least get to know the reason why?"

Brodick led them to the top of the rise before he pulled up his stallion.

"My mother was betrothed to McQuade but he lost her contract in a game of dice to my father."

"That's absurd." But it was exactly the sort of thing that she'd heard tales of at Warwickshire.

"Nae in Scotland, it isnae." Brodick grinned in the face of her astonishment. A wicked gleam twinkling in his eyes. "Didn't I claim ye as boldly?"

She shook her head, caught between the need to reprimand him and laugh because he spoke the truth.

"You're a devil, I'll agree to that much."

His expression changed, darkening with passion. "Be careful what words ye place on me. I might decide to live up to them."

"I can hope."

A tic appeared on the side of his jaw. Hard need glittered in his gaze. Anne stared back at him, boldness firing her blood. An insane urge to taunt him flowed through her.

"Yet hopes will not satisfy me. I simply need more."

"Yer a bold wench. Careful. Act so brazen and ye'll reap the crop ye've sown."

Her mare pranced in a circle, feeling the emotion. "And what might that be . . . my lord?" She drew his title out, knowing full well that it would frustrate him.

He glared at her, but the look in his eyes was not angry, it was demanding. "Maybe ye need a taste of what a raiding Scot does with his captured prize."

"That is only if you can catch me."

She slapped the reins, giving the mare her freedom once more. The animal dug into the soft spring ground, bolting forward. Leaning low over her neck, Anne laughed as she hung on tightly. Excitement surged through her veins as she looked back over her shoulder.

Brodick was hot on her heels. Just like a raider, intent on making her his captive. His midnight eyes glittered with determination as his stallion snorted. He bared his teeth and let out a yell that heightened her excitement.

Turning back around, she urged the mare forward. They raced up a hill and into the wooded patch. Her heart was hammering inside her chest, the blood speeding so fast through her veins it was hard to hear. She had never felt so alive.

She heard Brodick, heard him closing the distance between them. His horse surged up beside hers, the noses of the two animals becoming even. A hard arm snaked around her waist, pulling her across the distance between the animals. The ground was still flying past beneath her and her breath caught for one wild moment as she was on neither horse.

Brodick tossed her all the way across his saddle, her head sailing right over the body of the animal. He pressed a hard hand into her back as he pulled up on the reins. His stallion rose onto its hind legs, pawing at the air. A crazy shaft of need went through her clitoris, the sensitive bundle pulsing.

"Now what have I caught here?" Brodick dismounted in a quick motion, standing near her head. He grasped her hair, pulling it just enough to send little nips of pain across her scalp. In the oddest manner, she found the sensation arousing.

"A bonnie lass ripe for ravishing."

His brogue thickened, hinting at his enjoyment of the moment. He pulled her from the horse, letting her feet touch the ground. His hand remained in her hair, holding her captive.

"Aye, I'm going to enjoy having ye at my mercy."

His mouth pressed down on top of hers, demanding submission.

She didn't yield.

Reaching down, Anne touched his bare skin where his kilt stopped. His tongue stabbed into her mouth, stroking across her own. Sweet need filled her, her own tongue tangling with his. Her hand slid up until she felt the sac at the base of his cock. Boldly cupping it, she teased him with her fingers.

"*Christ.*"

"Are you so sure who will be ravishing whom, my lord?" She gently squeezed and his lips curled back to show her his clenched teeth. "Maybe you should think again. It does appear that I hold the trump card."

"I admit that yer telling me what to do, in private, is beginning to grow on me."

She curled her hands around his staff. "Is it now?"

"A bit. But ye can nae put that card down without losing its power."

A challenge coated his tone. A challenge she was in the mood to answer. Kneeling in front of him, she pushed his kilt up. The wide belt that held the pleats in place made a perfect place for her to tuck the end into. His cock was erect, the head swollen and ruby red. Running her hand up to the top of it, she teased the slit on its head with a fingertip. Seeing the thick pole in daylight didn't make her blush. A deep enjoyment filled her as confidence kept her eyes open, even enjoying looking at it.

"Now about playing the card in my hand . . ."

The wicked delight he'd given her had planted its seed in her mind. Leaning forward, she licked that slit, intent on giving him the same pleasure.

"Sweet blessed virgin."

Satisfaction filled her, stiffening her confidence. His hand stroked over her head as she worked her hand up and down his cock once again. Leaning forward, she added a long lap to the head. The hand in her hair clenched, telling her that she was succeeding. Opening her mouth, she closed her lips around the girth.

"Ye can tell me what to do all ye like as long as ye keep sucking me."

His hips thrust toward her mouth, pushing his cock deeper. She relaxed, allowing it to penetrate. He tasted good, a slightly salty fluid weeping from the slit. But his skin was warm and male, filling her with hot need. He held her head in place, his hips pulling back before thrusting forward once more.

"Tease the underside of the head with yer tongue."

His brogue had thickened further. She complied as he slid deeper into her mouth. She heard him take a ragged breath when her tongue touched his cock. She lost track of time, intent only on drawing more harsh sounds from him. His grip tightened, pulling her hair, and she didn't care. The little nips of pain combined into a desire that seeped into her. Between her thighs, her clitoris begged for attention. She felt her passage heating, clamoring for the hard flesh inside her mouth.

"Enough." He pulled her away from his cock. The grip in her hair tightened to keep her obedient to his will.

"My seed willnae be spilled in your sweet mouth, lass. Nae today. I plan to ravish ye properly." He knelt down, holding her head steady so that his breath brushed across the wet surface of her lips. "With a hard fucking."

Reaching down, she grasped his cock again. Her fingers slipped along its hard length easier now that it was slick from her sucking. He drew in a sharp breath, his eyes closing as she worked her hand up and down his cock.

"Are you sure, my lord? You appear torn. Quite indecisive."

The muscle on the side of his jaw twitched. Working her hand faster, she listened to his breathing increase. "Maybe the captive will ravish you, after all."

He chuckled but it wasn't a pleasant sound. Determination flickered in his eyes as he thrust his cock up into her hand, shuddering in delight.

"I think ye have forgotten who yer master is. I'm just the man to remind ye."

He pushed her head down, while sitting back on his haunches. She ended up across his thick thighs, her head over one side. He tossed her skirts right over her head as he clamped a hard arm over her back.

"Aye, ye need a wee bit of discipline."

"Brodick!"

She braced her hands on the ground, trying to push her body off his legs. She might as well have been trying to move a mountain. He held her down as he yanked the tail of her chemise up as well. Cool air hit her bare bottom, brushing across the fluid that seeped from her passage. She felt the touch of the sunlight and the brush of the breeze on her bottom. Her skin began tingling in anticipation.

"I could become used to the sight of yer ass waiting for my hand."

"I could not! What if someone is watching?"

"Then they shall see what a fine wife I've made out of ye. There are men aplenty that didnae think I might get my English bride to suck my cock."

"Brodick . . ." She pushed against the ground again.

He chuckled, a warm hand rubbing her exposed bottom. "What bothers ye, lass? The fact that I'm intent on smacking yer ass or the fact that I havnae started yet?"

"That's an absurd question. Let me rise."

He smacked one cheek, drawing a gasp from her. The sensation was surprising. It bolted up her spine but also centered on her clitoris. Need tightened around her as a second slap landed on her opposite cheek.

"Some women enjoy it. They claim it makes their clitoris hotter. I've a mind to see if ye are one of them."

His hand rose and fell again. A whimper crossed her lips because she couldn't contain everything anymore. Being spanked should have horrified her, but all she could do was think about how close his hands were to her wet passage. Each smack jiggled her clitoris, pushing her closer to climax.

"Now, there's an interesting sound." He smacked her bottom once more before rubbing a warm hand over the smarting flesh. "I wonder. Do you like being pressed into submission?"

He stroked his finger down between her thighs and she jerked. There was too much sensation now, and her body refused to remain still.

"I believe I need to investigate just how much ye enjoy my discipline."

He touched the opening to her body. Circled it with one fingertip. A moan rose from her lips as his finger slid in easily, aided by the welcoming fluid easing from her passage.

"Aye, ye are enjoying it." He thrust a finger into her, stroking the sensitive skin inside her. "So am I."

He worked two fingers in and out of her, little wet sounds reaching her ears.

"But I'm more in the mood to get back to ravishing my prize. We've played enough."

He flipped her over. Her body lay across his thighs for one moment, allowing her to look at his expression. Pure devilment danced in his eyes.

"Now let's get to that fucking I promised ye I would demand from ye."

He picked her up, moving her to the ground. There was new, sweet grass there to lie on.

"Now to ravish ye properly, I need to lift yer skirts and nae take the time to undress ye." He caught a handful of her skirts and tossed them up onto her chest. He moved between her thighs and pulled them up on either side of his hips. "We'll have to wait until tonight to make love naked."

A tender look crossed his face, but only for a moment. Hard need replaced it as he looked down at her spread flesh.

"Now there's a sight, yer body spread for my use. Yer slit all glistening in welcome. Nae raiding man could ask for better. I might take to spanking you every day."

"You shall not."

His body weight pressed down on her. He kept her legs tightly held over each of his broad shoulders. His hard cock touched her opening, nudging into the wet entrance. His eyes glittered with determination.

"I shall have ye, as often and in as many ways as I please." He thrust forward, his cock pushing deep. He felt too large, too hard, but her body eagerly took him.

"Wife."

She hissed at him, defiance burning inside her. It combined with the excitement, heightening her passion. Her body wanted him, wanted him to take her. Balling her fingers into a fist, she hit his shoulder.

"You're a fiery one." He captured her wrist. Stretching her arm above her head, he pinned her hand to the ground. His hips didn't move. Her passage was full of his hard flesh, aching for motion, but he remained still. Grabbing her free hand, he pressed it above her head as well.

"Better. That's what a captive should look like while she's being ravished."

"Except that you aren't doing anything but sitting on me." Anne sniffed in disdain. "Quite boring, I must say."

One dark eyebrow rose. His lips curved slightly up, mocking her. "Maybe I like the feeling of your sweet body clasping me."

Well, it wasn't enough for her. She struggled against his grip, needing to move. He laughed at her efforts, holding her in place, his cock rock-hard inside her.

"Yer body was made for me. I think I could spend hours just enjoying the way yer passage grips my cock."

"Ohhhh . . ." She bucked, finally achieving some movement. Pleasure spiked up her sheath but it only made her crave more. She needed deep thrusts to relieve the hunger gnawing at her. The hard length lodged inside her was unbearable, teasing her with what she needed while remaining motionless.

"Get off me!"

"Or get on with fucking ye?"

His expression dared her to demand what she wanted.

"Yes!" She bucked, the twist of need making her frantic to get him to comply.

"Do ye want me hard and rough?" His voice was steel edged, his nostrils flaring.

"*Yes!*"

He growled and released her wrists. Propping his elbows on either side of her head he twisted his fingers in her hair holding her prisoner once again.

"Then ye shall have it."

His first thrust sent the air out of her lungs. Her entire body moved as he drove his cock into her. It was hard, but pleasure filled her.

"Wrap yer thighs around me." His breathing was harsh. He gripped her hair tighter, his hips working to drive his swollen length back and forth rapidly. She clasped him with her thighs, locking her ankles to hold on tight. Little whimpers crossed her lips because she just couldn't contain all the sensation. Pleasure rippled upwards from each strong thrust. One wave collided with the one in front of it because he was moving so quickly.

"*Yes . . .*"

Only that single word made any sense to her. There was nothing but the friction of their flesh, only the pleasure shaking her in its grasp. Her back arched, her sheath tightening. Her lungs refused to work as pleasure exploded. She felt as if she was falling away from the edge of a cliff and it was the most euphoric thing she had ever experienced. The delight rippling out to her fingertips and toes. Every inch of her body pulsating with satisfaction.

Brodick shuddered, his cock pumping its hot seed into her body. He snarled against her neck, grazing the skin with his teeth. Anne dragged a breath into her starving lungs. Her fingers hurt from the tight grip she had on his shirt. Every bit of her strength suddenly drained away. There was only the deep satisfaction washing along her limbs. It settled into a pool around his cock. Uncurling her fists, she smoothed her hands over his shoulders. His torso quivered, his breathing ragged.

A soft kiss landed on her neck, soothing the bite. He trailed more sweet kisses along the sensitive column and along her jaw until he reached her lips. He kissed her softly but deeply, taking his time to lick her lips before pressing her mouth open for a deeper kiss. The hands in her hair released their hold, his fingertips gently massaging her scalp.

"Did I hurt ye?"

His voice was muffled against her cheek. In spite of the ache from her hips being spread so wide, she shook her head. He sighed, raising his body off hers.

"I got a wee bit carried away."

He stood up, looking very much like the raider he'd played at being. 'Twas a truth that he was every inch a warrior. Strength was etched into his body, forged just like his sword. The long weapon was still strapped to his back and had been there the entire time.

"I am glad of it, my lord." Rolling over, she stood up. Her skirts fell down to cover her thighs. Her passage was sore, but she would not lament it. She had enjoyed herself full well. "Even if my words will make you arrogant."

He was already arrogant but it was something she seemed drawn to. No softly worded flattery had ever turned her head. Brodick's bold demands turned her into a wanton.

He watched her, an unreadable expression on his face. Anne lifted her chin, giving him strength back to match his own. The wind whipped up, bringing a chill. Casting her eyes towards the horizon, she noticed the dark thunder clouds rolling in from the coast.

Brodick shook his head. "Ye're a distraction, madam. I dinnae think I've ever been so intent on a woman before."

"You say that as though it is to be lamented."

He turned to sweep the area behind them, doing it in a polished, confident manner that further enhanced his appeal. She'd never encountered a man who impressed her the way Brodick did.

"Maybe I've nae decided about that yet." There was a hint of mischief in his eyes. "Some men think falling in love with their wives is a fate worse than death."

The word love stunned her. Her father loved her. She loved her mother and siblings. Yet love between a man and a woman was something that was denied her by her bastard heritage. To allow her heart to soften would be to invite heartache.

She knew it and still her heart swelled. She suddenly felt so happy, she wasn't sure her feet were still on the ground. Brodick was watching her face, his expression carefully guarded. His lips twitched up as she failed to mask her emotions.

"Aye, lass, look what ye've gone and done. Stolen me heart. I'm going to have to take ye back to my castle and keep ye forever, else wither away for want of ye."

He winked at her. " 'Tis the Scot raiding way. We keep what we steal."

He left to retrieve their horses. A stricken look took command of her features as she hugged her arms around her.

Love. It was amazing and more precious than she ever might have imagined. No girlhood dream could have prepared her for the feeling.

The years of Philipa's scorn had never once felt like such a burden as they did right then. Her knees practically buckled, her shoulders wanting to throw the weight off. Her stomach was knotted with nausea so thick, she had to suppress the urge to retch.

Love . . . both gift and curse. The faces of her family tugged at her while her heart longed for the man riding toward her. If she remained with Brodick, loving him, she had to abandon the family who loved her to a cruel fate.

She had no idea what to do. None at all.

Brodick pulled his horse up when Sterling came into view. His body became still for a moment as he stared at one of the towers.

"We've company."

"Indeed?"

He nodded. Raising one hand he pointed toward the far north tower. "See the banner? 'Tis nae mine or Druce's."

Peering in the direction he pointed, she glimpsed a blue and green banner dancing in the wind.

" 'Tis from court."

His voice went serious and it was something she understood full well. Even a titled earl was subject to the will of his king. Brodick kneed his mount forward, and her mare picked up her hooves to follow.

Brodick swung from the saddle the moment they reached the yard. He reached up and plucked her from her horse before the mare even came to a stop.

"Take a nap. I'll have to finish ravishing ye later."

A nap indeed.

Anne laughed at his jest but he was already striding away, intent on joining his secretary who was standing on the steps waiting for his master. Anne had seen the man a few times, the large leather bag slung across his chest a telling thing. She knew what was in it—letters, books and, most importantly, the seal of the house. He appeared at each meal with the bag and she had not seen him even once without it.

He lowered his head as Brodick got close, moving forward so that their words would not drift.

A cart creaked as it entered the yard, two oxen pulling it.

"There ye are, lass." Helen's voice was full of cheer. She had to wait for the team to be held steady before another man unhooked the gate placed across the back of the cart. Helen climbed out, shaking her skirts and tartan when she was standing on the ground.

"Me daughter had a strong son, she did. 'Tis me first grandchild. They baptized the boy Ian."

Brodick's sister was also in the cart, although Fiona looked frustrated as she climbed to the ground. A dark-coated mare followed the cart and the animal nuzzled Fiona the moment she stood up. Brodick's sister stroked the animal's muzzle with confident hands, speaking softly to it.

"You enjoy riding?"

Fiona looked guilty for a moment but her hands remained on the mare. "As much as I'm allowed."

"Fiona, behave." Helen shot the younger girl a stern look. Fiona didn't appear contrite, only stubborn.

"There are many who believe riding will toughen my womb, twould make me sterile. I'm nae allowed very much time on my mare."

Anne watched the way the girl pouted, clearly feeling as though life was unfair.

It was that, Anne agreed. "There are many in England who say the same thing."

Fiona humphed. "Ye did not need to say that. Helen is already firm in her belief. I dinnae like riding in the cart."

Helen frowned at her. "Don't act so young, Fiona. If a lass gains a bad reputation, who will have ye? Think, miss, ye'll want to have yer choice when the time comes for marriage."

"I'm nae interested in marriage." Her hands stroked the mare lovingly. "At least nae now and 'tis only riding. It's nae as if I were asking to go riding out under the moon."

Helen frowned. "Nae gentle lass should talk about such things. You just leave the moon riding to the fallen women who dinnae have someone to keep them from that hard path. It might sound exciting, but be very sure, lass, that it's a rocky road to set yer life on."

"Your brother took me riding today. I must say, I understand your fondness for it."

Fiona smiled, all sweet forgiveness now that Anne appeared on her side. "Beware, Sister, Helen will blister yer ears for it. She is all aflutter about babies."

"I will nae. Once yer wed ye can ride all ye like because the womb doesnae toughen once yer sharing yer husband's bed." Helen shook her head. "Listen to ye, young miss. How could ye know everything at sixteen?"

Fiona smiled, as vexing as Cullen often was. "I know that I love to ride."

Anne laughed, unable to help herself. Helen rolled her eyes, but still grinned good naturedly.

"Tell me about your trip. How is your daughter?"

Helen happily clasped her hands together to begin speaking of her family. Anne let the sound of Helen's joy surround her. There was much at Sterling worth loving.

Especially its master.

Brodick looked formidable that night. Anne entered the eating hall and a prickle of worry went down her nape at the hush in the air. Even Cullen, who normally was so carefree, appeared years older. Druce was busy crumbling a round of bread, his jaw working quickly while his thoughts appeared to race.

Brodick nodded to her but continued to brood over a tankard. Cullen broke the heavy silence.

"He's a bastard."

Druce grunted, sounding like he approved, while continuing to chew more bread. Brodick's expression darkened further.

"That is nae the issue at hand. His bloody uncle has the ear of the King. We have to be careful how we answer his charges."

"The bloody raiders burned a dozen homes." Cullen looked ready to draw his sword.

But Brodick tempered his brother's ire with a calculated shake of his head. "I spent five weeks running them back to their nest. No one knows it better than I, but they've gone and complained to the King making it sound like we have been raiding them. Jamie is nae tolerating that from any clan. That's why he sent his men here to make sure it's known far and wide that he's watching."

" 'Tis nonsense. The McQuades were on yer land." Druce

washed the bread down with a huge swallow of small beer. "I'll ride with ye to court."

Brodick nodded, but his expression was still dark. His gaze touched hers and he winced.

"I'm sorry, lass, but 'tis poor company ye have to sup with tonight."

"For good reason, it sounds like."

His lips twitched, just the slightest amount. One of his hands covered hers. His fingers were warm, sending a tiny ripple of enjoyment up her arm.

"Protecting McJames' land is a fine reason, to be sure. Yet I'm nae looking forward to riding to court."

There was a disturbance at the far end of the eating hall. All three men grunted, hissing under their breath as a party of five men appeared and demanded some of the retainers relinquish their seats to them. Although wearing kilts, these men had doublets on and their tartans were blue and green. Never mind that there were seats aplenty a bit further across the room. The McJames' retainers looked to Brodick for direction, but it was clear they wanted to give the newcomers a taste of their fists.

Brodick jerked his head and the retainers set their expressions. They rose from the benches, moving to empty ones. The newcomers smirked with their victory before assuming their seats and loudly calling for service.

"You have guests." Anne watched them with growing disdain. "Rude ones at that."

Brodick grunted. "Aye. The sort of company I can do without."

Druce cut a hard look towards the men. "We all can. Damned royal hounds. Here to make us dance to Jamie's tune and all because we were defending our own land."

They bellowed again, beating their tankards against the table-top. Not a single maid looked their way.

Anne stood up, disgusted by their behavior. Brodick's hand shot out to clasp her wrist. She gasped because he normally controlled his strength with her and this grip was hard, unrelenting.

"Where are ye going?"

"To show them that no woman of this house is intimidated by their arrogant snobbery. As well as to stop that racket before the children learn ill manners from their poor example." She pulled her arm gently, keeping her eyes steady. "I'll not have them gossiping about Sterling hospitality."

Brodick released her, pride shimmering in his eyes. She lifted her chin, enjoying the praise. Their guests beat the table again. With a determined stride, Anne covered the distance to them. She hooked a full pitcher out of Ginny's hands. The younger woman gasped, but Anne had no time for her.

"You will have to stop beating those tankards against the table if you would like them filled."

Her English accent silenced all five of the men. They wrinkled their noses, one of them muttering something in Gaelic.

Leaning over the table, Anne splashed small beer into one tankard before the man holding it noticed her intentions. He jerked it away from her pitcher, sending a small wave of the dark brown liquid onto his shirt.

A ripple of amusement went down the long tables.

"You should be more careful with a full mug, sir." Her tone was carefully controlled but there was a subtle set down in it.

One of the other men hit the table with his tankard. "How long do I have to wait anyway?"

Anne smiled sweetly at him, years of serving Philipa finally becoming useful.

"Forgive me, I was distracted by your companions' clumsiness."

"Damned English." He peered into his mug frowning. "Likely poisoned."

Dropping the pitcher, Anne snatched the tankard from his hand. She quaffed a healthy measure of it and slammed it onto the table in front of him. The thump of the tankard hitting the table bounced around the hall because it was so silent.

"May I refill your tankard, sir?"

Amusement began to fill the air, Brodick's retainers breaking into loud laughter.

Helen suddenly appeared, the model of good hospitality with a tray of cut cheese and new spring leaves. She placed the tray with a great deal more force than needed.

"I do hope ye remember to tell the King how the mistress herself filled yer tankards with her own hands."

"So ye be the English heiress." The one nearest her ran his eyes down her length, pausing for a moment on the swell of her breasts. "I see yer nae so hard to look at. That's a bonus considering McJames had to fuck you to get yer dowry."

Anne felt Brodick's eyes on her; the hall had gone quiet again. She could feel the tension drawing tighter.

"Helen, please instruct the cook to heat some bathing water. Our guests need to remove the dirt from themselves now that they are indoors again. It is only polite, after all, to not drip filth at the table."

Anne turned her back to find the rows of McJames' retainers eyeing her with respect. They slapped their thighs with one hand, filling the room with noise. She carried herself with dignity through the men and into the kitchen.

"Och now, ye put them in their place right nicely."

Helen laughed, but her eyes fell on Ginny. Anne turned toward the older woman.

"Do not worry, Helen. We all listen to gossip. You should hear some of the things I have been told about Scots women." The maids working on the long table slowed down, tilting their heads toward her to listen. Even Ginny looked less defiant as she waited to hear what Anne had to say.

"Indeed. I understand that Scots women ride naked and pick their teeth with the points of their dirks." She paused for a moment, raising a hand to shake a single finger. "Yet, I always did wonder if that might leave wind burn on their skin as well as thinking, where do they store the dirk when they are naked? And how do they manage to pick their teeth with a sharp dirk while riding and not slice their lips? It seems rather complicated."

The women looked at her, stunned. Helen suddenly laughed, her cheeks turning red.

"Yer a rare one indeed, Mistress," Helen shot Ginny a firm look, "to be able to ken that some things are not as they seem. Hearing it doesnae mean you know enough to judge."

There were several mutters of approval. Even Bythe nodded agreement. She watched from her post near the stoves, keeping a watchful eye on her ovens.

"There's hot water aplenty if yer in the mood for a bath, Mistress."

"Thank you." To refuse would have undone the fragile truce she'd just forged. Helen nodded once more, approving of her. The tension in the kitchen dissipated, giving way to soft banter once more.

It was work well done, Anne decided. Something she might be proud of because not everyone could handle the prejudices of centuries. Maybe that was the true use of Philipa's sourness. Serving the woman had taught her patience.

She had done well, if she did think so herself.

More importantly, she had not shamed Brodick. That was

the true reward and she hugged it tight as she followed Helen towards the bath chamber.

Very tight.

"Och look at that puppy dog look of affection." Cullen moaned.

Brodick threw a broken loaf of bread at him. "Yer daft to joke about her. Fate has blessed me and I've no desire to tempt her to take it back because I'm nae grateful."

He was too. His wife was taking command of Sterling. She was doing it with kindness, something that was far too rare in English noblewomen. He could sit and watch her for hours, absorbing the way she moved, the way she dealt with difficulties without temper.

Aye, fate had been kind and he was grateful.

Chapter Eleven

"Oh now, don't ye look lovely." Helen fussed over the fire, poking it when it was blazing very well already. "I suppose I should leave ye to awaiting yer husband. Good night."

Await her confession . . .

Anne swallowed roughly, trying to maintain her resolve to do as she'd promised herself she would. She had to do it. Find the courage to trust in the love he'd offered her.

There was no more time for her. Besides, she did not have the heart to deceive him further. She could not do that to the man she loved.

But the candles burned low and the fire became a bed of coals blanketed by thick ash. The warm coverlet lulled her into slumber long before the chamber went dark.

Anne awoke at dawn, a sleepy yawn on her lips. She was the only one in the bed, the sheet beside her still smooth. A patch of scarlet caught her attention even in the dim light. Moving from the bed, she pulled the window curtain to let the rising sun shine in. A piece of silk was carefully folded around a box, a parchment sitting on top of it that bore the wax seal of the Earl of McJames. Her hand shook when she reached for it. The wax snapped in the chilly morning air, the sound as piercing as a pistol shot.

Dearest wife—
With regret I must go to court by royal command.
Be very sure that it took a King to summon me from
yer side.
Write to me . . . Yer letters will strengthen me.
Brodick.

She traced his name with a finger. Never once had she had a love letter. Today she did.

Brodick.

Only that name that she used in their bed. It was a sweet intimacy that touched her heart. Setting the letter aside, she unwrapped the silk to find a lady's writing desk. It was smooth and crafted with skill. Two hinges allowed the top to lift up. Stored carefully inside were sheets of paper. A small pottery jar with another piece of expensive and rare cork stood there. Two bone quills lay near the ink well. There was a scarlet strip of wax and a small brass seal along with it. Lifting the seal, she choked on a sob when she noted the rampant lion of the McJames. There would be very few of these seals because they represented the earl. Each one would be carefully guarded.

It was a gift worthy of the mistress of the manor.

Anne carefully closed the lid. She finally understood her mother completely. Ivy Copper was in love and that emotion blinded her to every insult or slur the world cast at her. She could no more stop loving than she could cease breathing.

"Och, I thought I heard ye moving about." Helen lacked her normal joy this morning. "I see ye found the lord's letter. He was most distraught at leaving ye. But those toads from court wouldnae hear of waiting. Kept him up most of the night arguing with him over this and that until the earl just mounted his horse and rode, wanting to end the matter the soonest. He wrote that letter with his own hand."

That was a gift of intimacy. A man of Brodick's station normally did not write his letters himself. She had written most of Philipa's. There had been a time when a part of the value a noble bride brought to her husband was her knowledge and finesse of being cordial with all the other great houses. She would carefully dip her quill and pen letters that maintained friendships with all the correct people.

Helen bustled about, pointing the two maids with her toward tasks. "Still ye'll have to get used to it. Being an earl means answering to yer king. Ye must have learned that in yer years at court."

Anne lost her focus, losing track of what Helen was saying. Her stomach rolled violently, sweat beading her forehead. There was no mastering the nausea this morning. She flew towards the garderobe, the contents of her belly rising.

Anne was trembling when Helen gently pulled her off her knees.

"I don't know what happened. I don't feel ill."

Helen led her back across the chamber, using a wet cloth to soothe her brow.

"I see now why ye had naught but stale bread in yer chamber." Helen looked up, snapping her fingers at one of the maids. "Fetch some bread and be quick."

The girl smiled so broadly all her teeth showed. "Aye, right away."

Anne stared at the empty doorway, trying to understand why the girl was so happy. Sickness in the castle was cause for alarm.

"Such a shame the lord was called away." Helen was practically dancing. "But better now than when yer time comes."

"My time?"

Helen turned, confusion on her face. She stared at her for a moment before a similar bright smile covered her face. "Och now, I forget that yer so newly wed. But a blessed union it is. You havenae had any monthly curses since leaving England, have ye?"

She hadn't.

Anne felt her eyes go wide. If she hadn't just retched, she would now. Philipa's ugly, evil, twisted face filled her thoughts. For sure she was breeding. Being a maiden didn't mean she was ignorant of the facts surrounding a woman's body. The kitchen at Warwickshire was often ripe with talk about pregnancy and its symptoms. How else had she learned of French kisses? Despair filled her because now there was an innocent babe to think of as well.

But it was replaced by the sight of Brodick waiting in the yard for her. The way he stood so proud and strong. Giving him a child was the greatest gift she might ever bestow on anyone. He was worthy of that.

But he wanted Mary's child, not a bastard half-sibling's child.

"Och now, look at ye. 'Tis a happy time. I've waited so long to see this day. I cannae wait until your belly is plump and round."

Helen chattered away while Anne tried to feel the tiny life growing inside her.

"We needs get the seamstresses to plying their needles at once. No more long stays for you."

Helen turned to reveal a creamy sheet of paper laid out squarely on the writing desk. The ink well was carefully placed in a small cutout made for it so that it would not spill while the cork was removed.

"You must write to the earl. Once a fortnight his messenger will bring you a letter and you may send yers back with him. He'll be so very happy to learn of the babe."

"I shall write, but not just this moment."

Helen shook her head, turning to replace the cork in the jar of ink. "Och, listen to me. Yer belly is heaving. 'Twill pass. We'll send the lads for Agnes."

Anne placed a hand over her mouth, horror filling her. She could not condemn her child to being bastard born.

If she remained at Sterling, that would be what happened. Tears trickled down her cheeks as she looked at the writing desk. She could not confess who she was. Not now.

Not ever.

Two weeks later a letter arrived as Helen promised. Anne didn't think she had ever been so happy to receive anything. To be sure, her sire never wrote to his wife when he was away at court. For that reason, she had tried not to expect a letter. Brodick was at court after all, and he had important things to attend to. All wives had to endure being second to the monarchs.

There was much to do and she threw herself into the fast pace of spring. There was planting and early harvest, lambs being birthed and soap to make now that the weather was good enough to use the large iron caldrons. They built fires beneath the huge pots and stirred the soap with boat paddles. Time had dragged on, in spite of her best efforts to fill it. She still awoke at night, searching the bed for Brodick. She told herself a hundred times to stop thinking about him, stop longing for him, that it was impractical and even insane to love him.

Her heart refused to listen.

Instead she impatiently saw to making sure the messenger was fed and new clothing brought up for him. She paced while he lingered in his bath, refusing to ask for the letter before she had shown the man good hospitality. When at last the night was creeping over Sterling, he untied his leather bag and handed a sealed parchment to her.

"Oh now, yer nae to read that here."

Helen whisked it out of her grasp before she closed her fingers. "Helen!"

"Nay. Ye listen to me. Wait. 'Twill be much better if ye wait to read it in yer chamber."

Anne frowned. She did not want to wait. Helen smiled gently at her.

"Follow me, mistress, and I'll show you how to read a letter from yer true love."

Her face transformed into a tapestry of sensitivity. Her eyes shimmering with a knowledge that was both deep and sultry. It was not about mistress and maid. It was a moment when Anne looked into the eyes of another woman who understood love for a man.

Helen held the letter up, beckoning her towards her chamber. The maid left the parchment on the bed as she removed her clothing, leaving her in only a chemise. Spring was well on its way to giving over to early summer so the air was warm. The fire kept the stone floor inviting for her bare feet. Helen removed the pins from her hair, brushing it out. But she didn't braid it as she normally did.

"There now. That's the way to read the letter. Just as ye would welcome him at night."

Helen replaced the brush on the vanity. The two maids with her pulled the bed curtains to close the sides. Sitting on the foot of the bed, Anne fingered the seal. Helen sent the maids away, pausing to extinguish the candles. She left a single one burning on the vanity. Its yellow flame danced over the sheet of paper she had laid out on the writing desk. The quill sparkled in the candlelight, looking magical.

"Enjoy it, mistress, and make sure ye write him back. The carrier will leave at dawn."

The chamber was left in deep quiet, the sort that allowed you to hear the crackle and pop of the wood as it caught fire. She heard the whistle of the wind outside the window. Anne still sat upright but Helen had tucked the coverlet around her.

The parchment crinkled as she broke the seal and opened it wide. The black ink danced across the page, in neat letters. She drank in the words, for the first time getting to know the man who had taken her from Warwickshire. They had never spoken of simple things. Brodick wrote of them now. Telling her about his likes and dislikes. That he preferred small beer to ale and heather to rosemary. The letter had many dates on it, like a diary. He would date the top of each entry, letting her know that he thought of her each night. Several drops of wax shone on the parchment, proving that he'd remained up past sunset to write to her.

The way they loved when together was exciting, their bodies creating heat and passion so hot it might even be explosive. But his letters were a different sort of intimacy. There was tenderness and trust as he shared things with her that were neither noble nor politically correct. They were often silly or whimsical. That endeared him more to her heart.

Crawling out of her cocoon, Anne went to the writing desk. It was as if he was there with her. As she dipped the quill into the ink, she felt the loneliness fade away for the first time since awaking to the news that he was gone. The sharp tip scraped softly against the paper as she returned it to the ink well over and over. She was careful to not smudge the drying ink, waiting to begin the next line until the candlelight no longer glistened in it. She did not care that it was a slow process. She lingered over her composition, savoring the next line. The candle burned lower as she began a second page, writing of small things just as he had, sharing who she was with him.

A tap on the door broke the mood. Helen held a tin lantern in one hand as she peeked in.

"I'm just finishing."

Blowing on the last line, Anne made sure it was dry before folding the parchment to conceal what she had written. Holding the wax over the candle, she turned it round and round until it shimmered then pressed it firmly onto the place where the edges of parchment met. The heated portion puddled into a round glistening circle of wax. Anne pressed the seal firmly onto it, holding it still while the cool metal drew the heat out of the wax setting it.

When she pulled the brass seal up, it left a mold of the rampant lion in the scarlet wax.

"Thank you for waiting, Helen."

" 'Twas a pleasure." She set the lantern down and went to the bed. Pulling the coverlet to one side, she waited for Anne to get back into bed. She went, enjoying the comforts because who knew when they might end. For tonight it was enough to simply enjoy.

Helen blew out the candle. She took the letter and left. The chamber was quiet and dark. But the babe inside her began to move. A tiny, soft motion like a flutter of butterfly wings inside her belly. Her breath froze in her lungs and the movement came again, confirming that she was not dreaming it. Laying a hand over her slightly thickened waistline, she cradled their child.

It would be born in love even if she had to see Mary cradling it. Many mothers gave up as much for their children. Tears fell onto the pillow as she refused to lament the ache in her heart. She would not repent for loving. Even if it broke her heart. To love was to taste life for the first time.

But her babe needed more than that. Her life was an example of what happened when you tried to pit love against the way the world was organized. Mary was the rightful mistress of Sterling. If Anne confessed to Brodick, she might remain as his leman, but her children would lead the same life she had when Mary was found out and was forced to take her position as wife.

But if she returned to Warwickshire and allowed Mary to pretend that her babe was hers, her child would enjoy all the benefits of legitimacy. Brodick would keep the dowry land.

She wiped the tears from her eyes. It would be done. Yet not until right before the babe was due, because Brodick would come for her. Bonnie had seen it. So she would have to deceive him for the sake of their child. It was the greatest gift she might give her son.

That thought lulled her into sleep. Brodick's face was there in her dreams.

The Scottish court

Arriving at court was not an easy thing. Brodick spent five days just finding a place to lay his head. With the king in town, most of the better homes were rented and he didn't keep a town house. His father had avoided court as well. Riding hell-bent toward the royal castle hadn't gotten him any closer to seeing his king. His clothing had to follow, making it longer still until he was at last ready to present himself at court.

At least the royal hounds were off his back. They left him the moment he began setting up house. The city was teeming with people. The different clan tartans denoted other titled men. Some clansmen still clung to their plain wool kilts without plaid striping. Not all clans had adopted the newer kilts.

It was a full fortnight before he was ready to appear at court.

Showing up any earlier would have been a waste of time. The first thing he needed to do was send a formal message to the King's chamberlain advising the man that he'd arrived as summoned.

James Stewart had been raised by courtiers. His mother had long ago lost her head in an English castle. It was an ironic twist of fate that left him the heir to Elizabeth Tudor's throne, since she had signed his mother's execution order.

But that didn't seem to matter much now. Brodick walked into the main receiving hall to find it bursting with ambassadors from all over the world. They were dressed in fine clothing, attendants trailing them. Foreign languages bounced around the hall—Portuguese, French, Italian and even Spanish. His temper strained against his control as he viewed the number of men waiting to see the king. This was the outer hall. They weren't even in the main court yet. James might keep him waiting for a month if he was of a mind to do so.

"It seems we Scots have gained a wee bit o' favor since I was last here." Druce looked around, his face pensive. "Now that's a change."

"It explains why Jamie is so concerned with raiding these days."

"Aye, it does."

Brodick watched the blending of new fashion with Celtic tradition. Kilts were still worn by at least half the men but now there were velvet slops and Venetian pants as well. Many of the ambassadors wore lavishly decorated short capes that shone with gold and jewels. He and his men were wearing doublets with sleeves, the green wool a mark of the McJames clan for a century. But he didn't think even being in the presence of his monarch meant he should have sewn gold baubles onto his clothing. Such frivolity was for women and fops who eyed young men for trysts.

"But I must admit that I'm a bit surprised at the fashion on display."

His brooch was gold and set with twin rubies for the lion's eyes. It had been his father's and someday it would be worn by his son. On his right hand was a signet ring with the seal of the Earl of McJames. It did not leave his hand unless he handed it to a man willing to defend it with his life. That was a promise his father had extracted on his death bed.

Druce scoffed at him. "I'll remain a happy man in my kilt."

"Agreed."

They all froze as McQuade came into view. The man stood with his retainers, frowning at the great number of men waiting to see the king. The royal guards kept the door barred while everyone awaited the call of the chamberlain announcing their name. Without that, they stood waiting.

"Thieving mongrel McQuade."

"Easy, Cullen. We're here to defend the fact that we nae started the fighting."

This time.

Brodick had to give the man his due; there had been a few nights that he strayed onto McQuade land. But he didnae fire the homes of the farmers.

Druce slapped Cullen on the back. "What's the matter, lad? Don't ye like the look of yer future father-in-law?"

"Did I miss something important?" Brodick watched his brother bristle but he clamped his mouth shut for a change.

The chamberlain stamped his white staff against the floor three times. The brass plate on the bottom of it echoed through the hall. Everyone fell silent.

"Oyee, oyee,oyee. His Majesty will receive the Earls of Mc-Quade and McJames."

A sound of frustration rippled through the men who did not hear their names. Several waved scrolls under the nose of the chamberlain, trying to get the man to notice their pleas. He stood straight, staring forward.

"At least Jamie's nae in the mood to see us cooling our heels."

Brodick moved forward, eager to see his king and quit the court. He had no ambitions that included remaining for any length of time among the schemers. The only favor currying he wanted to do was back home with his sweet wife. He'd gladly spend every night seeking her favor.

The guards uncrossed their pikes, allowing him and his men into the inner hall. It was decked out with the banners of the royal house. Here there were ladies wearing velvet and silk gowns. Their faces were painted but not the ghastly white of the English court. They still looked ridiculous to his eyes, their cheeks bright red and their lips the same shade.

Brodick lowered himself to one knee, Cullen and Druce mimicking him. He swung one fist against his left shoulder.

"Yer Majesty."

James Stewart was an interesting cross between Scots and European style. He was seated on a throne at the end of a red carpet.

"McJames and McQuade, join me in my private chambers. Two men each."

McQuade slid Brodick a sinister smile. The older man knelt on one knee the same as he had. The king stood and left the throne room. Brodick stood up, eyeing his nemesis.

"Ran crying to the king, did ye, McQuade?" Brodick smacked his lips. "Always knew ye were a whining bastard when ye lose. Like yer father before ye."

The older man's face turned ruddy. "And yer the son of a thief that waits 'til a man is in his cups to challenge him to a game of wits."

Brodick smirked. "My father often said I look a lot like me mother. Since ye knew her, do ye agree?"

McQuade spat on the floor. "She was mine."

Cullen scoffed at him while stroking a lock of his lighter hair that was the same shade as their mother's had been. "Nay, man, we're living proof that she was had well and good by our father."

McQuade smiled. "Well, now we'll be seeing just who has the last word."

He moved toward the king's private chambers, his spurs clanking against his boots. Druce patted Cullen on the shoulder once more.

"That had a nice ring to it."

Cullen smirked. "Ye think so?"

"Oh, lad, aye." Druce tilted his head to the side. "I think ye're going to be quite the family when ye make good on that threat to tame Bronwyn."

Cullen glared at Druce, his fingers tightening into a fist. There wasn't time for more as they came into the king's presence and hit a knee once more.

"Rise."

James Stewart eyed McQuade first. The older man lifted his chin, stubbornly resisting the look from his monarch to soften his stance.

"McJames, tell me why ye wounded several of McQuade's men last month."

Brodick resisted the urge to grin. James might be dressed like a European king but beneath his pants he was pure Scot.

"Because I caught them burning some o' me farmers' homes."

" 'Tis not so."

Druce stepped forward. "It is. Saw it with my own eyes."

The king held up a hand. He looked at Druce.

"Ye swear that?"

"On the title of Bisbane. I was at Sterling for the celebration of my cousin's marriage." Druce pointed a finger at McQuade. "I rode out with Brodick and saw the torches myself."

McQuade didn't look repentant. Quite the contrary, the man's face lit with satisfaction. The king grumbled beneath his breath.

"What am I going to do with ye, McQuade?" Jamie sat down and propped his hand on his knees. He rested his chin against one palm while considering McQuade and his men.

"The eyes of the world are on Scotland. We've no time for raids and quarrels long past settling. Man, that woman is long ago wed and her sons grown to men."

McQuade shook his head. "I want a portion of the dowry returned. That will satisfy me."

"Ye married a woman with a good dowry."

"But no land. 'Tis the two-hundred measures of land I'm wanting. They were promised to me." McQuade was yelling by the time he finished.

"No chance o' that happening." Brodick wasn't much calmer. "Ye dragged me here for no reason. Yer men were raiding and I sent them back to ye whining like their master."

"Enough."

Jamie stood up. He pointed at McQuade. "Ye've wasted my time, man, and I'll nae thank ye for that. That land went with the heiress. There will be no arguing with what a father settled onto his daughter thirty-five years ago. I suggest ye look to arranging a good match for yer sons if it's a larger holding ye want."

"But that bastard just took an English bride who will double his land yet again." McQuade shook a tight fist in the air. "I want that land."

"I said nay." Firm authority rang out of the king. He looked at Brodick.

"Ye claimed yer bride?"

Brodick lifted his chin as high as McQuade's, but with a far different emotion. "Aye, three months ago."

The king didn't respond for a long moment. McQuade began to shake his fist again.

"Ye see?" McQuade stepped closer to the king. "The man is power hungry. He's setting himself up to challenge ye."

"That's nae true." Brodick glared at McQuade. "Watch yer insults, man. I'm nae a traitor and willnae hear any man say I am."

"Enough!"

The king's guards reinforced their monarch's order with lowered pikes. McQuade shook with his rage, but the man stepped back in the face of cold steel leveled at his belly.

"The pair o' ye will remain with the court for the summer. I've not the time to deal with yer fighting."

"I've got a new wife that's breeding."

The king lifted an eyebrow. "If her belly's full, she dinnae need you anymore. Ye'll stay."

Brodick clenched his fists. Even the guards behind his king didn't settle his temper. Jamie waved a finger at him. "I've need of ye, McJames. This court is full of tale-spinning lords who want to keep raiding each other over things that can never be changed. Yer clear thinking will be welcomed."

"My King—"

"I've spoken, man." Jamie's voice rang with a royal decree. "And ye will serve me for the summer. I'll send ye home in time to see yer son born."

McQuade snickered.

"And ye, McQuade, will remain in the outer hall awaiting my summons."

"Yer Majesty—"

"Ye have that correct, man. I am yer king and I nae appreciate ye spinning tales in my ear like I'm some lack-wit. There's men out there who have waited months to have their issues settled. Quarrels that can be resolved, unlike the question of a bride who was lost decades ago. Good God, man, stealing a bride is as Scottish as a kilt. Ye should have planned things more secretively if ye didnae want someone to try and lift her out of yer keeping before the consummation."

Jamie lifted his chin, looking every inch the king.

"Go and ye had better be waiting in the outer hall when I summon ye."

" 'Tis an insult, even coming from me king."

Jamie pegged him with a hard stare. "And 'tis also better than being locked into shackles for bearing false witness against a fellow lord."

McQuade snapped his mouth shut. He glared at them both before staring at the points of the pikes. He lowered his head before storming from the room.

"That man is going to hound ye until he's dead." James shook his head and reached for a goblet. He took a long drink from it, his guards resuming their positions of vigilance behind him. "No doubt his sons have been raised to detest ye as well. 'Tis a good thing ye didn't let him get wind of yer impending nuptials. He'd have stolen the bride if he'd known."

"He might have tried."

Jamie laughed. "Aye. He'd have done that sure enough."

The king snapped his fingers and a servant offered goblets to them all. Brodick took it but he wasn't interested in the French wine. He had no taste for the strong brew. It made mush out of a man's thinking. Jamie scoffed at him.

"McJames prefers small beer."

Brodick let the servant take the goblet. "Ye remember." He was slightly impressed. The last time he and Jamie shared a drink was a full ten years past.

"I'd have been dead years ago if my wit wasnae sharp. There's plenty o' men that dinnae want me succeeding the throne of England." The king waited until the servant returned with another drinking vessel. This one was a tankard far better suited to small beer. Druce looked ready to weep until he noticed the second servant with two more tankards.

"I really do need ye, man. We've delegations from every royal house on the continent. This is a summer when Scotland needs her earls at court." James pegged him with a firm look. "I need ye here, and I'll keep McQuade on a leash so you'll nae have to worry about him harassing yer people."

"What about the man's sons?" Druce asked.

The king nodded. "I'll summon them to wait with their father. A few months cooling their heels in my outer hall should teach them to carry tales. But I'll nae promise that it will keep them from raiding ye in the fall."

"I need no help with running him back to his own land." Brodick looked at Druce and Cullen. Both smiled unpleasantly. The king grunted.

"But I need ye, man."

To serve his king was an honor.

But that meant not returning to Sterling . . .

Brodick hid his disgruntlement behind the tankard. He'd judged older men harshly because they wanted nothing more than to return home. Look at himself now. Young lads didn't know what they were missing. He hadn't until he was forced to leave it behind. Still he was blessed and needed to remember that.

The only thing that vexed him still was the fact that his wife hadn't told him about their child. Her letter was sweetly written, more than he'd expected salving the wound that was left when he rode away from Sterling.

But it didn't contain the news that she was carrying. That had come in a second letter written by Helen. He didn't feel any remorse over commanding the maid to write him in se-cret. There would be no surprises when he returned home this time. He needed to know that his wife was cared for. Needed to know that she was not wasting away to a sack o' bones.

Something felt wrong but he couldn't place it. Just that inkling of a feeling that tingled down a man's neck when he knew he was being watched.

But for the time being, he would serve his king. It was the McJames' duty.

England, four months later

"Mother, I'm bored! I will go insane if I am forced to endure much more of this confinement."

Mary Spencer snorted while she paced in a wide circle. She wrinkled her nose and picked at her sleeve.

"And I detest this wool. It stinks like a sheep. I want my vel-vet dress back. It has been forever since that Scot took Anne away."

"It has been only seven months." Philipa sounded tired. She cast a strained look at her child.

"Seven and a half months. The summer is waning."

"Still not enough time has passed."

Mary groaned long and loudly. Philipa rubbed her forehead. She was sick unto death of the demands of men, no longer caring if the church preached that it was her place to shoulder such. Mary huffed and sat in a puddle of wool skirts, her ex-pression unhappy.

"Don't fret, my lamb. We've almost bested this marriage your father negotiated. A few weeks more is all."

"What if Anne isn't with child?"

Philipa frowned. "She had better be."

She had better be.

Philipa felt her temper heat. Oh, she would enjoy letting her wrath fall on Ivy Copper and her litter of bastards. She'd wanted to drown them all the day they were birthed. Anne had better be with child. A son. She didn't dare risk leaving the girl with the Scots household too long. Servants talked. Even when you whipped them.

Philipa sighed. It was certainly difficult to make it through life's hurdles. She would just have to endure like her daughter for a few weeks more. She frowned, considering how long Anne had been treated as the mistress of a house. It was possible the bastard might forget her place. Even the threat against her family might lose its sharp edge when she was safe and pampered so far from Warwickshire.

Something would have to be done about that. Something to drive it deep into her heart. Philipa paced, considering her methods.

Yes . . . something very frightening to a girl.

Sterling, one month later

Surcoats were evil.

Anne snarled as she tripped on the edge of her loose gown. Grabbing two handfuls of the fabric, she lifted it out of the way of her feet. Now that her belly was swelling large, she could not wear her skirts. Without a waistband, the fabric puddled on the ground every time she bent over, even a little bit. It was frustrating because she felt wonderful and didn't want to be slowed down by the loose garments needed for her ripening figure.

"Get on the other side of the flock, Ginny. Hurry."

Anne ran the opposite way, flapping her surcoat in the wind to get the geese into the pens. It was time to wash them and remove the thick down that had grown over the winter. Now that it was full summer, the feathers could be thinned. There would be enough time for it to grow back before winter returned.

Anne ran and headed off a large gander. The animal honked at her, flapping his wings.

"Get on with you. I want a down comforter to keep me warm. You will never miss the feathers, I promise." Raising her hands, she sent the bird back toward the pens on the riverbank. Water made it much easier to remove part of the down.

Her baby kicked. Anne lowered her arms to softly stroke her rounded tummy. She was as ripe as a fall pumpkin, her child pushing her womb out. The bells began to ring. Her heart accelerated as she looked toward Sterling. A cloud of dust was rising on the road and she peered at it, willing her husband to ride out of it.

"Mistress, ye need to get within the castle walls."

One of the captains was always with her when she left Sterling. Anne looked up to see the man frowning at the approaching riders.

"Forgive me, ma'am, but we needs to go now."

There was a solid ring of duty in his voice that didn't hint at any argument from her. He reached for her hand and helped her into the cart the man insisted she ride in. Her mare having been denied her the second Helen told all at Sterling that she was with child. Ginny and the others were left to deal with the geese. But for her, she was returned to Sterling in haste. Brodick had kept his promise to have her accompanied anytime she left the imposing walls. They rode through the gate well before the riders reached them. Helen stood on the steps waiting for her.

"There ye be, ma'am."

"Is it the earl returning?" Her voice was full of anticipation.

Helen shook her head. "The lord doesnae have the bells rung on his return. He claims 'tis an honor he has yet to earn."

A shiver went down her spine. Her babe kicked hard as she lifted her chin and watched the gate. The riders drew in close enough to see and the banner of Warwickshire flapped boldly in the afternoon sun. Horror flooded her, stealing her breath as they filled the inner yard. But the worst was yet to come. The man leading them yanked his helmet free and shook out his long hair.

It was a face that she wished she might forget.

Cameron Yeoman was an evil man. One of a handful of men Philipa employed to keep the staff in hand at Warwickshire, the man often gained compliance with his brute strength. He flashed a sneer at her, his gaze settling on her distended belly. The tip of his tongue appeared on his lower lip, swiping back and forth across it a few times.

"Good day to you, ma'am. Your Mother, Philipa, sends her greetings."

Anne paled. She felt the blood draining from her face. Cameron waved a horse forward and she heard a faint tinkling of laughter. Her sister Bonnie rode confidently up beside Philipa's strong man. Her cheeks were red, a haunted look in her eyes.

"I brought you a letter. The mistress commanded me to bring it to you."

Anne moved down the steps as fast as possible with her belly so large, unable to see her sweet sister so close to such a monster. More than one maid at Warwickshire had suffered his rape. The man was a monster, often beating a girl even after she bent to his will. Bonnie reached into a leather pouch and pulled a folded parchment out. She shuddered but hid it almost in the same moment that it shook her slight frame.

Anne took the letter, but was more intent on getting her sister away from her escort. Cameron stared at her belly, a twisted smile on his lips.

"Dismount, Bonnie."

"Hold." Cameron held up a hand. Bonnie flinched but froze with her hands tight around the saddle horn.

Captain Murry, charged with her protection outside the gates, had shifted away, leaving her at the mercy of her visitors. Work was resuming around them. Even Helen had joined several women working on washing wool. Everyone seemed to be granting her privacy to talk to her guests, thinking it a kindness.

Cameron swung a leg over the head of his horse. He moved close enough to keep his words between them.

"Your sister stays on that mare." He reached into his leather doublet to pull another letter from it. His smile grew. "This is a proxy marriage, giving me full rights to your sweet sister. You can say anything you wish but no man in this castle will deny me the rights to my wife."

"*No . . . She's but fifteen.*"

"Aye, you heard correctly. I confess that I like the young ones best." Depravity danced in his eyes. He licked his lower lip, enjoying the horror the gesture bred in her.

"Find a way to take a ride with me and leave your guardians behind or I'm going to enjoy the trip back to Warwickshire. Your sister won't." He sniffed. "But every wench has to learn to take a man inside her at some point."

"I think I shall just have you thrown out like the filth you are, while keeping my sister safely at my side."

Cameron raised an eyebrow at her. "Maybe you'd better read that letter in your hand before you open your mouth. I really don't care. Your sister is mine if you choose to stay. You can't keep me locked away forever, and slapping me in shackles won't dissolve my marriage. My men are really looking forward to getting to watch me consummate it. I might even share."

Anne ripped the seal open. She didn't want to read Philipa's words, didn't want to give the woman any of her time ever again. But seeing Bonnie in his care was too much. She could not abandon her to Cameron. He'd do it, all of it and more.

"Your brothers will be sailing for the New World if you don't return with me."

That was a death sentence. All of the brave men and women who had set out to found Roanoke had disappeared, their fate unknown in the vast wilderness that was Virginia. But the Privy council was determined to see an English colony in the new world. They sent ships every few years, and few of them returned.

The letter in her hands confirmed Cameron's words but it went on snagging her attention.

> *Do you really believe that your child will be welcomed any more than you are at Warwickshire? Return and let your babe be accepted as Mary's. The world will see the child as legitimate. It's a gift that will see him enjoying all of the comforts that you have sampled as the mistress of Sterling. Think about that before hiding behind the Scottish border.*

Philipa was horrible, but she wrote the truth. Even if Brodick did not cast her out, her child would bear the stain of being born bastard.

It didn't have to be.

She trembled, rubbing her belly with a soothing hand. Her throat had tightened, making it difficult to breathe. Anne forced the lump down. She had to do the best for her baby. The in-

nocent growing inside her could be as respected as his father
or as scorned as she.

She could not place her own life above her child's. There
could be no joy in her heart if she knew her happiness was
purchased through the sufferings of her siblings.

"There is a valley below the castle, out of sight of the walls.
Wait for me there."

Cameron grunted, but Anne stepped away from him, not
wanting to hear anything else he had to say. Climbing the
steps, she lifted her chin.

"I am sorry to hear that you cannot stay for supper. Thank
you for your service in bringing Bonnie to me."

Cameron scowled but covered his displeasure when Helen
moved up beside her.

"The young miss is staying?"

"Indeed she is. Captain Murry, will you help her dismount?"

The captain turned and walked swiftly across the yard. He
reached up toward Bonnie. Her sister swallowed another whimper as she placed her hand in the man's. Relief showed on her
face. The captain led her away from the mare, while Cameron's
men looked at their leader. He stared at her while tucking the
marriage license back into his doublet. He patted it in warning.

"I understand that Warwickshire is as busy as Sterling. I bid
you good journey."

Anne glared at Cameron. His gaze moved to Bonnie. Lust
danced in his eyes but he tossed his head when Anne stepped
slightly in front of her sister.

"True." He swung up into the saddle. Aiming a hard look at
her, he turned around, grabbing the reins to Bonnie's mare.
He and his men quit the yard quickly.

"He'll come back for me." Bonnie's voice was hollow. "He
promised . . . promised to do terrible things to me."

"Do not think of it," Anne whispered in her sister's ears as Helen watched them. The senior maid frowned.

"Ye look as though ye didnae sleep a wink last night, child."

Anne welcomed the distraction. "Aye, it does seem that traveling does not agree with young Bonnie. Will you please take her to the bath house, Helen? I believe she needs a bit of comforting from your skilled hands."

"But . . ." Bonnie began.

"Hush now, Bonnie. There is no one better than Helen. She has taken such good care of me. I feel almost guilty."

Helen beamed under her praise. She proudly took Bonnie's hand.

"Follow me and we'll see you feeling fresh and new."

Anne followed them up the steps but continued on up to the second floor chamber that had been hers for so short a time.

She would never forget it.

Tears stung her eyes and she let them fall. She knew what she had to do. In her heart she knew that it would be better to face Philipa than watch Bonnie ride away with Cameron. The Church held more authority than either Queen Elizabeth or King James. The proxy marriage license would be respected in either country. Even if the captain of the guard disliked the union, he could not prevent Cameron from taking Bonnie. At least not without a mark on her to prove that the man was a beast.

Aye, Cameron was as evil as Philipa. Both knew how to choose their threats well.

She looked at the bed and more tears fell. But this time she was happy. Running her fingers across the coverlet, she smiled for the joy that she'd known there. No one could ever wipe it away from her mind. Grasping one of the pillows, she shoved it beneath the coverlet. Pulling on the bedding, she rumpled it to look as though she were sleeping. Jerking the bed curtains closed, she left only a small opening at the foot of the bed.

She needed time to make it far enough away from Sterling. The McJames' retainers would not cross into England without their lord.

Sitting down, she wrote a last letter to Brodick. Telling him at last about their child and how happy her heart was to carry his babe. She sealed the letter, confident that her babe would return to Sterling and his rightful place.

That was the greatest gift a mother might give. It was the thing that prompted many a noble daughter to marry without love. The knowledge that her child would have a better life.

She wrapped another surcoat over the one she was wearing and left. The yard was full of busy labor. But it was the young McJames' captain that she had to escape the watch of now. He was instructing a younger lad with a bow, showing the boy how to aim. They let the arrow fly and it soared over the stable. With a good-natured laugh, the captain climbed onto the roof to seek the arrow out.

Anne hurried out of the gate while he was distracted, searching along the thatched roof for the arrow shaft. If fortune favored her, he would never know that she had descended from her chamber. There were many on the road. Carts full of newly cut grass and goods. She was merely one more walking with the others, her woolen surcoat blending with the tartans of the others.

The bells did not ring. She kept walking, hugging to her heart the knowledge that Bonnie was safe. Her child kicked and she walked faster, determined to see him born legitimate.

Helen peeked into the chamber that night. Lifting a hand to her lips, she cautioned the maids to be quiet. Pointing them

toward the fireplace, she stepped lightly across the floor to retrieve the letter.

Bonnie stood quietly on the steps, waiting to be told what
to do.

Helen did not worry that the mistress had retired early. Her
time was growing near, the babe taking more of her energy.
News from her mother had no doubt made her teary as well.
Tomorrow she'd try to keep the mistress away from herding
geese. Soon it would be time to have Agnes moved into Sterling. The arrival of first babes was always hard to anticipate,
but if the mistress was taking to her bed, the time must be
growing near.

Motioning to the maids, she hurried them from the chamber. The fire popped and crackled. Helen shut the door to
leave the mistress in peace.

"Och now, she's sleeping already. I'll see to settling ye and
ye may spend tomorrow chatting."

Bonnie let the kind hands of the maid shepherd her to a
bed. Horror and fatigue made it impossible to think. All that
mattered was that she and Anne were sleeping someplace far
removed from Cameron. She fell into a fretful sleep.

Cameron pressed his men to ride through the night. The
trip was faster because a good amount of it was downhill.
Anne did not care for she wouldn't have slept anyway. Not with
having witnessed the unseemly lust in Philipa's lackey's eyes.
Instead, she noticed the stark difference between her two jour-
neys. Brodick's retainers with their honest service and Cameron
with his bullies. She had willingly stayed near the kitchens at
Warwickshire because Cameron's group of men were known
for debauchery. Philipa never reprimanded them because they
did her bidding, no matter how foul.

They crossed onto English soil shortly after dawn. Anne

tightened her hands on the saddle. By night, she'd be standing in Philipa's presence again.

Sterling

Helen screamed for the first time in years. She ripped the
bed curtains as she tried to find her mistress. It made no sense!

The maids flew from the chamber, their shrieks awakening
the manor. Retainers rushed in from the yard, hesitating for a
moment when they realized the commotion was coming from
the mistress's chamber.

"The mistress is missing."

Helen shouted, pulling on her hair. "I dinnae ken. She
mussed the bedding to look as if she were there. I should have
checked."

"You cannot blame yourself." Bonnie's soft voice froze everyone in their tracks. She stood at the door, her face shining
with tears. "Philipa has always hated her more than any other."
She shuddered, hugging herself. "But my sister is the kindest
soul, always thinking of others first."

Captain Murry gripped her by the upper arms.

"Tell me where the mistress is."

Bonnie recoiled from his touch, her heels sliding on the
stone floor as she tried to escape. Panic held her features as
she pushed and struggled. The man looked confused by her
reaction.

"Don't touch me. Please don't touch me." Bonnie's voice
was a thin wail that stirred pity in everyone in the room.

"I'll let ye loose if ye tell me what goes on here."

Bonnie bobbed her head up and down. The captain released his grip on her, careful to do it slow enough so that she
didn't fall in a heap. He placed his body between her and the
door, making it clear that he would get what he wanted.

"Philipa has ordered her back to Warwickshire else she will set our brothers to sea for the New World."

"That's insanity. There is nothing across the ocean save death for those foolish enough to sail toward it." Helen shook her head and even made the sign of the cross over her body.

"That's why Anne went. She knows that Philipa means to do it if Anne does not return."

The Captain held up a hand for silence. "Did ye say brothers?"

Bonnie nodded. "We are two sisters and three brothers born to the Earl of Warwickshire's leman. Philipa sent Anne in her daughter's place to conceive a child because Mary did not want to marry. Anne was ordered to return when she was with child or Philipa would turn our mother out. When Anne still didn't return, Philipa grew angry and sent Cameron here with new threats to force Anne to obey her. Philipa married me to Cameron because she knew Anne would protect me, as she always had." Silent tears glittered on Bonnie's cheeks.

There was silence. Helen grew pale but she suddenly snarled like a angry bear.

"Captain Murry, fetch the mistress back."

The captain seemed unsure. He looked at Bonnie and back to Helen.

"If she is nae the Earl of Warwickshire's legitimate daughter, she's nae the lord's wife."

"Nae his wife? Are ye daft, man? She's round with his son."

"His bastard." One of the maids spoke the words. Helen rounded on her like a storm.

"She was pure when the lord took her to his bed. She is also the Earl of Warwickshire's daughter. Mark my words. It will be the legitimate daughter who suffers for nae taking her place. The earl's wife stood there and sent her as the bride. They are both daughters of the earl, the proxy will hold up in court because our lord was deceived. The Church will annul the first proxy and then the lord can marry the mother of his child."

Captain Murry nodded slowly. "I see yer thinking, Helen, but there are those who will nae agree."

"There is no time for debating now. Ye need to ride after her." Helen wrung her hands.

The captain shook his head. "No time at all. They're too close to England by now. The mistress planned this well enough. I might have caught her if she'd been discovered missing yesterday." The captain shook his head, his hand tightening on his belt. "We need the earl to settle this matter. They'll nae even open the gates for us at Warwickshire, much less admit to such a deed now that the proof is in their hands."

"That babe will be born inside a fortnight."

Murry paused at the door. "Then I shall ride through the night to alert the lord."

He quit the room, his men following close on his heels. There was no hint of reluctance in any of them. Helen looked at the chamber, tears of sadness in her eyes.

"Och now, how did such a thing happen?"

"Love is a curse." The same maid spoke once more. "My sister has a bastard because of falling under love's spell."

" 'Tis not always a bad thing." Helen just wished that she believed her own words, but they sounded hollow. The entire chamber echoed with emptiness. She felt the chill of it creeping across her skin.

Chapter Twelve

Warwick Castle

"You are disgraceful."

Philipa spoke slowly, allowing each of her words to fall and impact before the next one crossed her lips.

"Clearly you care for no one save yourself." The mistress of Warwickshire pulled a letter from her writing desk. She snapped the paper against her palm.

"Your sire did not return for quartering day." Triumph shone in Philipa's eyes.

Anne stood steady. She stared straight at Philipa, refusing to lower her eyes. She would not be giving blind respect to the lady of the manor anymore. Philipa frowned when she remained steadily staring her in the face.

"It is a good thing that I had the forethought to marry your sister to a man who will keep her in check. The very fact that you penned this letter proves that you and all your siblings are tainted with the lack of respect that your mother has shown me by giving my husband sons."

Anne smiled softly. The expression angered the mistress of Warwickshire, turning Philipa's face red.

"My sister is in Scotland."

"What?" Her lips twisted into an ugly scowl. "I commanded that she return."

"If I only cared for myself, I would still be at Sterling, far from your reach."

"Watch your mouth, girl, I am your mistress."

Anne didn't back down "Not any longer, you aren't. You sent me away, gave me to another noble. My loyalty belongs to Sterling's master now."

A flicker of fear crossed Philipa's face. She looked stunned by the emotion, her lips working without sounds for a few moments, her hands closing into fists.

"You shall obey me, *bastard*."

"Or what?" Anne wasn't as sure as her voice sounded, but she was finished holding her tongue. Being obedient to Philipa had not rewarded her with fairness as the Church preached. Keeping to her place would never mean anything if the woman she offered her loyalty to did not remember her duty to her own servants. That was the lesson she'd learned from Brodick. He was a leader because he considered it a duty, not just tribute given to his name, something he received but did nothing to earn.

"I shall have your mother put out."

Anne didn't waver. "It is no longer winter." Philipa gasped at Anne's audacity. "Yet maybe it is better that you should. When she reaches the next shire, there will be an end to this farce. I do not think my sire will be pleased when he learns of this deception."

Philipa stuck her finger out, trying to impose her will with the stern gesture. "You will do as you are told, *bastard*."

Anne simply laid a hand on the top of her belly. Philipa looked at it hungrily. For a moment she resembled someone addicted to wine, all weak-willed and unable to stop her own destructive behavior.

"I carry the Earl of Alcaon's child. If you are just, you shall dissolve my sister's marriage and send my brothers to serve at court with their sire to, possibly with God's good will, better their lot."

A lump tried to form in her throat and Anne suppressed it. She did what was most important for her babe. Sacrifice was the proof of a mother's love. "You shall not have my child for nothing. My brothers know nothing of this. Send them today."

"Or what . . . bastard?" Philipa smirked. "Hmm? You have so much to say, but I am mistress here. The gates only open when I say they shall."

A moment of uncertainty filled her and Philipa must have sensed it. She smiled, the expression unpleasant.

"I have heard that in Scotland being born bastard means very little. But this is England . . . *bastard*."

A sharp slap hit Anne's face. Philipa did not stay her strength. Anne's neck whipped to the side with the force of the blow.

"Here, you will keep to your place. That had better be a male child."

Philipa paced back across the chamber. She sat in an ornately carved chair, arranging her skirts as if she were royalty. Mary moved to stand behind her mother. They looked every inch the noble, powerful women they believed themselves to be.

But they didn't compare at all to Brodick.

"You shall occupy my solar until your time comes. I will be gracious and allow your mother to attend you."

She paused to gloat with a few amusing sounds sent toward her daughter.

"Of course you many persist in this defiance and your child will be born exactly as you were . . . illegitimate."

"I am here." What else was there to say? Philipa did know

what she was speaking of. The world was not forgiving and it was not interested in how things happened. Born out of wedlock, her child would be a bastard.

"Exactly. There is some part of you that is not mesmerized by the lust that Scot no doubt stoked inside you." Now Philipa's expression turned to one of revulsion, her lips thinning with distaste. "I had little doubt that you'd enjoy his carnal demands. You are very much like your mother.

"Still, it is what was needed." Philipa reached for a goblet. She took a long sip, fully expecting everyone to wait on her while she pampered herself.

"You will remain in the solar. That is the only way that we shall be able to make everyone believe that Mary has birthed that child."

"But how long, Mother? I'm tired of being locked up."

Philipa frowned. "Has the world gone mad? Why is there no respect in either of you? Here I am working so diligently to make everyone happy and both of you argue with me."

Mary pouted but she didn't look like a child who knew she was defeated. Instead her face brightened with her desire for retaliation.

"You will have to remain in bed after the child is born, Mary, acting your part as the one recovering from childbirth. It sounds to me as though you might put that time to good use learning to be thankful that you do not have to face the pain of labor. She might die before pushing the child into the world and then we shall have a true mess to sort out."

Mary's nose wrinkled. "You mustn't die, Anne."

"I shall endeavor not to."

Mary shrugged while rolling her eyes, clearly unconcerned with anything more than what she wanted. The child inside Anne kicked as if he understood that he was being fought over. Anne refused to weaken. Her son deserved to be born to the full station he had been conceived under.

May Brodick forgive her.

"What has that woman's spite done to you?"

Ivy Copper entered the small solar, but she only had eyes for Anne. She swept her daughter from head to toe and back to swollen belly.

"Never once might I have suspected that she would do so horrible a deed." Ivy flew across the room, folding Anne into her embrace.

"I have missed you, Mother."

And she had. But the steady beating of her mother's heart was sweet reassurance. Life. That was what she had left Warwickshire to ensure. It was also what she'd brought back with her.

"It was not awful. He is a good man."

Her mother made a low sound. She stepped back to fix Anne with her mother's eye.

"Please tell me that you did not fall into love's trap. Anne, I warned you about it. You are saddled with the burden of having my tender heart. Both you and Bonnie."

"But it's not a burden, Mother."

Ivy sighed, but a smile decorated her lips. She cupped both sides of her daughter's face, tenderness in her voice. "Well, sweet Anne, you have gone and done it now. Placed your hand into the foolishness of love. I can no more scold you for it than stop loving your father. Forgive me for setting such a poor example for you."

"Do you still love him, even now?"

"You mean at my age?" Ivy turned, looking around the solar. "It's the truth that I do."

Her mother surveyed the chamber. It was round because it

was the top of one of Warwickshire's towers. There were costly glass pane windows here because it was Philipa's solar. There were three expensive chairs near the windows, their backs and arms ornately carved. A tapestry loom stood threaded and waiting for the lady of the house to work. Anne had never known Philipa to labor at such a task.

She ran a finger over the fine threads. The sunlight danced over them. They almost glowed.

"Silk."

"Aye," her mother confirmed. "Your father has always done right by Philipa. He denies her nothing."

There was a note of envy in her mother's voice. Anne smiled at her.

"He never gave her his love. That has been yours alone."

"Just look what that's done to you." Ivy shook her head. "She used me against you, didn't she?"

"Love is not one-sided, Mother. You have made sacrifices for me as well."

Ivy frowned. "It is not the same, Daughter. This was evil."

Anne sighed. She gazed out the window and realized that it faced north. Out there was Sterling. Her child belonged there with the kilts and long swords strapped to the men's backs. Warwickshire was not home. There was no feeling of warm joy here, no comfort.

"I believe that good has already begun to unravel Philipa's work. I left Bonnie in Scotland, away from Philipa's reach. It was not a bad experience, Mother. If that is sinful, I am guilty."

Ivy only shook her head. "I am not in any position to counsel anyone on the foolishness of love." Her mother laid a hand on her daughter's swollen belly. "Yet I did wish that your first child would be born in less turmoil."

"I returned to make sure of that. This child will take his place even if I must allow Philipa to continue her foul scheme.

If I speak against her, my babe will be illegitimate. There is no other way. Just as I could not watch Bonnie leave Sterling with Cameron. She is safe now. Brodick is a good man; he will not allow Cameron to take her."

Anne felt confidence surge through her. She would not fail. There was naught but a curtain hung in the arched doorway between Philipa's room and the solar. Philipa frowned as she strode into the room. Hatred blazed from her eyes when she looked at Ivy.

"I shall have satisfaction for every year that I have been forced to endure the shame of you giving my husband children."

Cameron stepped into the room, grinning.

"Step outside this solar, and you shall face harsh consequences."

Ivy glared at the mistress, her face displaying her contempt for the first time that Anne could recall.

"Wipe that look off your face . . . slut." Philipa shook a finger at Ivy. "I am mistress here. You are nothing but the light-skirt my husband used to ease his lust."

"I am much more." Ivy raised her chin, defiance filling her voice.

The mistress of Warwickshire didn't appear to know how to deal with the silent refusal of both women to lower themselves. Philipa shook with rage, her face turning red.

"You'd better remember."

The curtain hit the wall when she left. Cameron followed her.

"You owe me for the service of fetching her back, since I don't get the younger one now."

Philipa argued as Ivy shook her head. But Anne smiled. She had diverted one plan and she would succeed in making sure her child was born to his rightful place. She sat at the loom, gently working it to make sure it was oiled. She needed to create. Her hands fairly itched to begin working. Selecting a thread, she began to weave it.

"I shall show you what he looks like, Mother."

Anne worked at the loom, willing her memory of Brodick waiting for her in the spring sun onto the growing tapestry. She did not quit until the last rays of light vanished. At dawn she began again. Her back ached but her son kicked. The only thing that she lamented was not being able to fill the chamber with fresh air. She walked around the room to ease the strain in her lower back, but always returned to her tapestry, determined to finish it.

Determined to see Brodick's face again, even if it was no more than silk.

The days stretched out and Anne didn't really notice how many passed. She was intent on her tapestry, working hard to finish it. Her mother wrote a list and gave it to Mary, who grumbled about fetching things like a servant. Ivy remained firm.

Cameron had to haul a birthing chair into the solar himself. He dropped it with a sneer.

"Women's work."

The man left as Ivy laughed at him. "Selfish man." She ran a hand over the sturdy chair. The seat was cut into a large horseshoe shape. Such a chair allowed the mother to bear down while having her body weight supported by the chair. It was quite a modern convenience.

Lady Mary threw a book across the chamber.

"Mother, there must be some concoction that you can get old Ruth to fix that will make that baby come today."

"Stop whining, Mary. For the final time, you shall wait." Philipa glared at her child. "We have but one chance to secure you in this marriage without risking your life. That child needs to be healthy and strong. Not forced into the world before his time."

Mary pouted.

Philipa's eyes narrowed. She glanced behind her toward the curtain. Seeing that it was smoothly draped, she waved Mary toward her. Her daughter shrugged and closed the space between them.

"Ruth fixed this for me."

Philipa raised her hand and showed a small glass jar. Inside was a jumble of leaves and strips of bark. Philipa placed it on her vanity table.

"Seeped in wine, it will send the drinker into a sleep they never awaken from."

Mary gasped, but a look of savage enjoyment crossed her face. She reached out to touch the jar. "Once the baby is born, we'll mull some wine and give it to both of them."

"Exactly." Philipa looked behind her once more. When she was assured that Ivy and Anne did not hear, she patted her daughter's cheek. "No more fits from you. It will all be done shortly."

Mother and daughter shared a smile that was pure evil. The jar sitting on the vanity awaited its moment of use.

Scotland

"Good God, man, ye look exhausted." Druce stood up, offering his chair to Captain Murry.

The McJames' retainer didn't take the chair. He offered Brodick a quick pull on the corner of his bonnet before speaking.

"The mistress was taken back to England."

"What?"

It was impossible to tell which man spoke first. Brodick,

Cullen and Druce's voices all bounced around the small town house together. Brodick held his hand out, authority rippling out of the gesture.

"Why did ye allow that?"

"She snuck out of the castle, made her bed look as though she was in it."

A deadly look passed over the earl's face.

"There's more my lord and it isnae good."

Brodick listened as Captain Murry explained the details. He shook his head, unable to absorb the deception completely. Who plotted such a thing?

There was a snort of laughter from the other side of the room. James Stewart hit the table top as his amusement grew.

"I didnae think the English had such cunning in them." He chuckled and raised his tankard towards Brodick. "Well, my friend, I suppose ye'll be wanting yer leave. 'Tis yers. Go fetch yer wife back."

"Yet is she yer wife, my lord?" Captain Murry lowered himself before the king before turning to ask the question.

"She sure as hell is, man! She's carrying me son." Brodick was on his feet. He reached for his sword and tied it into place with stiff motions.

"Aye. I agree with that." Druce nodded his head and reached for his own sword.

The king looked pensive for a long moment, too long for Brodick's taste.

"She's also the Earl of Warwickshire's daughter and his wife sent her with me. Told me that was the bride I'd come for."

James Stewart raised an eyebrow. "Yer too passionate by far, man, but 'tis the truth that I envy ye."

The king stood, the two men-at-arms with him, keeping close to their master. "I agree that the marriage is valid. But I'll ask ye this, do ye want a woman that lied to ye?"

Brodick stared at his king, his mind replaying that first meeting.

"She didnae lie to me."

James raised an eyebrow.

Brodick clenched his fists. "She said nothing at all. That bitch of a countess should be flogged for abusing her position so greatly."

James snorted. "Aye, I see yer thinking there, man." He nodded. "Go fetch her back and I'll see that the wedding agreement is honored."

There was nothing more to be said. Brodick quit the room with Druce and Cullen on his heels. Their men hurried to saddle the horses. Leather snapped in the autumn morning air. Bridles and reins were secured while a few meager supplies were strapped to the horses. Brodick swung up into the saddle, his heart pounding.

What have ye done, lass?

He didn't care. He was the McJames and she was his. According to the laws of both her country and his, and by right of possession. If he had to take her back, he would. Leaning over the neck of his mount, he urged the animal forward.

His . . .

Chapter Thirteen

Warwick Castle

A nne awoke in a surly mood. It was odd the way she noticed her own ill temper. She was not hungry and did not
care for what was offered to break her fast, either.

She sniffed at herself because what did it matter what was
served to them in their prison if she was not hungry? With a
huff she paced around the solar. Anne stopped to pick at the
finished tapestry, the silk thread having brought Brodick to life
in stunning display. She fingered his dark hair. Her mother
was abnormally quiet this morning, slowly knitting on the
round. Looking back at the tapestry, she felt a shiver race
down her spine. It was almost as if she heard him riding towards her.

Which was foolish.

He'll come for you . . .

Bonnie's sweet words echoed from her memory. It seemed
so long ago that they had shared that last moment together.
One short season, and so many things were changed. Her entire body quivered as she recalled watching her sire depart
that morning. Sweat popped out on her forehead as she heard
Bonnie talking about the child she would birth in the fall.
Through the windows, she could see the scarlet leaves. Bun-

dles of barley were standing in the fields, drying in the last of the warm weather.

She was so lonely, the sight of the tapestry made her want to cry. She paced around the room, hating the stone walls. A chill raced down her back and then her entire spine turned warm. She stopped as a cramp tightened along her hip line.

Her surcoat was too warm. Opening the buttons that closed the top of it, Anne laid it over the foot of the bed. It was still much too hot in the solar. Her body shuddered as another cramp moved through her. A rush of warm fluid down her thighs made her gasp.

"Well, I thought it was that time."

Her mother calmly knelt and wiped up the puddle. The cloth she used turned pink.

Ivy stood up. "Don't worry, Anne, that is the way it goes. It is normal."

She didn't have time to argue with her mother's calm statement. Another cramp began and this one was much stronger. Leaning over, Anne braced her hands on her thighs while the pain moved through her.

"Breathe, Anne. Long, deep breaths. You must for the child."

The curtain suddenly moved, Lady Mary looking in.

"Is it time?"

Ivy glared at the girl but Mary didn't wait for an answer. She smiled, greed brightening her eyes.

"Mother, Mother . . . it's time."

There was a scuff of shoes against the stone floor. Philipa peered into the room as Anne straightened up.

"Good. Very good. I'll get the cook to keep the water at hand." Philipa nodded. "Mind your screams, girl. Make too much noise and I won't be able to make the staff believe that your child is Mary's."

"Now is not the time for threats."

Philipa was stunned by Ivy's words. She pushed her lips into a line of disapproval but Ivy was not intimidated.

"We've work to do here. Birthing is not an easy task."

Philipa bit back her words. "No, it is not." For a mere moment there was a glimmer of compassion in her face but it died quickly and the curtain dropped back into place.

"Bitter, poisonous woman," Ivy said as she began arranging the items she'd had brought to the room. "Take no notice of her, Anne."

Anne couldn't have, even if she'd wanted to. She was held captive by her own body. The day bled away as she walked around the solar, stopping for each cramp. She shed her under gown, only able to tolerate her chemise. Even her stockings irritated her legs. The stone floor was cool beneath her bare feet. She sighed as she paced more, at last free of the overwhelming heat.

"It's time . . . it's time."

Mary twirled around the room, adding a few dance steps into her motions. "Oh, Mother, you were so right."

Philipa basked in the admiration from her child. Contentment mixed with a sense of achievement inside her. Mary would never have to endure the things that she had been forced to when her father ordered her to marry. She had succeeded in giving her child a better life than her own.

That was the greatest gift a mother could give.

"Here now, Toby, lend a hand."

Joyce scolded her son when she caught him watching the guards in the lower courtyard. The clang of swords drifted in through the window, drawing his young attention. He'd watch them train all afternoon if she allowed it.

"Mother, can I be a knight?"

"If a saint or two looks kindly on you, blessing you with

strength and skill. Mayhap." Joyce kissed the top of his head, smiling with a mother's joy. "We'll have to place you in the captain's path and see that he gets a good look at how tall and strong you are growing. You shall have to look him straight in the eye, though, so that he knows you have courage."

Toby grinned, showing off the gap where his front teeth had fallen out.

"But that's for later. The mistress will be having her comforts and there is supper to get on the tables. For now, you earn your keep in the kitchen like your mother."

Joyce turned to apply her tongue to the hands that had begun working slowly as the morning faded away. Clapping her hands, she shook her long wooden spoon at her staff. Lazy wenches, they took advantage of her good will when Toby was in the kitchen. Aye, they slowed down knowing that she was soft toward her youngest child.

"Get that wine mulled before the mistress calls for it. I'll see you bent over in the fields if you get me summoned to her chamber because you're dreaming the day away."

There was a clatter of copper pots as the coals were poked and the wine set to heating. Toby waited for it, carefully balancing the tray as his feet moved swiftly toward the mistress's chamber. He lifted the heavy door knocker and let it fall onto the door. It seemed to take a long time for the heavy panel to open.

"Mulled wine, Mistress."

"Yes, yes. Well don't stand there while it cools."

With wide eyes, Toby scurried into the room, trying not to stare at the opulent furnishings. To his young eyes, the decorative wood carvings on the bedpost looked like something from Chaucer.

"Don't forget the soiled tray. Its scent is foul."

Forcing his gaze onto his task, Toby gathered the soiled

linens that were lying on the table. Dropping them on the soiled morning tray, he made sure to take the heavy silver goblet, too, so that it might be cleaned. He was just picking up the tray when he spied the small glass jar sitting near a book. It was full of spices and clearly belonged in the kitchen. He sat it among the used napkins.

A low moan drifted in from behind the tapestry curtain. He looked up with curiosity, wondering who was in the solar.

There was a crash from behind him. The mistress frowned as her mulled wine lay spilt on the floor. She glared at it for a long moment before waving her hand.

"Clean it up and bring me some more."

Using the linens, Toby mopped up the wine before retreating from the chamber. He sucked in a deep breath, grateful to be on his way back to the kitchens. The mistress's chamber might be full of beautiful things, but it sure made the hair on the back of his neck stand up.

His mother was missing when he returned to the kitchen. Molly looked up as he brought her both silver goblets.

"The mistress wants more mulled wine."

Molly shrugged, reaching for the wine. "Stay and wait for it to heat. You'll have to take it back. I must mind the porridge."

"Can I watch the knights practice while I wait?" Toby shifted from side to side as he waited to be granted permission.

"Aye."

Toby skipped toward the window, a happy smile brightening his face.

While the wine heated, Molly cleaned the tray, pausing when she found the small glass jar. Pulling the stopper from it, she sniffed it. The odor wasn't pleasing, but clearly the mistress had sent it with Toby to have it mulled in her wine. Why else would she want more wine so soon? Dumping it into a cloth, she gave it a twist and sat it in the warming wine. It was some manner of relief from the ache that had kept the mistress in her chamber for the last week. It must be nice to have the silver to pay for such comforts.

"Toby, the wine is ready."

The boy shuffled his feet but left the window to take the tray to his mistress. She answered the door quickly this time, waving him in.

"Leave it and go."

Toby did her bidding gladly, skipping down the hallway once the task was finished.

"Mother? Hurry. I think it's time." Mary sounded terrified, her voice echoing from the second chamber. She stood in the doorway, holding the heavy curtain up.

"Quiet down. If anyone sees you, this has all been for naught." Philipa paused and took a long sip from the goblet. The warm wine soothed her nerves so she took a few more, draining most of it.

"*Mother.*"

"Do compose yourself, Mary. You aren't doing any of the work. Try to have a bit of dignity." She passed the silver goblet off to her daughter. "Have some wine. It will calm you."

Mary frowned at her mother's words but lifted the goblet to her lips. The wine was warm and she greedily drank every last drop.

"Good. Now where is this babe?" Moving through the doorway, she heard the muffled groans as Anne labored. Ivy crouched near her daughter as she sat in the birthing chair. A rag was between her teeth to keep her screams from reaching beyond the chamber.

"It's coming, dear, push. Push hard."

Philipa watched as the baby slid from its mother. The tiny

body glistened as Ivy gripped it by the ankles patting the back firmly. With a shake the arms began to flail and the chest filled with air. A thin wail filled the chamber.

"Turn it around, woman."

Ivy cast a frown toward Philipa as she cradled the child's neck and held it up so that Philipa might see the sex. A small penis was well formed between the baby's legs. The child turned red as he squalled.

"Well done. You see? Everything is in order and now I am pleased."

Anne was leaning back on the birthing chair, her body shivering. Philipa turned her back on them. She smiled at Mary, fixing the hair that had escaped from its braid.

"There now, dear, you see? Everything is just as I told you it would be."

Mary smiled. "You are always so right, mother."

"A few more days and you may then present your son to everyone. We'll write to your father."

Mary smiled. "And I may return to court?"

"Yes, my dear. It is important that that Scot doesn't catch up with you for many months. You will have to be clever and avoid him." Philipa waved a hand in the air. "I doubt he'll ride so far into England."

She did not know Brodick.

Anne cradled her son. Even if Philipa's scheme was foul, the product was beautiful.

"Riders ho!"

The Captain of the Guard cried out as the bells on the walls began ringing. Philipa lost her smug, satisfied look as she rushed toward the window.

"Christ's wounds! It's your husband."

The McJames' banners flew proudly in the afternoon sunlight, bearing down on the gate. The earl himself was leading the pack of retainers, five times the number that had arrived to fetch Mary.

"Stay here, Mary. Let no one see you or that baby."

Philipa grabbed a handful of her skirts and ran from the room. Anne stared at the empty doorframe. Not once had she ever seen the mistress of Warwickshire run.

Mary wrung her hands. "Give me the baby."

Ivy grabbed a broom. "Get out."

"You forget your place, slut."

Ivy turned the broom with a practiced hand, and swung it in a circle using both hands.

"Oh, I know my place. I know how to beat you senseless with this broom if you don't get away from my daughter and grandchild."

Ivy stamped the broom on the hard stone floor. Mary flinched at the sound, her face turning pale.

"Stupid girl." Ivy shook her head. "Your father should never have allowed you to be raised so weak. I am going to have a word with that man when he returns. You may count on it."

Mary's eyes grew large and round. Ivy pointed at her. "Stay out of my way, girl. There is women's work to see to. I've no time for your childish ways."

Mary looked shamed for the first time that Anne could recall, her cheeks red and her eyes glittering with unshed tears.

Anne shivered but the bells made her heart swell. Her mother wiped her forehead with a cool cloth. Her son nuzzled against her breast, rooting about for a nipple. Every muscle twitched and it was an effort to hold the infant. But she was happy. So pleased that it felt like sunshine was shining out of her.

She'd given Brodick a son.

There was no greater gift that her love might bestow.

Heavy fatigue pressed down on her as her mother tended to her, cleansing away the last stains of the birth.

"Your husband is here, riding into the courtyard," Ivy whispered, but Mary screeched in outrage.

"My husband. He is my husband. She is a bastard."

Ivy stood up, her temper overriding her good sense. Anne grabbed her mother's wrist, trying to restrain her.

Ivy shook her daughter's hand off. "I'll have none of this. Do you hear? I've suffered in silence for my entire life, but no more."

Anne smiled at her mother "Well now, he's a fine, healthy boy."

Anne gently hugged the tiny body close to her chest. "Like his father."

"Aye, I see that." Ivy took the baby to the copper basin. She gently washed him, cupping the water in her hand to pour it over his head. He didn't cry, but wiggled while making soft cooing sounds. Her mother finished and wrapped the infant in swaddling so that only his face and upper arms were free.

She laid him in the cradle before turning to help Anne. Soon she was settled into the bed and Ivy handed the baby to her.

"He'll want your breast, if he's anything like your brothers."

Anne didn't have time to lower her chemise. There was a scurry of feet in the outer room.

"Stop! These are my private chambers. You have no right to invade my rooms, you . . . Scots!" Philipa bellowed in outrage as the sounds of footfalls echoed between the stone walls.

"I'll tell you who has rights, madam. I have the right to see my wife. Now stand aside or I'll knock ye to the floor. But I will find where ye have hidden her."

Brodick sounded dangerous, but he also sounded sweeter

than any sound she'd ever heard. Anne clutched her son close, tears easing from her eyes.

"Brodick! I'm here!"

The curtain was ripped half off the rod as her husband erupted through the doorway. His face was a mask of fury, his sword in hand. He swept the room before charging towards her.

"I swear I wish I had the strength to beat ye for placing yourself in such danger." He cupped her chin and his fingers shook. "Look at what ye reduce me to, lass. I'm but a shell of a man in yer grip."

The baby hiccupped and Brodick dropped his sword. Anne wasn't sure what surprised her husband more; the sight of their newborn son or the clatter of his sword. He ignored the dropped weapon, reaching instead for the edge of the cloth wrapped around the baby's head. With a single finger he gently pulled it aside to peer at the tiny face.

"I've given you a son." Her voice was laced with tears, tears born from happiness. "Just as I know you wanted."

"No!" Mary screamed, stomping her feet. Brodick turned, his kilt flaring out. The sword was back in hand before the fabric settled.

Mary's face was red, her eyes bulging from her head. "That's supposed to be my baby. Mine. I'm a countess."

"Ye're no wife of mine." Distaste colored his words.

Philipa stood frozen in the corner. "Oh, but she is, my lord, and you'd do well to listen to me. You have your son. My daughter is the only daughter with a dowry. You must keep Mary as your legal wife or lose what you married for. As for that bastard, you may have her for a leman. Look how strong she is. She'll give you all the children you want and Mary will bring you the land you desire."

"I can't believe what I'm hearing." Cullen stood behind Philipa, his face a mask of disapproval.

"I wish I didnae believe it, but the proof is plain." Brodick lowered his sword but stood in front of Anne, shielding her from Philipa.

"You can keep yer dowry. The woman I love is worth far more than any land."

"But you need the land, Brodick." Anne reached for his hand, unwilling to see him lose what he wanted. "It is still yours and your son's."

"I'll not have that creature on my land." He pointed at Mary. She tossed her head, looking down her nose at him.

"I certainly do not want to go to Scotland. Why do you think my mother sent that bastard in my place?"

Druce reached out to close his hand around Mary's nape. She squealed but he granted her no mercy. "And the world calls us Scots the uncivilized ones."

He flung Mary into the outer room without any remorse. Anne heard her half–sister's shoes scuffing against the floor. Druce pointed at Mary through the arched doorway. "Keep a hand on her and a gag if she starts talking again. We've heard enough from that one to last a lifetime."

There was a grunt from the retainers in the other room before Druce turned to face Brodick. "She was making me head ache."

"Mary is your legal wife." Philipa shook her fist in the air. "My daughter. Not that bastard girl."

Philipa looked at the baby, hunger brightening her eyes. She made a lunge towards the bed but froze when Brodick raised his sword, the deadly point even with her heart.

"Ye'll nae touch my family, woman. Make no mistake about it, I'm nae a forgiving man when it comes to what I consider my own."

His words were as strong as the steel in his hand. "I swear I'll run ye through, noblewoman or not."

"Sounds like a fair plan to my way of thinking." Cullen wasn't joking this time. His voice was as hard as his brother's. "Ye deceived every McJames and we nae take kindly to that."

"Leave her for her husband. 'Tis his duty to sort out this mess." Brodick didn't lower his sword until Druce took hold of Philipa. She snarled but the Scot shook her like a rag doll.

"Have done, madam," he growled at her, towering over her.

"The marriage won't stand. You'll get nothing if you bring my husband into this."

Brodick sneered at her. "I've already dispatched a message to yer husband, woman. He needs to get home and take his estate back under his command." He moved toward her, his sword still unsheathed. "But there's one thing that ye had best be clear on. I'll nae have any other but the mother of my son."

Philipa screeched. Druce pulled her from the room as she ranted and raved.

Brodick turned then, his midnight eyes pegging Anne with a hard look. He reached up and slid his sword back into its sheath without shifting his attention away from her.

"Cullen. I want a full guard on this room."

"Aye."

"And keep a watch on that pair until the Earl of Warwickshire returns to take them in hand."

Brodick froze for a moment, the tapestry catching his eye. His face softened for a moment as he stared at it. He stiffened, shooting a hard glance at her.

"Everyone else, leave." Brodick stared at her. "I need a moment with my wife."

Everyone left the solar, but all Anne noticed was the word *wife*. Brodick looked as formidable and unrelenting as he had the first time she'd laid eyes upon him. Fierce determination flickered in his eyes as he considered her.

"Good God, woman. I'm going to take to spanking you once a week."

The bed shook as he closed the distance between them with such determination. His body was large and welcomed. She didn't feel overwhelmed by his frame anymore. His strength gave her comfort. She caught the hint of his scent and it made her sigh. The few months away from him now felt like an eternity. She reached for him, just her fingertips making contact with his chest. A soft sigh passed her lips and he flinched.

"I swear I'll nae be soft with ye. Murry is going to trail ye like a hungry colt and I'll nae tell the man to give ye any peace. It's the truth that I'm going to tell him to bring along a few other men to make sure the job of guarding ye is done."

He suddenly scowled. "What is yer name?"

"Anne."

He snorted, but cupped her chin. "Why did ye leave Sterling? Why did ye place yerself in harm's way?"

He was such a proud man. Her cheeks colored as she cringed on hearing what her flight had reduced him to. By leaving Sterling, she had left him.

"Because I love you." His large body shook. "I couldn't steal the dowry from you. It was the only way." She hugged the baby tightly. "The only way to keep our son from being born illegitimate." She took a ragged breath. "Like his mother."

She tried to look down but Brodick's grip was solid. His eyes flickered with frustration.

"Och, I dinnae know what to do with ye, woman."

The small bed shook as he leaned further across it, his hand sliding over her cheek and into her hair. "Tis ye I love, no matter the details of yer birth."

"But the dowry—"

"Will still be mine." He cupped the back of her head. "Ye are the daughter of the Earl of Warwickshire and 'twas his wife that presented ye to me and my men. Ye were pure and ye have given me a son. That's the best definition of wife that I've ever seen."

The earl was speaking, the hard authority in his voice edging his words. But his face softened and the hand resting on the back of her head softly soothed her.

"Leave the legalities to me, lass. I'm nae blind to the reason why ye fled. What I want to know is, why didn't ye run to me?"

Need glistened in his eyes, so sharp and needy, that tears fell down her cheeks.

"I love you, Brodick. I couldn't see you disappointed even if it meant I had to sacrifice my own heart. I love you too much for that."

A smile appeared on his lips. The hand in her hair tightened. Pleasure shone from his eyes and she knew without a doubt that life would have been miserable without him.

She wasn't even sure she would have survived very long.

" 'Tis glad I am to hear it . . . Anne."

A tiny smile graced her lips as he spoke her name.

Her name.

Their son nuzzled her breast in his sleep and a shudder shook her body. She was suddenly so tired, her eyelids felt heavy. Her arms shook around the baby.

"Take . . . take the baby . . ." Her voice shook. She couldn't seem to stay awake, her body sinking back into the bedding. Her entire body ached now and she wanted to escape it in slumber.

Brodick lifted his son from her arms and she smiled as she surrendered to her fatigue.

* * *

Brodick had never held so tiny a babe in his life. He wasn't even certain he'd seen one so young before.

"Cradle him, my lord, or he'll fuss and wake my daughter. She needs rest now."

Druce had a hand on the woman, keeping her in the doorway. But she spoke softly, mindful of Anne's need for rest. Her face looked similar to Anne's. She lifted her arms, showing him how to hold his son.

"Are ye Anne's mother?"

There was a harsh note in his voice that she didn't miss.

"Yes, and I knew nothing of this until Philipa locked me in this solar with Anne." She shrugged, but Druce didn't release her until Brodick nodded approval. Leaving the bed, Brodick moved toward her to allow his wife to rest.

"I'd have turned myself out before seeing my own child suffering for my choices." She shook her head sadly. "But Anne has a pure heart. It's better than I deserve for allowing her to be born out of wedlock."

"I dinnae care."

Anne shifted, muttering in her sleep. Brodick stepped through the doorway, Anne's mother following.

"You're a good man then. 'Tis grateful I am to you."

Brodick grinned as the baby opened his puffy eyelids, showing off blue eyes. Brodick could feel the heartbeat against his forearm, could see the tiny chest filling with the breath of life. It was by far the most touching experience he'd ever had.

"Then there is something you may help me with, madam." Brodick looked at Druce and Cullen.

"Assemble the staff and retainers. Bring Mary. I'm going to make sure there's no doubt about the fact that she didnae birth this child."

It was harsh, but no more than the noble daughter deserved.

"As you say, my lord." Ivy lowered her head before leaving the chamber.

Druce grinned. "Well now, let me look at the laddie."

Cullen joined him as they chuckled and teased him about being old enough to have a family.

If having a family meant he was old, he was content with his lot.

Anne awoke in Brodick's arms. He cradled her body as surely as he had their son.

"Easy, lass, I'm sorry to disturb ye, but ye'll nae be sleeping in that room that served as yer prison."

Anne didn't have any energy to reply. Her hand pressed against his chest and she smiled when she felt his steady heartbeat. A few moments later he swept her into another room. One of the large chambers that had been empty for as long as she could recall. Her sleepy brain awoke as she noted all the fine touches added. Carpets and scented candles. She could smell rosemary in the air now. It was always used after a birth to help the mother gain strength. No one knew why, only that it had always been that way.

"This is a much better bed. One that disnae look at walls that ye had to see as a prison."

Brodick settled her in a lavish, double-sized bed with a canopy and curtains. The fireplace was lit with a cheery blaze that warmed her nose. A cradle was placed at the foot of the bed but she heard her son fussing as her mother brought him into the room.

"Here now, Anne, your son is hungry."

Brodick pushed a few plump pillows behind her back as Ivy

placed the baby in her arms. Ivy looked at Brodick for a moment.

"I'm nae leaving, woman. This is something I've been waiting to see for three years. Me family."

Anne gazed into his eyes when Ivy settled the baby near her breast. There was nothing but happiness, nothing else at all.

If that meant she was insane, so be it.

She was in love.

Chapter Fourteen

The bells rang near noon the next day. The riders approaching rode with the banners of the Earl of Warwickshire. Brodick boldly met the man on his own front steps. The older man didn't lack any strength. He dismounted and yanked his riding gauntlets off with a snarl.

"Where's that bitch I'm married to?"

His voice bounced off the walls. Everyone froze, never having heard the master of the house publicly curse his wife.

The earl looked up. "McJames, I owe you a great deal for ferreting out this scheme. I swear I'll do right by the dowry." He climbed the steps, stopping to offer his hand to Brodick.

Brodick stood for a moment, feeling the eyes of the estate on him. He clasped the man's wrist and there was a mutter of approval from those watching.

"I suppose ye'll nae be cross with me for locking yer wife and daughter up. I wanted to make sure they didnae manage any more mischief before ye arrived to deal with them."

"I'd not have cared if you drowned them like the demon felines they are."

"I'll leave that task to you." Brodick walked into the castle with the earl. They climbed the stairs to the mistresses' chambers where two of Brodick's men stood guard.

"But there is someone I'd like ye to meet first." Brodick opened the door slowly, taking care that the hinges didn't squeak. The Earl of Warwickshire followed him inside frowning when he faced Ivy.

His leman smiled as bright as summer. She lifted a hand and motioned him forward. "Come my dear and see our first grandchild."

The color drained from his face but Brodick didn't think the man weak. He understood.

"Anne has a babe?"

"My wife has given me a son."

The earl suddenly smiled. He slapped a hand on Brodick's shoulder that sent him forward a step.

"Well now, that's grand news!"

Ivy shook a finger at him. "Hush. Anne needs her rest."

"I'm not sleeping, Mother." Anne shouldered her way through the curtain drawn across the doorway. She cradled her child, a soft smile curving her lips.

"Here Father, come and meet your grandson."

Tears shimmered in her father's eyes. Anne gently placed the baby in his arms. Brodick slid an arm around her waist, taking up some of her weight. She patted his hand reassuringly. "I am well."

He didn't listen. Her husband scooped her off her feet in one smooth motion. "I did warn ye that I intend to drive ye insane with my protective attitude."

He carried her back to the bedchamber. Anne frowned at him when he settled her back into bed.

"I have never been idle."

"And ye have never had a babe before either."

Anne wanted to be cross but she looked past Brodick at her parents. The earl cradled her son while his forehead touched her mother's. Joy radiated from them, warming the entire room. Her throat tightened and so did the arm Brodick had around her.

"Love is a beautiful thing, lass." Brodick's words were thick with emotion.

Her father turned to look at her, his gaze touching on the man that held her.

"Well now, Anne, my girl, you have made me proud."

Her father walked into the room. He settled the baby back into her embrace.

"Young Brodick, I see you make a good husband for my daughter."

"I intend to spend many a day trying, sir."

Her father nodded. "Glad I am to hear it."

No one would let her out of bed, so they spent the afternoon talking and getting to know the new baby. It wasn't until the sun began to set that her father's expression turned dark. He placed a kiss on Anne's cheek.

"I must see to my wife." His words were grave but sad as well. His body was tense as he left the room. Brodick followed.

The Earl of Warwickshire shoved open the door to the chamber where his wife and daughter were imprisoned.

"Philipa . . ."

The chamber was silent. Brodick scanned it, looking for the women. They were already in bed. Moving closer, he and the earl peered at the pair of unmoving forms. There was only a whisper of breath in them, the skin of their faces pasty white.

The earl touched Mary's face, moving her eyelid up to look at her eye.

"Poison, if I'm not mistaken." His voice had the unmistakable ring of familiarity with that evil vice of assassins and taunted lovers.

"Nae by my hand." Brodick shook his head. "I'd have run them through and taken credit for my own deed."

The earl looked pensive. "I believe you." He searched the room, lifting the used goblets and sniffing them.

There was a cough from the bed. Mary opened her eyes. The earl walked toward her.

"Tell me, daughter, what ails you?"

Mary drew a deeper breath in order to speak.

"Mother got the hemlock . . . from the village . . . for Anne." She sighed. "It was left on the table and . . . the . . . boy took it . . . by mistake . . . for our afternoon . . . wine."

Her eyelids fluttered but she lifted them and stared at her father. Mary reached for his hand.

"It was not his . . . fault. Mother . . . plotted murder . . . and . . . I agreed . . . We have . . . reaped . . . what we . . . sowed." Her fingers clutched at her father's hand. "Forgive me. I repent . . . my . . . sins . . . please, Father . . . bury me in hallowed . . . ground . . . I . . . beg for your pardon . . . I repent . . . God have mercy . . . on me . . . ."

Her voice trailed off as her eyes closed. The earl laid her hand on her chest, slowly shaking his head. He reached out to stroke a hand over her head.

"I'm sorry I failed you, child. I knew your mother was bitter but I didn't think she'd turn you so spoilt. I thought her love for you would keep her sane. I was wrong. Forgive me, Daughter."

Mary's hand clutched at the bedding. She held it tight for a moment before her fingers went lax and her breathing grew soft once more. She never opened her eyes again. Her mother died before she did, but Mary followed before sunrise. The Earl of Warwickshire sat by their bed, slumped in his chair.

Ivy appeared at dawn. She stood in the doorway, the rising

sun illuminating her. Henry Howard, fifth Earl of Warwickshire, stood up and went to her. A woman of common birth, she was the keeper of his heart. He took her hand and pressed a kiss onto it.

"Will you marry me, Ivy?" He squeezed her fingers. "Make an honest man of me and bring legitimacy to our children?"

"I will."

Tears shimmered in her eyes but one fell down his cheek first. Tucking her hand onto his arm, he strode from the chamber leaving his blue-blood marriage behind.

"Get back in that bed, Anne."

His wife scowled at him. Brodick sent her a stern look in return.

"I am going to my mother's wedding, Brodick."

And nothing was going to stop her. "For every time that I have heard the word bastard flung at me, I will crawl to church if I have to, Brodick." Her entire body ached but she kept moving. She suddenly frowned.

"But I need some money to bribe the clergymen since I haven't been churched yet. They won't let me into the sanctuary."

Brodick scowled. "This country has traditions that are insane."

Anne grinned. "I suppose it is a good thing we plan to live in Scotland."

He didn't look amused by her words. " 'Tis a good thing that all yer countrymen will be getting a Scots king. No allowing ye into church just because ye had a babe? What is the point of marriage, might I ask ye?"

Anne flinched when she bent over to pick up her shoes. Her husband swept her off her feet a moment later, placing her back on the foot of the bed. Brodick lowered his large body to one knee and slid her shoe into place himself.

"Och well, I can see why ye need to be there."

He didn't sound very contrite. But he placed the second shoe on her foot and helped her into her loose grown and surcoat.

"But no dancing."

He turned to pick up their son. Brodick refused to allow the infant or herself out of his sight unless Druce or Cullen was with her. The man was keeping his promise to have her guarded but it wasn't something she could become angry over. He did not trust Warwickshire and its staff. She could not blame him.

She took solace in his presence, enjoying every second of it. The burdens of life would steal him away soon enough. For now she would cling to his arm and watch her mother's wedding. Ivy made the most beautiful bride Anne had ever seen. The reason was simple.

She was in love.

Be it curse or blessing, Anne did not know. But she suffered the same affliction, cheerfully following in her mother's example. Brodick held her heart and if fate was kind, she would never cease loving him.

Never.

Be sure to catch WATCH OVER ME by Lucy Monroe,
available now from Brava . . .

"**D**r. Ericson"

Lana adjusted the angle on the microscope. Yes. Right there. Perfect. "Amazing."

"Lana."

She reached out blindly for the stylus to her handheld. *Got it.* She stared taking notes on the screen without looking away from the microscope.

"Dr. Ericson!!!"

Lana jumped, bumping her cheekbone on the microscope's eyepiece before falling backward, hitting a wall that hadn't been there when she'd come into work that morning.

Strong hands set her firmly on her feet as she realized the wall was warm and made of flesh and muscle. Lots and lots of muscle.

Stumbling back a step, she looked up and then up some more. The dark-haired hottie in front of her was as tall as her colleague, Beau Ruston. Or close to it anyway. She fumbled with her glasses, sliding them on her nose. They didn't help. Reading glasses for the computer, they only served to make her feel more disoriented.

She squinted, then remembered and pulled the glasses off again, letting them dangle by their chain around her neck. "Um, hello? Did I know you were visiting my lab?"

She was fairly certain she hadn't. She forgot appointments sometimes. Okay, often, but she always remembered eventually. And this man hadn't made an appointment with her. She was sure of it. He didn't look like a scientist either.

Not that all scientists were as unremarkable as she was in the looks department, but this man was another species entirely.

He looked dangerous and sexy. Enough so that he would definitely replace chemical formulas in her dreams at night. His black hair was a little too long and looked like he'd run his fingers through it, not a comb. That was just so bad boy. She had a secret weakness for bad boys.

Even bigger than the secret weakness she'd harbored for Beau Ruston before he'd met Elle.

She had posters of James Dean and Matt Dillon on the wall of her bedroom and had seen *Rebel Without a Cause* a whopping thirty-six times.

Unlike James Dean, this yummy bad boy even had pierced ears. Only instead of sedate studs or small hoops, he had tiny black plugs. Only a bit bigger than a pair of studs, the plugs were recessed in his lobes. The had the Chinese Kanji for strength etched on them in silver. Or pewter maybe. It wasn't shiny.

The earrings were hot. Just like him.

He looked like the kind of man who had a tattoo. Nothing colorful. Something black and meaningful. She wanted to see it. Too bad she couldn't just ask.

Interpersonal interaction had so many taboos. It wasn't like science where you dug for answers without apology.

"Lana?"

The stranger had a strong jaw too, squared and accented by a close-cropped beard that went under, not across his chin. No mustache. His lips were set in a straight line, but they still looked like they'd be heaven to kiss.

Not that she'd kissed a lot of lips, but she was twenty-nine. Even a geeky scientist didn't make it to the shy side of thirty without a few kisses along the way. And other stuff. Not that the other stuff was all that spectacular. She'd always wondered if that was her fault or the men she'd chosen to partner.

It didn't take a shrink to identify the fact that Lana had trust issues. With her background, who wouldn't?

Still, people had been know to betray family, love and country for sex. She wouldn't cross a busy street to get some. Or maybe she would, if this stranger was waiting on the other side.

The fact that she could measure the time since she'd last had sex in years rather than months, weeks or *days*—which would be a true miracle—wasn't something she enjoyed dwelling on. She blamed it on her work.

However, every feminine instinct that was usually sublimated by her passion for her job was on red alert now.

The temperature's rising in Karen Kelley's HOW TO SEDUCE A TEXAN, out this month from Brava . . .

S he hit another pothole.

Dammit! They came out of nowhere. As soon as she got home, she'd need to take her car in for realignment. And she'd send Marge the bill.

She topped a rise and slammed on the brakes, the car fishtailed, spewing a thick cloud of dust behind her. Her heart felt as if it had taken residence in her throat. She skidded to a stop, barely missing the cow that languidly stood in the middle of the road looking unconcerned that it had almost been splattered across her windshield.

Nikki's heart pounded inside her chest and her hands shook. She closed her eyes and took a deep breath. When she opened them again, the black and white cow looked at her with total unconcern. This was so not how she wanted to start her vacation slash investigative reporting.

"I almost wrecked because of you." She glared at the cow. Her cold-eyed, steely glare that she'd perfected over the years. If it had been a person rather than a dumb animal, it would've been frozen to the spot.

The cow opened its mouth and bellowed a low, meandering, I-was-here-first moo.

She didn't think the cow cared one little bit that it had almost become hamburger. Damned country. She'd take city life and dirty politicians any day.

"Move!" She clapped her hands.

The cow didn't get in any hurry as it lumbered to the side of the narrow road and lowered its head. The four-legged beast chomped down on a bunch of grass, then slowly began to chew.

She shifted into park, then waved her arms. "Shoo!"

Nothing.

She honked the horn.

Nothing.

The hot sun beat down on her. A bead of sweat slid uncomfortably between her breasts. She judged the narrow road, wondering if she could maneuver around the cow without going into the ditch.

Before she decided to attempt it, another sound drew her attention. She glanced down the dirt road, shielding her eyes from the glare of the sun as a cloud of dust came toward her. The cloud of dust became a man on a horse.

Correction. A cowboy on a horse.

Hi-ho, Silver, the Lone Ranger, she thought sarcastically.

But the closer he got, the more her sarcasm faded. The Lone Ranger had nothing on this cowboy. Broad shoulders, black hat pulled low on his forehead . . .

Black hat. Bad guys wore black hats. Right? Things were looking up.

At least until he brought the horse to a grinding halt and dust swirled around her—again. She coughed and waved her hands in front of her face.

"Bessie, how the hell do you keep getting out?" he asked.

His slow, Southern drawl drizzled over her like warmed honey, and she knew from experience warmed honey drizzling over her naked body could be very good. Sticky, but oh so sexy.

Did he look as good as he sounded?

She shaded her eyes again at the same time he pushed his hat higher on his forehead with one finger. Cal Braxton's tanned face stared down at her. His cool, deep-green eyes only made her body grow warmer with each passing second.

So this was the infamous playboy star football player. The man who had a pretty woman on his arm almost every night of the week—at least until Cynthia Cole had come into his life.

"I almost hit your cow," she told him as she slipped off one of her high heels and rubbed the insole with her other foot. It didn't stop the tingle of pleasure that was running up and down her legs. He could park his boots by her bed any day.

"Sorry about that. Bessie thinks the grass is greener on the other side of the fence."

He pulled a rolled-up rope off the saddle horn and swatted the end of it against Bessie's rump. The cow gave him a disgruntled look before ambling down the road.

His gaze returned to her . . . roaming over her . . . seducing her. "Are you lost?"

"On vacation."

He easily controlled the prancing horse beneath him. "Staying nearby?"

"At the Crystal Creek Dude Ranch."

His grin was slow. So, he did have all his teeth, and they were pearly white. She ran her tongue over her dry lips.

"My brother owns it," he said. "I'm helping him out. It looks like we might be seeing a lot of each other. Name's Cal—Cal Braxton."

His thumb idly stroked the rope. For a moment, she was mesmerized as she watched the hypnotic movement.

"You know, you shouldn't drive with the top down in this heat," he said.

She almost laughed. It wasn't the heat from the sun that had momentarily stolen her wits. Cal was good. Ah, yes, he knew all the moves that made a woman yearn for him to caress her naked skin. And he made those moves very well.

No hero comes close to MIDNIGHT'S MASTER, the latest from Cynthia Eden, out next month from Brava . . .

"Throw her out, Niol. You want the vamps to keep comin', you *throw that bitch out.*"

The tapping stopped, and, because the vampire had raised his shrill-ass voice again, the nearby paranormals—because, generally, the folks who came in his bar were far, far from normal—stilled.

Niol shook his head slowly. "I think you're forgetting a few things, *vamp.*" He gathered the black swell of power that pulsed just beneath his skin. Felt the surge of dark magic and—

The vamp flew across the bar, slamming into the stage with a scream. The lead guitarist swore, then jumped back, cradling his guitar with both hands like the precious baby he thought it was.

The sudden silence was deafening.

Niol motioned toward the bar. "Get me another drink, Marc." He glanced at the slowly rising vampire. "Did I tell you to get up?" It barely took any effort to slam the bastard into the stage wall this time. Just a stray thought, really.

Ah, but power was a wonderful thing.

Sometimes, it was damn good to be a demon. And even better to be a level ten, and the baddest asshole in the room.

He stalked forward. Enjoyed for a moment the way the crowd jumped away from him.

The vampire began to shake. *Perfect.*

Niol stopped a foot before the fallen Andre. "First," he growled, "don't ever, *ever* fucking tell me what to do in *my* bar again."

A fast nod.

"Second . . ." His hands clenched into fists as he fought to rein in the magic blasting through him. The power . . . oh, but it was tempting. And so easy to use.

Too easy.

One more thought, just one, focused and hard, and he could have the vamp dead at his feet.

"Use too much, you'll lose yourself." An old warning. One that had come too late for him. He'd been twenty-five before he met another demon who even came close to him in power and that guy's warning—well it had been long overdue.

Niol knew he'd been one of the Lost for years.

The first time he'd killed, he'd been Lost.

"Second," he repeated, his voice cold, clear, and cutting like a knife in the quiet. "If you think I give a damn about the vampires coming to *my* place . . ." His mouth hitched into a half-grin, but Niol knew no amusement would show in the darkness of his eyes. "Then you're dead wrong, vampire."

"S-sorry, Niol, I—"

He laughed. Then turned his back on the cringing vampire. "Thomas." The guard he always kept close. "Throw that vamp's ass out."

When Thomas stepped forward, the squeal of a guitar ripped through the bar. And the dancing and the drinking and the mating games of the *Other* began with a fierce rumble of sound.

His eyes searched for his prey and he found Holly watching him. All eyes and red hair and lips that begged for his mouth. He strode toward her, conscious of covert eyes still on them. He could show no weakness. Never could.

I'm not weak.

He was the strongest demon in Atlanta. And he sure as hell wasn't going to give the paranormals any cause to start doubting his power.

His kind turned on the weak.

When he stopped before her, the scent of lavender flooded his nostrils.

She looked up at him. The human was small, to him anyway, barely reaching his shoulders so that he towered over her.

She was the weak one. All of her kind were.

Humans. So easy to wound. To kill.

He lifted his hand. Stroked her cheek. Damn but she was soft. Leaning close, Niol told her, "Sweetheart, I warned you before about coming to my Paradise."

There was no doubt others overheard his words. With so many shifters skulking around the joint, a *whisper* would have been overheard. Shifters and their annoyingly superior senses.

"Wh-what do you mean?" The question came, husky and soft. Ah, but he liked her voice. And he could all too easily imagine that voice, whispering to him as they lay amid a tangle of sheets.

Or maybe screaming in his ear as she came.

He cupped her chin in his hand. A nice chin. Softly rounded. And those lips . . . the bottom was fuller than the top. Just a bit. So red. Her mouth was slightly parted, open.

Waiting.

She stepped back, shaking her head. "I don't know what you *think* you're doing, Niol—"

He stared down at her. "Yes, you do." He caught her arms, wrapping his fingers around her and jerking Holly against him. "I told you, the last time you came into *my* bar . . ."

Her eyes widened. "Niol . . ."

Oh, yeah, he liked the way she said his name. She breathed it, tasted it.

His lips lowered toward hers. "If you want to walk in Paradise, baby, then you're gonna have to play with the devil."

"No, I—"

He kissed her. Hard. Deep. Niol drove his tongue right past those plump lips and took her mouth the way the beast inside of him demanded.